DEEP BACKGROUND

A NOVEL

RICK TREON

Black Rose Writing | Texas

ISBN: 978-1-68433-167-3
PUBLISHED BY BLACK ROSE WRITING
www.blackrosewriting.com

Printed in the United States of America
Suggested Retail Price (SRP) $18.95

Deep Background is printed in Book Antiqua

Praise for Deep Background

"Compulsive and hard to put down ..." –David William Pearce, author of *Where Fools Dare to Tread*

"*Deep Background* is an intense thriller. I would recommend this book to anyone who loves dark suspense." –Kim Black, award-winning author of *Little Black Dress*

"An impressive, realistic, dark thriller with an unnerving conclusion ... *Deep Background* is entertaining, eye-opening reading." –*Lone Star Literary Life*

"Highly recommended." –*Viewpoint Books*

"An intelligent, textured and taut thriller ... Treon hits a home run." –*Best Thrillers*

"A truly engaging story ... I highly recommend Deep Background." –Stephen Kanicki, author of *The Seven Experiments*

"Anyone who picks up *Deep Background* will be keenly looking forward to another thrilling read." –*The Big Thrill*

"I guarantee, if you are into suspense, this will be the book for you." –*Authors Reading*

For my parents, my sister, and everyone we consider family

DEEP BACKGROUND

CHAPTER ONE

In two years, Lucky Levi had developed an affinity for skinny bitches. The drink, that is. Vodka, soda, and lime, a low-calorie cocktail that helped him fit in his suits despite drinking at hotel bars far more frequently than a person should. And, if he only wanted to appear tipsy for the sake of female company, he could discreetly tell the bartender to hold the vodka.

Levi Cole, chief investigative reporter for the *Dallas Daily Star*, also enjoyed flying to the East Coast, staying in fancy hotels, and sleeping with women like Emily Greene. She worked in Atlanta for Georgia Barrett, who hosted cable's second-most-watched primetime news program. And as the mid-term elections drew closer, Levi had become a frequent member of the show's discussion panels, which meant more opportunities with Emily.

"Are you ever going to tell me how you got that dirt on Lockwood?" she asked as she put her hand on his bare forearm. Like all the other times they'd been together, Levi had rolled up his white shirtsleeves and loosened his tie after appearing on the show.

"You're cute, but you know I can't reveal—"

"My sources," they said together.

"So, I'm just cute?"

"No," Levi said, leaning in. Emily was, as it happened, skinny. And blonde. And tall. As she had been during those previous encounters, Emily was wearing what she had once called her "good" perfume. Maybe a little too much, but with his senses dulled and his inhibitions waning, it was in the sweet spot.

"But," Levi continued, "I like to try and keep it professional when

I can."

"And when you can't?"

Emily had gotten comfortable enough with Levi to skip most of the small talk. Levi took another sip of his drink and leaned in closer, his lips just brushing Emily's left earlobe.

"Come see for yourself."

• • •

Emily tripped and nearly fell into the doorframe as they made their way into Levi's suite. He had been guiding Emily by the small of her back, allowing him to keep her on her feet. *Good catch. That would've killed the mood.*

"Scotch or vodka?" Levi asked, opening the minibar.

"Scotch."

"My kinda girl."

"Woman," she said.

Levi turned around just in time to see Emily drop her black bra. She was still wearing the black skirt from earlier that night when Levi had been on Georgia's show to weigh in on national politics. He used to wonder why they cared what he thought. He didn't know the politicians, nor did he have any unique insight. Or did he? It didn't matter, so long as they kept booking him.

"My mistake," Levi said before putting down the liquor and walking toward Emily. He paused just before their lips touched. Her eyes were swimming, and she couldn't focus on him. *Whatever. It's fine.* He kissed her before taking her right hand and moving toward the bed. Emily tried to follow but tripped again.

Shit. When he was in college in Austin, Levi and his friends were diligent about making sure they never went too far. Don't put yourself in that situation, and no trouble can follow. Levi hadn't had to worry about it since the night he graduated from The University of Texas. After getting his free shot at every bar on Sixth Street, Levi found himself dancing with a petite brunette in her little black dress. As they made their way out of the club at closing time, Levi asked if she was going home with him. She said yes. His buddies said no.

But now, alone in a hotel room with a woman he'd slept with before, he had no such guidance. Could he ask her what she wanted to do, if she felt okay at regular intervals? That might work, unless she was blackout drunk, at which point it wouldn't matter how much consent she gave.

No matter how badly he wanted to sleep with Emily, Levi knew he would do the right thing and preserve his ability to face his reflection in the morning. He knew what it was like to sleep with Emily. He didn't need to do it again tonight. Levi also reminded himself that he was a public figure. He needed to keep his name below the headlines, not in them.

"Come here. I think it's time for bed," Levi said.

"Finally."

"No, I mean time for you to lie down and sleep. I'll get you a ride home in the morning."

Emily pouted for a moment, but then stumbled toward the bed and curled up next to Levi, still in his pants and shirt. *Lucky Levi my ass.*

• • •

Coherent thoughts escaped Levi as he pulled the anvils from his eyelids and slowly pried them open. How long had he been asleep? He picked up his buzzing cellphone and saw the time. Who was calling him at 12:30 a.m. on a Saturday? Tim Edwards. *Fuck me.*

CHAPTER TWO

Hot bile crept up Levi's throat as he digested the typewritten letter.

To whom it may concern,

Please find enclosed a DVD with several video interviews regarding the reporting of Levi Cole over the last four years. In these interviews, sources quoted by Cole detail his misquotation and misrepresentation of facts. As you will see, the only accurate work he has done during his tenure with you is his reporting on the Lockwood scandal.

I trust you will use this information to serve the public interest.

Cheers.

Tim Edwards, the managing editor of the *Dallas Daily Star*, retrieved a laptop and opened it when Levi finished reading. Publisher Christopher Applegate and a corporate lawyer were also seated at the long table in the executive conference room, and everyone watched for ten minutes as the first source spoke. A voice offscreen asked a high school football coach questions about a story Levi had written more than two years ago. The coach detailed how Levi had misquoted him during a preseason interview. The quote had been part of a flowery lede detailing how two-a-days made men out of boys and prepared them for both football and life.

"I never said that. All I said was that these practices are hard every year and that sometimes it helps kids decide whether or not they really want to play. I liked his version better, though. My wife cut out the story and put it up on our fridge at home."

Edwards stopped the DVD. "That would be enough right there, but there are five of these interviews. I had to sit through an hour of that shit."

Over the years, Levi had convinced himself he wasn't a shoddy reporter. He hadn't written outright lies. Fudges, maybe. Sensationalized anecdotes and polished quotes—things busy reporters sometimes do but never talk about, especially in sports and features—all to tell a greater truth. That story had earned him praise. The coach was as redneck as they come, and to quote him directly would've made Levi, and the *Star*, look bad. And, just as the guy had said on the DVD, he was grateful Levi had made him sound intelligent in one of the state's largest newspapers. Everybody won. That's why he'd done it. A few victimless cases of journalistic malpractice during a time when he needed to catch a break. Levi had been in a bad way when he started at the *Star*, as low as he'd ever been. Of course, neither Edwards nor Applegate had known Levi then. Now, Levi was top of mind. Lockwood had put him on their radar—on everyone's radar—and anything before that hadn't mattered.

Until now.

"You know what comes next," Edwards said. "We're going to have to run retractions for just about everything you've ever written. We don't even know where to begin."

"Hold on now," the lawyer said. "I've watched this DVD, too. None of the people sounded angry. None said they were going to sue. In fact, that guy isn't the only one who thanked Mr. Cole."

"So? We printed inaccuracies and misrepresented sources, and we know about it," Edwards said. "If it ever gets out that we found out about this and didn't fire Levi, and print retractions, we're through as a newspaper. Readers will never trust us again."

"And what do you think happens if we run a retraction to every story our chief investigative reporter has ever written?" the lawyer asked. "What do you think happens to all those awards we won for the Lockwood stories? He wasn't the only one who reported on that."

"That doesn't matter," Edwards said. "We can't bury this."

"You know, I never thought I'd agree with a lawyer," Applegate said. "But I don't want to have employed the next Stephen Glass or Jayson Blair."

Levi saw his chance. The bosses didn't know who'd sent the letter and DVD. He did.

"Why don't you just let me leave," Levi said. "I'll be out of here. When someone asks why I stopped writing stories, all you have to say is you can't discuss personnel matters. I'll stick my head in the sand, come up for air on TV in a week or so, and announce that I decided to go freelance again."

"Do you think whoever sent this is just going to let us sit on it?" Edwards asked.

"I do. This note is from the same anonymous source from the Lockwood stories."

"You said an old friend turned you onto Lockwood," Edwards said.

"I lied."

Edwards pinched the bridge of his nose.

"The original note was also anonymous, but it was addressed to me, personally, when I was a freelance sports and features writer," Levi said. "This is about me. Plus, this new letter says that the Lockwood reporting is good. This person wanted me to expose Lockwood. He won't want you to put that reporting into question."

Levi had become a professional bullshitter, but this time he was selling the truth.

"I'll buy that," Applegate said.

Edwards shook his head. Levi had known Edwards for a few years now, and they'd never seen eye to eye. Edwards was cordial enough but had politely declined the time Levi had invited him out for drinks. He didn't change Levi's copy much, but he never gave Levi positive feedback, either. Levi had concluded that Edwards was jealous. It's the only explanation that made sense. The implausible alternative was that Edwards didn't respect Levi's talent.

"Alright then, it's settled. I'll coordinate with HR," the lawyer said. He turned to Levi. "As of right now, you are no longer an employee of the *Dallas Daily Star*. To help keep this quiet like we just discussed, I won't have security escort you out. But I will need you to leave immediately. Per company policy, we'll pack up your personal items — discreetly of course — and send them to you. What's your address?"

Levi started to give them his Arlington address, but as he thought about having complete freedom for what he hoped would be a brief period, another great idea struck. "Just send everything to Bison Ridge, Texas," Levi said. "204 Broadway."

Levi had no reason to stay in the Metroplex. He rarely spent more than a night or two in his condo during election season. He'd been touring the network Sunday morning shows and participating in cable news discussion panels next to reporters from the *Times* and *Post*. The *Star*'s bosses preferred him on the road, sitting among journalism's heaviest hitters, promoting the paper's national political coverage. He was their traveling East Coast bureau chief.

Levi used to feel like a fraud. Those other reporters had covered the White House. They'd met U.S. presidents and foreign leaders, and most had broken major national and international political scandals. Levi—along with Edwards, Applegate, and a few others at the *Star*—knew how underqualified he was to be in their presence. But when he started getting booked more frequently, Levi realized none of that mattered. He was charismatic, had an easy smile, and his stories had affected real change. And, according to those respected reporters, Levi had "changed the course of American political history."

Levi's nausea had passed by the time he'd left the building and removed his tie. Not that he deserved to avoid a life sentence in journalism jail, but Lucky Levi had once again emerged unscathed.

CHAPTER THREE

Kat Hallaway's eyelids popped open at the sound of the dinging elevator, which had rudely ended her five-second nap. The third floor's trophy case greeted her as always. She ducked her head and hurried past the *Amarillo Morning Standard's* 1963 Pulitzer Prize medal for public service.

"Kat, I need you for a sec."

Shit. Greg Bishop had summoned her in his signature style—yelling at her from his desk through the glass walls of his office, which was decorated with framed front pages hanging on the wall and a coat rack in the corner wearing a lonely navy blazer. Nobody ever mentioned it, but the paper's managing editor also had management-for-dummies books stacked up on the side of his L-shaped desk.

"What brings you in on a Saturday afternoon?" Kat asked.

"Shut the door, please," he said.

"I've got to sit down and start writing."

"I only need you for a minute."

It was never a minute with Bishop. In his world, every story every reporter ever worked on was essential to the paper. There were always more sources to interview, more background to dig up. Bishop was intelligent and cared about the craft of daily journalism, but it was fucking exhausting.

Kat's assignment had been to write a bullshit feature about a local pumpkin farm as it prepared for Halloween and Thanksgiving. She clenched her jaw and wondered what sage advice Bishop could give about that piece of essential journalism—the B section centerpiece, which was more about the cute kids in her photo than the text surrounding it.

"You're the boss."

"I know I haven't been here long, and I haven't done a lot to get to know everyone, and I apologize for that," he said. "But, I've started reviewing the staff's past work. You've done some impressive stuff here."

"Yep. Two-time Reporter of the Year," Kat said. It seemed like a lifetime ago, but Kat had once been the pride of the University of Missouri School of Journalism. In addition to those awards, the Texas Associated Press Managing Editors had given her a third-place Investigative Report award and an honorable mention in the Breaking News Report category.

"It's been about four years since you've won anything, though. Judging by your submissions, I'm not surprised. And, I don't know if you've checked the board out there, but your page view numbers are low."

Kat sighed. Bishop was right. The dismal sum of her combined clicks from stories, videos, and photo slideshows mocked her every day from the whiteboard at the newsroom's back wall. Despite covering the area's prominent crime stories and trials, the name Katherine Hallaway remained glued to the bottom of the ever-shrinking list. She never bothered with taking and editing video, or providing extra photos for slideshows, unless explicitly told to do so. The night reporters, however, were eager to record endless footage and snap countless stills of the graphic and deadly wrecks they covered. They were young, most were unmarried, and none realized the pitfalls of working off the clock. They wanted to seem like team players and thought their loyalty would be rewarded. Maybe that worked in other industries. Movies and TV continued to spin that story, the same one Kat had heard when she was young and had the scanner-hound beat. That was before "page views" and "web traffic" had become more important than journalism. J-school Kat wouldn't have stood for it. Hungover Kat didn't give a shit.

The Web department updated the board on Monday and Thursday mornings. It was a source of public humiliation disguised as a way to give bonuses. The first bonus came at a weekly page view threshold—Kat didn't know or care what it was—then there were monthly winners. The most dedicated ambulance chasers could earn a whole three hundred extra dollars a month if they "earned" all the available bonus money. If a reporter hit their monthly threshold three consecutive months, another bonus. Hitting it all twelve months meant a New Year's bonus. Kat imagined it was like working for a high-pressure sales company, right down to that damn whiteboard—though at any other business, there'd be at least one more zero at the end of the monthly pot.

"I'm not sure what you want me to say." Kat leaned back in her chair. She knew she was underperforming. She didn't care.

"I didn't bring you in here for a lecture." He leaned toward Kat and lowered his voice. "I wanted to tell you that more layoffs are coming in December. At least that way, people will be able to spend a long Christmas break with their families."

"Again? It's only been, what, eight months since the last round? Do you know who's getting laid off yet?" Kat's volume increased with each question.

Bishop held up a hand to stop the rapid-fire questions and checked to make sure the paper's only remaining copy editor wasn't watching them. "I just found out earlier today, so I don't know who they'll let go yet. But, for better or worse, corporate has an objective way to figure it out." He motioned to the board.

Kat's nostrils flared. "Are you trying to tell me I'm fired if I don't get my page views up?"

"Look, I shouldn't've even told you about the layoffs, but I don't want to lose a reporter with your potential. And I absolutely cannot discuss personnel issues. All I can do is tell you the same thing I tell everybody else: You need to generate more web traffic."

"Yeah, let me get right on that." Kat jumped from her seat and flung open Bishop's door, muttering a string of curse words that would make a sailor blush. A knot grew inside her stomach, feeding off the anger and fear. She didn't care about this job anymore, but she loved her son too much to jeopardize her family. Kat was her family's breadwinner.

And, though she wasn't making nearly as much as she was worth at her best, Kat earned enough, and getting laid off would have severe consequences. Kat's clip file would contain stories that were either old or boring, neither of which would land her a job that paid enough to support her household. She had no other marketable skills, which would mean starting at the bottom if she had to switch industries.

Kat sat down at her desk and started writing. This story wasn't going to save her, but she had to start somewhere.

CHAPTER FOUR

Kat treasured Sunday mornings. Their family did not go to church—she'd been agnostic since college—but it was the one morning she had with both her husband, Bill, and three-year-old son, Michael. Kat spent Mondays with Michael, but Bill worked bankers' hours at a local print shop. Bill had chosen perhaps the one bachelor's degree more useless than hers—philosophy. He should've gotten a master's and Ph.D. so he could teach, but Bill was not ambitious. They'd also married young, and Bill had agreed to let Kat start her career and choose where they lived after college.

"You want to give it a try this morning?" Bill asked. It was his weekly joke. He was the cook of the family and made breakfast on Sundays. Kat had tried to duplicate his buttermilk pancakes, but they were never fluffy enough, and there was never the right amount of vanilla.

"I would, but I'm too busy cuddling." She and the boy were on the microfiber couch streaming kids' videos on her phone. When the pancakes were ready, Michael hurled himself off the couch and ran like a crazy person to the kitchen. Kat smiled as a social media alert popped onto her screen. She tapped the blue-and-white lowercase letter, which informed her the Vista County Emergency Operations Center had just started a live video. She was off the clock and enjoying her favorite part of the week, but Kat replayed her conversation with Bishop. Even if the timing was terrible, she had to chase everything. Only one reporter was on-call for major accidents or breaking news in Amarillo. Vista County was in the *Standard's* coverage area, but not close enough to the city for this to show up on local scanners. The story was hers if she acted quickly.

Kat scrambled to find a notebook and pen. She could write a story from here and email it in, then get to her pancakes. She watched as a stout man wearing a beige collared shirt and bronze star entered the screen, a pasture of dead grass and barbed wire behind him. Below his brown cowboy hat was a thick mane of black hair, dark aviator glasses, and a bushy black beard. The sheriff was holding a press conference with no press, cutting out the middleman. *This is where all my damn Web traffic is going.*

"Hi there everyone, I'm Vista County Sheriff Shawn Nichols. I just wanted to let everyone know what all the fuss was about near Bison Ridge this morning," he said before unfolding a piece of paper and clearing his throat, a bit too dramatically. "At approximately 7:15 a.m. this morning, a Vista County Sheriff's Office deputy discovered the body of a teenager in a pasture about two miles northwest of the Bison Ridge city limits. Emergency crews are working right now to determine what happened. The name of the girl is being withheld, pending notification of next of kin. That's all we have for now. We'll keep you updated when we know more."

Kat finished writing her notes and found her laptop. She would send an email straight to the web department—the poor souls who were essentially on-call 24/7—and copy in Bishop. The story wouldn't look like much in print, but it would be on the paper's website, app, and social media within the hour.

Subject: BREAKING NEWS, post and distribute IMMEDIATELY

Teen's body found near Bison Ridge

The body of a teenager was found Sunday morning about two miles northwest of Bison Ridge, according to Vista County Sheriff Shawn Nichols.

The female was discovered by sheriff's office deputies at approximately 7:15 a.m., Nichols said Sunday during a live internet video announcement. Her name is being withheld, pending notification of next of kin.

— Katherine Hallaway, Morning Standard Staff

Sadness and excitement played tug of war with Kat's heart, but in the end, she smiled. Five minutes of work that would generate thousands of page views today and continue through Monday morning. The hard part would be keeping the momentum long enough to keep from being fired.

"What was all that about?" Bill asked as Kat walked to the kitchen table.

"Had a story fall into my lap."

"Oh yeah? What happened?"

"A teenage girl was found dead near Bison Ridge. I'll have to do a lot of follow-ups. I'll probably go there tomorrow. Can you miss work, or will we have to find a sitter?"

Bill froze, two pancakes balanced on his spatula just above Kat's plate. "You're going to go to Bison Ridge?"

Kat craned her neck to look up at Bill. He was tall, over six-five, and reminded her of a thinner Ichabod Crane.

"It'll be fine," she said. "There's nothing there for me now but this story."

• • •

Levi smiled as he pulled into the Jolly Travel Center. The name would've been enough to cheer him up, but it was also a gateway to his hometown. He'd stopped there dozens of times going to and from college. It had become a ritual, and he would always time his fuel and restroom needs accordingly. The last time he'd gassed up in Jolly, Levi had been on his way to Dallas, trying to put the Texas Panhandle in his rearview for good.

He'd lasted four years.

Levi had driven straight to the *Daily Star* and surprised his old editors by talking his way into the newsroom using the badge he'd kept from his days as an intern. They offered him a part-time freelance gig covering high school sports again. A few old friends had let him couch surf. His parents and friends had agreed to clear out his apartment in

Amarillo and store his things in their respective garages. He told them to keep it all for themselves, not that there was much to divvy up. A fifty-inch TV, the futon he'd inherited from an uncle, a queen bed, old clothes, and other inconsequential items.

Levi's phone buzzed as he flopped back into the driver's seat of his black Kia Optima.

BREAKING: Teen girl's body found near Bison Ridge

CHAPTER FIVE

Levi chomped on his gum as Ace Anderson stood on the Vista County Courthouse steps. Anderson's short, wavy blond hair remained perfectly in place despite the Panhandle wind. His white collared shirt had been robbed of its tie, and the sleeves had been rolled up his ropy forearms. The tall, blue-eyed U.S. House representative from Texas' 13th District flashed his signature smile and waved to the crowd before beginning his stump speech—likely the first of several on a Monday during the final stretch of his first re-election campaign. A wholesome scene for those who didn't know better.

"I'd like to thank y'all for coming out this morning," Anderson said. "I had planned to start today's speech with a joke about this weekend's game against my Diamondbacks. Instead, I'm going to talk for a minute about the tragedy that has rocked your community. Our community. As I'm sure many of you are aware, I knew RayLynn. As editor-in-chief of the high school newspaper, Miss Gutierrez had been working on a story about me that would've run today in her *Buffalo Nickel* and in the *Vista County Courier*. She was a wonderful, talented, beautiful young woman, and we're all going to miss her."

Levi had gone to the courthouse, which stood tall in the middle of Bison Ridge, looking for more information about the girl's death. The political circus had been an unwelcome distraction, but it was worth seeing Anderson again to get confirmation that RayLynn Gutierrez was the deceased. Levi's mother had filled him in the night before, but having a second source before entering the courthouse was helpful. Levi had also gotten some additional nuggets to use later. While Levi thought writing about Anderson was a waste of ink, RayLynn was ambitious and already stringing for the *Courier*.

And as a promising young journalist, Levi was sure RayLynn would be upset by a sitting congressman using her tragic death as a segue into a speech about "urban" crime's infiltration into "God's country." The same folks who cried yesterday were clapping and yelling in a mindless populist frenzy. Dog whistle politics at its worst, though Levi reluctantly gave Anderson a bit of credit for using the whistle rather than a megaphone like many politicians in rural America.

Levi snuck one last glance at Anderson before making his way to the side entrance of the red-and-brown brick courthouse. The last time Levi saw him in Bison Ridge, Anderson had been wearing a Yucca Diamondbacks football jersey, yelling taunts over the roar of five-thousand silent fans.

· · ·

Levi had never considered Sheriff Shawn Nichols a close friend in high school, but they were in the same graduating class. More importantly, they'd been members of the Stampede. Once teammates, always teammates.

"The prodigal son returns," Nichols said.

"You quoting the Bible now?" Levi asked.

"Nope. *Twister*."

Since high school, Nichols had spoken in pop culture quotes, mostly movie and TV lines. He'd usually pause and wait for someone to name the title. It was a fun game—when it wasn't annoying.

Levi walked into Nichols' office, past a glass door with his name below the word SHERIFF into a warm workspace, which was anchored by a sturdy wooden desk and matching bookshelf filled with a mix of law enforcement manuals and classic literature. It reminded Levi more of an old den where two men should discuss politics and worldly topics.

"I don't know if you read the paper this morning, but you've picked a terrible time to drop in," Nichols said as he sat back down behind his desk.

"Actually, that's why I'm here."

"I thought you were some big-shot political reporter in Dallas now. Everybody's been talking about you being on TV. But, if you're here covering the story, I'm just going to have to give you the runaround like all the other media."

"I'm not here as a reporter. I'm here to ease Sharon's mind. She called my mom—you know how that goes. She just wants me to come and make sure you're working hard on her granddaughter's behalf." Levi took no pleasure in this lie, but he needed a reason to be there. And, for all Levi knew, Sharon Smith would have asked him to talk to Nichols. If asked, Levi knew his mother would cover for him.

The burly sheriff slumped his shoulders, and the charming spark disappeared from his eyes. There would be no more jokes this morning.

"News does travel fast here," Nichols said.

"Yep. But even if Sharon wasn't telling everyone, the esteemed congressman Ace Anderson just told his crowd outside."

Nichols smoothed his lumberjack beard and shook his head. "Fuckface Anderson. Goddamnit."

Levi smirked. It had been nearly twenty years since he'd heard that nickname, bestowed upon the future U.S. representative by the Bison Ridge High School football team. They thought it was the smartest thing ever. They were using the F-word, insulting him, ironically making fun of his obvious good looks, and still using his real name. Brilliant! They'd even used shoe polish to write FuckfACE on the back window of the rich boy's BMW during hell week Anderson's senior year.

"We're off the record, right?" Nichols asked.

"Of course."

"I'm serious. We've got to keep a tight lid on this until we figure out exactly what happened."

"I'm not writing a word." *Not a lie. Technically.*

Nichols pulled a nondescript folder from his right-hand drawer and slid it toward Levi. He opened the folder before immediately slapping it shut. Levi looked up at Nichols, who slowly nodded down at the folder. Levi opened it again, trying to just peek around the cover. A typewritten report was paperclipped to the left side, but Levi's eyes were drawn to a stack of crime scene photos on the right. The top image was a closeup of a girl's face. What was left of it, anyway. The picture stirred images of Emmett Till. Underneath he found a photo of RayLynn's naked body staged on the prairie. Her arms and legs formed a cross and the letters XXX were burned across her chest.

"That's RayLynn?" Levi asked, knowing it was a stupid question but finding himself unable to focus well enough to say anything else.

"Yeah. Sharon confirmed it was RayLynn because of her snake."

"Her snake?"

"The tattoo of a diamondback that runs down her right thigh. No mistaking that thing," Nichols said as Levi turned the photo sideways and leaned closer. "We all knew it was her, though. Sharon had called on Saturday and said RayLynn had been gone since Friday afternoon, but technically she wasn't a missing person. We didn't find her until-"

"Yesterday morning, before church."

"Oh yeah. I forgot everyone drove right by your parents' house."

Levi's mother had recounted the scene to Levi over dinner the night before. She said it was like a convoy of sheriff's office and Department of Public Safety pickups and SUVs. They'd driven down the block and gotten bottlenecked at the cattle guard that led to an oil lease near town. She said it took them half an hour to cross, which meant it took about five minutes.

"How far out there was she?"

"A deputy found her out where we used to go drinking after games. Kids still go there, so it was one of the first places we searched."

Levi flipped to another photo. He saw ligature marks on her wrists and ankles. RayLynn's hands and feet didn't look right, though Levi couldn't pinpoint why.

"They were pulled off."

"What were pulled off?"

"Her fingernails. All of them. Toenails, too. You probably noticed the holes in her palms and feet. Looks like someone took a large-bore drill bit to them. Given how her body was staged, we're assuming they're supposed to look like stigmata."

"Jesus," Levi said, before realizing his inadvertent pun. Despite himself, Levi couldn't keep from thinking, *See what I did there?*

"What kind of sociopath would do this?" Levi asked instead.

"Not a sociopath. Psychopath."

"Same thing, right?"

"Nope," Nichols said. "Sociopaths aren't careful. They're not smart like this guy. He didn't leave anything behind. Her whole body was doused in bleach."

"Guess all that law enforcement training's coming in handy."

"Not really," Nichols said. "This is my first murder."

Levi closed his eyes at the word. Murder. He'd come to the courthouse assuming the girl had died in an accident. His plan to use that tragedy for his own personal gain was wrong enough. But RayLynn had been killed by someone with a mental disorder who'd watched one too many horror flicks.

"I know we agreed we're off the record, and we are. But I have to ask: Why'd you show me this?"

"I wanted to let you know why Sharon was so upset. And to show you why I can't have you, or anyone else, interfering," Nichols said. "The Texas Rangers have already been out there, and they don't mess around."

"Understood. But Shawn, if they don't make some headway on this real soon, people here are going to be at your door with pitchforks. They don't understand or care about jurisdiction. To them, you're the authority here."

"Tell me something I don't know." Nichols stood and extended his right hand. "But next time, tell it to me over the phone."

"Yeah," Levi said as they shook hands. "I guess I'll let you get back to it."

He turned around and tried to remember how to get out of the courthouse. Levi had seen the devil's handiwork, and his mind refused to focus on anything else.

Chapter Six

Ace slammed the back door of a black Suburban and flopped down beside his chief of staff, Hunter Matthews. "Have I mentioned how much I hate this shithole town?" Ace asked rhetorically. "How the hell did you grow up here?"

"With difficulty."

Ace was not a natural politician and didn't care much for public speaking, but the good Lord had gifted him height—he stood nearly six foot six, impressively tall but not freakishly so—an athletic build, and one hell of a smile. People trusted him, and he used that to his advantage. Others, like old bosses and now Matthews, had learned to use this natural gift to their advantage.

Matthews was the politician and openly wished he didn't need Ace. But what God had given Matthews in intellect and cunning, he'd taken away from his physicality. Matthews reminded Ace of a mole—a short, overweight, nearly hairless creature with terrible eyesight.

"What's next?" Ace asked.

"A meeting with the mayor."

"That asshole. Why do we have to—"

"Why do *you* always have to question me? Just do what you're told. I'll do the thinking."

Matthews wasn't always such a prick. In fact, when they were in Washington and things were going well, he could be downright pleasant. But Matthews had been increasingly angry since they arrived in Vista County. Ace didn't mind coming back, but Matthews detested the place. Ace figured he would feel the same if he looked like Matthews and had gone to Bison Ridge High. Still, Matthews was being an extra-sharp prick. Ace thought about playing whack-a-mole and wondered how it would feel to smash those Coke-bottle glasses deep into Matthews' acne-scarred face.

"Hey, you don't get to talk to me that way," Ace said. "I'm in charge. Don't forget that."

"Without me, you'd still be hawking supplies in those dirty refineries, and you know it."

Ace was mad, but he knew Matthews was right. Ace wasn't sure how his father, a founding partner of one of the largest law firms in the state, had come up with the idea to team them up, but it was a genius move. Together they'd ousted a longtime incumbent by running on a combination of decreased regulation for the oil and gas industry, increased subsidies for agriculture, and strict immigration reform. Ace wasn't far right-wing, especially for the Texas Panhandle, but Matthews had written Ace a compelling script.

Ace had figured he would once again coast to re-election after winning the Republican primary in March, but the presidential race two years ago had changed everything. The day after Ace beat out his opposition, a third-party candidate claiming to be with the "New TEA Party" had thrown his grease-covered ball cap into Ace's ring. And, though he'd been campaigning for just seven months, Bobby Joe Carter—who owned a successful towing service and body repair shop in Yucca—was a real threat. He had backing from an ultra-conservative political action committee, All Texans Matter, whose acronym and ties to dark money were not lost on Matthews or Ace. ATM's platform featured congressional term limits, abolishing all taxes, complete deregulation of the markets, and no international trading. The PAC had been dumping money into TV and radio campaigns blasting Ace for his ties to "Big Oil," citing his old job as an outside salesman for a distributor of oil pipeline and refinery equipment. The idea that Ace was in the pocket of oil companies was a crock of shit and using Ace's sales background as proof was absurd. But people around here didn't seem to care. Red America was in the post-truth era, and the 13th District was scarlet. Any candidate to Ace's right was a legitimate threat, especially with ATM funding. If Matthews said he needed the support of a Podunk mayor to gain an edge, Ace had no choice but to trust him.

"Fine," Ace said. "But let's make it quick so I can get the hell outta here."

"Finally, something we agree on."

• • •

As he sat on a bench just outside the courthouse, Levi reconsidered his plan. RayLynn was supposed to have died from drinking too much or rolling an all-terrain vehicle. But murder? That didn't happen in Bison Ridge. People were occasionally murdered in Yucca, but those were usually drug-related killings. The last true murder in Vista County—one with a motive that didn't involve meth, opioids, or other illicit substances—was a revenge killing.

A small business owner in Yucca who often touted a by-his-bootstraps story started cheating on his trophy wife, with whom he had a son and a daughter. As the affair continued, the man's wife talked him into taking in his teenage nephew, whose parents had landed themselves in jail for dealing drugs. With the businessman constantly out of the house with his mistress, the wife seduced the boy. The husband, perhaps projecting his own cheating ways onto his wife, started getting suspicious. He set a trap for his wife and, upon catching her in bed with his nephew, killed them both. He then took their bodies to nearby Lake Meredith and burned them in a fire pit, though not nearly well enough. He was later convicted of the double-murder and, as far as Levi knew, was still on death row in West Livingston.

Stories like this are sometimes hyperbolized as they spread across small towns. But the basic facts of this case had been well-documented in an episode of a true-crime TV series. Levi forgot which one, but it aired on a channel formerly dedicated to learning. The episode was simultaneously a source of embarrassment and pride for Vista County residents.

When RayLynn's story was made into a TV episode, limited series or feature film, it would not be so well-received by the locals. In the meantime, the brutality of her death was causing a problem for Levi. To stay on his current path would mean getting involved in a criminal investigation. His involvement would be tangential, and he would do his best to remain out of the public eye this time, but Levi still disliked the idea. And, since he had yet to take any action, Levi maintained the option to walk away, to stand up, get in his car and drive back to North Texas. He'd leave Bison Ridge empty-handed, but his life would remain uncomplicated, which he treasured above almost anything.

Faced with no better alternative, Levi began walking toward his car. The parking lot, which had been so full he parked across the street at the local grocery store, was deserted except for a couple of municipal vehicles and a brown 1990s pickup. The wheel wells were nothing but rust, and the corners of a faded Missouri Tigers sticker curled up from the rear window.

•   •   •

Kat knew this game. The sheriff was in, but he was on a "very important conference call" and unavailable to talk to the media right now. She was usually not a patient woman, especially while getting the runaround from public officials. But, it was her day off, and she was not on deadline. All media staffs, including the *Standard*, TV news stations and blogs — which now called themselves "independent online news sources" — were at their lowest. Reporters in the region waited on news releases or called sources. Many organizations no longer authorized trips farther than Canyon or Bushland, essentially a twenty-mile radius, except for natural disasters like wildfires or tornadoes. Even those could often be covered using stringers, phone calls, and texts. Kat had become lazy like the rest — except when properly incentivized.

Kat mindlessly scrolled through her social media apps as she waited. She was a longtime addict by now. While most people she knew were on them, Kat and a select generation of J-school graduates had been hooked from the beginning. She joined the Website everyone on campus jokingly renamed "stalker.com" her freshman year. It was now one of the largest corporations on the planet. She started using a microblogging site her junior year, on the same day she learned what microblogging was. Her professor had said it would be one of the most essential tools journalists would need moving forward. They had all called bullshit. He was one of the smartest professors she ever had.

In that same class, Kat had invented the mobile tablet and e-edition. The professor had asked how news consumers would replace their physical newspapers in the next decade. Her proposal, which had also been laughed at by her peers, was a flat, electronic device that someone could lay down or hold, just like their newspaper. Some pointed out that the Sony Librie, the first modern e-reader, already had this function, though the graphics were shit. Kat's innovation would be in the ability to display the PDFs that were later translated into print pages. Readers would even be able to "flip through" the PDFs, which would have embedded hyperlinks to old stories and to the paper's homepages. In her future, the news organizations would buy the devices and lease them to subscribers. Her professor gave her an A on the project, though said she was clinging to the thought of the printed newspaper too much. A decade later, she still was.

Kat had reached the point where refreshing her feeds failed to show new content. She was about to start reading a true crime novel on her phone when the sheriff's secretary poked her head out.

"Sheriff Nichols can see you now, hon."

The office was old, though more impressive than she'd anticipated. She had spoken to Nichols on the phone a few times and seen him on the video, but she'd never met him. He kept writing in a manila folder as she sat down at the wooden desk. Kat pulled out her phone again and opened the recorder app before writing *Nichols* at the top of a fresh page in her reporter's notebook.

"Ms. Hallaway, a pleasure to meet you." Nichols looked up from his folder but did not smile or extend his hand. "We both know that there's not much I can tell you about this investigation."

"Any piece of information helps, sheriff," she said before tapping the big red button on her phone. "For instance, have you had time to notify next of kin?"

"Yes, ma'am." Nichols stared with intense cocoa eyes. After a few seconds passed, Kat realized she was going to have to ask precise questions.

"Does that mean you can release the victim's name?"

"RayLynn Gutierrez. Age sixteen."

"Would you mind spelling her name for me, please."

Nichols let out a dramatic sigh and opened another file on his desk. "R-A-Y, capital L, Y-N-N. All one word. Gutierrez is normal spelling."

"Thank you, sheriff. I assume the autopsy in Lubbock is not done yet?"

"No, ma'am."

"So, no preliminary cause of death to release."

"No."

"Can you give me any information regarding the circumstances surrounding her death?"

"No."

"Do you know if it was accidental or if foul play is involved?"

"I can't release that kind of information at this time."

Kat, who never hid her emotions very well, was quickly tiring of this game. "How can you be leading an investigation but not be able to at least tell me that much?"

"We are not leading the investigation."

Kat's eyes widened. If the Vista County Sheriff's Office wasn't in charge, there was only one other agency who could be investigating. "So, the Texas Rangers then. Are they treating this girl's death as a homicide?"

"You know I can't comment on an ongoing investigation, Ms. Hallaway. Especially if it's not mine to comment on."

It didn't matter that Nichols wouldn't answer. Around here, the Rangers usually didn't get involved unless county investigators were in over their heads, or if a teacher was caught fucking a student, so Kat already had all the information she needed from Nichols. "Who should I contact for comment?"

"I would suggest DPS Trooper Alex Correa. I assume you know how to reach him?"

"Yes, sir." Kat had to call Correa almost weekly. He was a spokesman for the Department of Public Safety who provided news releases and comments for major wrecks and crimes in the northern half of the Texas Panhandle.

"Will you be assisting with the investigation at all?" Kat asked.

"We will do anything we can to assist the Texas Rangers as they look into RayLynn's death," he said in a patronizingly over-rehearsed fashion. "And that's all you're going to get from me, Ms. Hallaway."

Kat finished writing and put a star next to the quote. "I appreciate your time, Sheriff Nichols. I'll let you know if I have any other questions for you."

CHAPTER SEVEN

From the moment she was introduced as the *Morning Standard's* new cops reporter, Levi tried not to want Kat. She joined the staff with much fanfare, including a cake and liters of Coke. He and the other sportswriters had even emerged from their cave to catch a glimpse of the new girl. They were all impressed with her body and youth. She caught Levi ogling her and winked when he managed to look above her neckline.

The days of her flirting with him were long gone. But he was determined to bring them back. In a small bit of fortune, Levi had dressed up for his meeting with Nichols. He had on a navy polo paired with dark Wranglers and had chosen his Swiss watch with the black alligator wristband. As Kat approached, Levi removed the Wayfarers from his face and sat them on top of his light brown hair.

"I see you're still driving Ol' Faithful." He flashed a smile and tried to disarm Kat, who'd seen him from a distance and was still cursing under her breath as she approached the pickup.

"I don't have time for small talk," she mumbled to the parking lot next to his feet.

"I saw the truck and wanted to say hi. Hi."

"Do you think things are okay between us now?" Kat asked before looking up at Levi through her black framed glasses. "You think just because we've texted each other a few times over the last couple of years that it's all good?"

"I thought we were at least on speaking terms."

"We've got nothing to talk about anymore. You made that decision for us a long time ago."

Now it was Levi's turn to inspect the weeds growing in the parking lot. "I take it you just came from talking to Shawn?" Levi wanted to let Kat know he and Nichols were on a first-name basis.

"Yeah. So?"

"I'm guessing he didn't tell you much."

"Like I'm going to tell you what he told me."

"I can help you with these stories if you'll let me." Levi looked back up at Kat. She seemed to be considering his offer.

"How?" she asked.

"Meet me at the high school this afternoon, a little before one."

"What for?"

"You won't be wasting your time."

"Like I trust you. Now please go so I can get back to work."

Levi nodded and started toward his car. "Twelve fifty-five. It'll be worth it. I promise."

• • •

Kat closed her eyes as she sucked on the last cigarette of her pack. She needed the nicotine more than usual. She was still in the courthouse parking lot, sitting in her front seat and trying to sort out the morning's revelations. She'd gone from frustration at the sheriff to excitement at the heightened profile this story would have now that it was a homicide. Her heart sank when she saw Levi waiting for her. But looking into his eyes and standing next to him had caused the rest of her body to go haywire.

It'll be worth it. I promise. Levi's words rattled around in her foggy cerebrum. Hadn't she told him something similar six years ago? If so, she'd been right. At least for a while. But Kat didn't have time to think about it all right now. She sat the cigarette in her pickup's ashtray and took out her phone. Kat had Trooper Correa's cell number in her address book. She wouldn't get much out of him, but if Kat could get him to just say the word "homicide," that would be enough.

"Katherine Hallaway. How's my favorite Amarillo reporter?" Correa was annoyingly chipper and always used her full name. She hated when others used it, but Correa spoke so enthusiastically that Kat had never corrected him. He had the perfect personality to handle the media.

"Hi, Trooper Correa. I'm fine, thank you."

"What can I do for you today? I didn't put out any new press releases, did I?"

"Actually, I just got done speaking with Vista County Sheriff Shawn Nichols. He told me the Rangers are investigating RayLynn Gutierrez's death."

Correa was silent for a few seconds, which never happened when they spoke. "I can't comment on something like that."

"I totally get it, and I just want to see if you can confirm two things for me. But it'll have to be on the record."

More hesitation. "Okay."

"First, can you confirm the Rangers are investigating her death?"

"Let me put it this way. The information you have is not incorrect."

Kat often wondered why officials tried so hard to provide non-confirmation confirmations. *Just say yes, you fucking weirdo.*

"Gotcha," Kat said. "Now that we have that cleared up, can you tell me if they are investigating it as a homicide?"

They both let the question linger. Correa finally relented after a deep breath. "Yes."

"Thank you. I will make sure to put a line in my story saying you can't comment any further on an ongoing investigation."

"Thank you," Correa said. "I'll send out a release when we *can* comment further. Until then, I can't say anything else. You know I'm not trying to be difficult, right?"

Kat knew he was being sincere and regretted cursing at him earlier, even if it was only in her head. She thanked Correa for the information and hung up, then opened the email app on her phone and began thumbing the story. She copied in Bishop.

Subject: HOT story for website, will fill in for print this afternoon

Officials ID girl found near Bison Ridge; DPS begins homicide investigation

By Katherine Hallaway

Morning Standard Staff

khallaway@amarillostandard.com

BISON RIDGE — Officials on Monday confirmed the identity of a girl found dead near Bison Ridge this week, and a Department of Public Safety spokesman said her death is being investigated as a homicide.

Vista County Sheriff Shawn Nichols identified the victim as RayLynn Gutierrez, 16, who was discovered Sunday morning just outside the small town about 70 miles north of Amarillo. Nichols said he did not have autopsy results Monday morning and could not provide a possible cause of death.

DPS spokesman Alex Correa said the Texas Rangers are leading the investigation and are treating Gutierrez's death as a homicide. He said he could not comment further because the investigation is ongoing.

Nichols also said he could not comment on the investigation, but said his office will lend support as needed.

"We will do anything we can to assist the Texas Rangers as they look into RayLynn's death," Nichols said.

Kat grinned as she hit send. It had been a while since she felt this excited. She used to break news on a regular basis. She had been perhaps one of the most sought-after reporters in the state. After her first Reporter of the Year award, Kat had been asked to the annual APME convention and awards ceremony. It rotated annually, and that year it had been held in Corpus Christi. She participated on a panel with two other female journalists to discuss their struggles in the profession, and recount how they'd risen to such heights. The other two were editors at some of the largest papers in the state. She felt out of place and wondered why they'd asked her there. She found out at the swanky dinner that night at the Texas state aquarium when they honored her with a second Reporter of the Year award. She didn't remember much about the "hospitality" portion of the itinerary that night in the hotel's seventeenth-floor suite.

A lot had changed after Kat learned she would be starting a family, and Kat hadn't resembled that reporter in years. Now she was faced with either finding that girl again or jeopardizing her family.

Then there was the Levi Cole of it all. But, if he could help Kat keep her job, it might be worth re-engaging with him. The time on her phone read 11:57. If she hauled ass, there would be just enough time.

Chapter Eight

Levi pulled out the last piece of sugar-free gum from his pack and checked his watch. 12:54. He had to go in a few minutes, with or without Kat. He'd have nothing to say without her. She was going to leave him looking like a damn fool. Again. Levi knew he deserved a measure of blame for what had happened between them. But she started it, and there's not a man alive who would've acted differently.

Levi had been helping the copy desk proof sports pages after covering a West Texas A&M football game in Canyon. Kat had walked into the sports office—she occasionally stayed right up to deadline on Saturday nights, when there was no shortage of alcohol-induced wrecks—and unloaded on him. That night's wreck had been worse than most. A drunken wrong-way driver on Interstate 40 hit a sedan head-on, killing his unbuckled three-year-old son and the other driver. Because the universe is twisted, the father survived. The drunk drivers always did. Perhaps living with what he did that night was poetic justice. Kat thought he deserved a firing squad.

After her rant, Kat leaned over Levi's right shoulder to read the lede to his game story and offer notes. He breathed her in. Not her perfume. Her. Levi's distracted brain told him it was just pheromones, nothing supernatural. It also reminded him that she was married. And a co-worker. He had the same internal dialogue every time she got this close to him. Small talk usually distracted him enough to get through it, but Kat wasn't having that tonight.

She leaned closer to his ear and ran a finger across the back of his neck. *Meet me at my desk when you're done.* Levi had to wait a few minutes before walking out into the newsroom anyway, so he finished proofing the pages. After he handed them to the copy deskers, Levi and Kat walked across the bullpen to the door that led to the back stairwell. Levi wondered if she'd ever taken other men up on their offers to cheat.

Rather than leading Levi into the bowels of the mostly unused building, Kat took him upstairs and into a room at the top of the steps. The door was short, and even Kat had to duck before entering and switching on the light. She called it The Hobbit Room. She'd found it trying to find roof access so she could smoke without going down to the sidewalk. *I always feel like I'm on display, you know, like some drug addict getting a fix instead of working.* Levi constantly teased her about quitting, but she always brushed it aside.

On the floor of The Hobbit Room were pillows and an old quilt. Some books were stacked in the corner beside a bottle of air freshener, which hadn't done enough to mask the room's smell. Kat dropped to her knees, then sprawled out on her stomach before rolling over to look up at Levi. *It's more comfortable than it looks. You should come down here. It'll be worth it. I promise.*

Women didn't seduce Levi. He was overweight—though there was enough muscle underneath to convince people he wasn't a walking heart attack waiting to happen—and back then Levi had found most of his romance on dating apps or at closing time. Kat would be, by far, the sexiest woman he'd slept with since college.

When thinking back like this, Levi always told himself he tried resisting. Whether or not that was true was irrelevant. He spread her knees before softly tracing her outer thighs, waist, and sides. Levi paused when they were face to face and dropped the weight of his hips against hers, allowing her to feel what he was thinking. He could smell her again. Kat wrapped her legs around his waist. The rest of Levi's blood rushed south.

• • •

Levi checked his watch again. 12:58. He pushed his door open and stepped out of the Optima trying to figure out what the hell to do now. He started for the front door of the school then heard Ol' Faithful's squealing serpentine belt.

"Thought you weren't going to show," Levi said as she slammed her door shut.

"Don't make me regret this. What am I doing here?"

"RayLynn, the dead girl, she was the editor of the student newspaper. We're going to talk to the class."

"Do they know I'll be there?"

"Not yet."

As Kat strode closer, Levi tried to decide if she'd changed clothes. At the very least she'd let down her wavy brown hair. It now hung below her collarbone and shoulder blades. She usually had it pulled back with all manner of torture devices—reason 259 Levi was thankful to have been born male—but he loved this look so much better, and she knew that. The black blazer was the same as at the courthouse, but he was convinced the white V-cut T-shirt underneath was different. They walked side-by-side toward the brick school, which had been built to mirror the courthouse. Levi opened the glass door leading to the common area and held it for Kat. She brushed past him quickly with her head down. He smelled her perfume. Had she been wearing it before?

As he regained his focus, Levi clocked a young brunette fingering her phone in the otherwise empty commons, her black skirt as short as she could get away with inside a school building.

"Dawn, so sorry we're late," he said.

"Mr. Cole." Her head snapped up with a beaming smile. "Don't worry about it. We're just so excited you're here, though the secretary didn't mention anyone else." Dawn sized up Kat and frowned.

"That's my fault. Dawn, this is Katherine Hallaway, a friend and reporter from the *Morning Standard*."

"Nice to meet you," Kat said, extending her left hand.

Dawn awkwardly shook her hand and looked at Levi. "We'd better get going. You realize that I don't have approval to let her interview any students, right?"

"Absolutely. We just ran into each other at lunch, and I thought your students would benefit even more from having a local reporter here, too."

Dawn nodded and led them down the main hall, which seemed much smaller than he remembered. Levi tried to remember his old locker number but came up empty. He hadn't thought much about high school since he left. There were a couple of friends he tried to keep up with for a while after graduation, but he hadn't had any real contact with them in years. He was "friends" with them on social media and liked their posts sometimes. That was enough. Maybe if things had gone differently back then, he'd have tried harder.

* * *

"All right, calm down," said Dawn Somethingorother. Kat had asked Dawn for her last name just before they walked into the classroom but had already forgotten it. She hoped it was written in her notebook.

"We have some very special guests with us today," Dawn continued. "First, we have Levi Cole, the renowned, award-winning journalist who all but single-handedly exposed the governor two years ago. Not only is he one of our most famous graduates, but Levi is the reason this class exists."

Dawn paused, and Levi flashed a bright, fake smile.

"And with Levi is his friend and former colleague from the *Amarillo Morning Standard*, Katherine Hallaway."

I'm an award-winning journalist, too, damnit. But, though she would never admit it, Kat knew she no longer had the more impressive resume. She didn't know how Levi had gone from a small-town sportswriter to regular cable news contributor and charming political pundit. She used to think people were incapable of change, but Levi could still make her question her beliefs, even in absentia.

"We are so fortunate to have Levi and his friend here today. It's not often we get to have a bona fide celebrity with us. So, let's don't be shy."

"Afternoon everyone," Levi said. "So, let's address the elephant in the room. We're all still grieving. Reporters, from Kat and me and you, all the way up to the *New York Times*, are a pretty small community.

Any time that group gets smaller in such a tragic way, we all get sad. They were sad in Annapolis, but the *Capital Gazette* put out a paper that night. Now you must keep doing your job. That's the way RayLynn would want it. You may not feel like what you do here is important because it's just high school, but it is."

Kat turned her head to face Levi. She almost didn't recognize him now. Levi had always loved to hear himself talk, even if he didn't have anything profound to say. But now Levi seemed genuinely confident and looked like he was born to be in front of a camera. That hadn't always been the case. Levi was at least fifty pounds lighter, with a thinner face that enhanced his square jaw and traditionally handsome looks. His face was clean shaven when she'd seen him on TV, but Levi now had that three-day, movie-star stubble he could never pull off before. She imagined how it might feel on her skin. Levi had also ditched his glasses. She examined his dynamic hazel eyes, which had always been his best feature — real ladykillers that seemed to change colors with his mood. She was jealous that everybody with a TV now had a chance to enjoy them. He wasn't wearing contacts, either. *He must've gotten Lasik.* Kat approved.

Levi's eyes were green as he spoke in front of the class. He was happy.

He turned his back to the students and walked over to Dawn, getting inappropriately close, Kat thought.

"I almost forgot," he whispered. "Could you go to the yearbook lab and see if someone can email RayLynn's most recent yearbook photo to Katherine? Just for a mugshot to go with her stories. It would mean a lot to me."

He motioned for Kat to join them. She dug through her purse for a business card and handed one to Dawn, who stood about six inches taller than Kat in her heels. Dawn looked down at the card, stalling while she contemplated leaving her class in their hands.

"Of course, Mr. Cole. Anything for you," Dawn said. "I'll also get permission from the office to let your friend interview one of the students, our assistant editor. But she's not here today. Mrs. Hallaway will have to call later."

Kat pictured Dawn leading Levi into a janitor's closet. *Slut.* But, at least she was a useful slut. After the door closed, muting the annoying sound of Dawn's heels, Levi turned back toward the class.

"Like I was saying, I know how bad this hurts right now. But journalists have to deal with death. Sometimes often, especially if you've got the police beat like my good friend Kat here. So, we're gonna talk about RayLynn's death today. Reporters play several roles when they cover a tragedy like hers. There are a lot of stories that can be written, but what do y'all think is the most important one?"

"Community reaction," offered a freckle-faced girl in the front row.

"Good guess, but no. That is important, but it's not what I'm looking for."

"Reporting the facts of how she died," said a beefy boy from the back.

"Close. But, despite the phrase, we're looking for a little more than 'Just the facts, ma'am.'" Levi paused for laughter, but none came. His audience was way too young to know "Dragnet," let alone the Joe Friday parody during which that phrase had been coined.

"All right, for time's sake, I'm gonna give you the answer. The most important thing we can do is find and report the truth."

"Isn't that what I just said?" beefy barked, causing some in the class to laugh.

Levi stood up straighter. "No. You said report the facts. I assume you meant as dictated by police, school officials, etcetera. But reporters don't always get useful information from authorities. Instead, we need to look for the *truth*, which is not always the same thing. In this case, if I were covering her story, I would be looking for the truth about who RayLynn was before she died. Telling your readers who someone was in their life can be as important as reporting how they died. Doing this requires a variety of sources. So, if we were to try and get to the truth behind RayLynn's story, who would we need to talk to?"

Levi turned to Kat and held up a black dry-erase marker. Kat cocked her head, but then the lightbulb turned on. She snatched the marker from his hand and began compiling her list of sources.

Kat looked over and caught Levi staring. She bit her lower lip and pushed her ass away from the wall. It had taken her a lot longer than it used to, but Kat's body was taking over. She tried to keep up with the names being tossed around by the students, but Kat's mind was busy imagining Levi coming up from behind her, one hand grabbing a fistful of her hair as the other slipped down her flat stomach until …

The sound of the classroom door opening brought Kat back to the present. She stayed facing the whiteboard, embarrassed that she was wet in front of a classroom full of high-schoolers.

CHAPTER NINE

Elliott Dawson read the text message from Trooper Alex Correa in the communications department blankly, as though he'd been told the sun had once again risen in the east.

Heads up. Vista Co. sheriff told reporter we're handling Gutierrez. Threw her bone, told her it was probably homicide, but no further comment.

Though the media, and by extension the public, was never supposed to know about his involvement until after an arrest was made, Elliott had enough experience to know something like this would demand attention sooner rather than later. Elliott had been with the DPS for decades, and with Company C of the Texas Rangers for the last five years. He worked out of the Dumas office and was available to nearby towns and rural counties. It wasn't exactly a metropolis, but homicides in his slice of the Panhandle kept Elliott busy enough.

But, as he studied the case file for RayLynn Gutierrez, Dawson felt like a rookie investigator. Of the homicides he worked, at least half were drug-related murders. Of the remaining fifty percent, most were either home invasions, domestic disputes, hunting accidents, or other accidental shootings. Elliott didn't have the exact numbers in front of him. But of this, he was certain—the number of sadistic, gruesome, ritualistic murders he'd investigated now stood at one.

Elliott was glad he hadn't thrown up on his full quill ostrich boots when he saw the body on Sunday. But now that the shock had worn off, the most worrisome aspect was how carefully the murder had been executed. With no fingernails or toenails, there was no chance to look for skin cells if she'd put up a fight, and the preliminary autopsy indicated her entire body had been doused with bleach. This case was on the fast track, so he'd have the full report in a day or less.

RayLynn Gutierrez had been staged in the pasture with no blood nearby, so his "crime scene" would not be of much help, either. There were indentations in the dirt indicating someone had carried her to the spot where a Vista County deputy had found her, but no shoeprints. The killer likely walked in socks or medical booties. The area was a known party spot among the Bison Ridge student population, so there were too many sets of tire tracks to bother trying.

In TV shows and movies, the genius investigator would find a clue in what was done to the body and how it was staged. That would lead to a Da Vinci Code puzzle that would identify the killer. While he was a proud member of the top investigative unit in the great state of Texas, there was no way on God's green Earth that Elliott would be able to do that alone. Elliott picked up the black receiver and punched the number to his superior, Lieutenant J. Henry Winters in Amarillo.

"Hi LT, it's Dawson."

"Heard you caught a bad one."

"Yes, sir. That's why I'm calling. I think we may need to call in someone with a little more expertise. Maybe someone who's worked a serial killer before."

"Serial killer?"

"Yes. I'll fax over the file tonight so you can take a look. I don't know if a serial killer may have done this, but ... well, you'll understand when you see it."

"Maybe. But Dawson, I don't want you to say the words *serial killer* again. Just saying that three times might summon a fed out of thin air. And you know how I feel about the feds."

"Yes, sir. I'll fax you that file as soon as we hang up. Have a good afternoon, sir."

Lt. Winters abhorred the FBI, especially now that they were considered dirty liberals out to help establish a one world government. Or something like that. Elliott tuned out Lt. Winters when he began ranting about politics. Elliott didn't get into all that very much, and since he'd never interacted with the FBI, he had no strong feelings either way.

Elliott walked out of his office with the file. "Loretta, can you do me a favor and fax this to Lieutenant Winters in Amarillo?"

"Of course." Elliott inherited Loretta, a civilian assistant, from his predecessor. She was in her fifties and had a GED, but Loretta was likely the smartest person in the building.

"Wouldn't it be easier to scan and email it to him?" she asked.

"You know Lieutenant Winters," Dawson said. "He's old school. But, if you're up for it, I could use a digital copy for my computer and tablet."

"Of course. Anything else?"

"Yeah. Could you ask around and see if any other departments have books about investigating serial or ritualistic killings that I could borrow?"

Elliott knew he would need all the help he could get. He'd never been a very ambitious man, but Elliott took pride in his work. He closed cases as efficiently as he could while still going home for dinner every night. When he watched detective shows and movies with his wife, Elliott always snickered when the investigators inevitably get so wrapped up in a case that they lose sleep and obsess to the point of getting suspended. They're always driven to drink and let their world devolve into chaos.

That fiction ignores the fact that those detectives have spent years building a career. Rising to the level of investigator in any department is difficult, and it's a status worth protecting. If those detectives burned themselves out like that once or twice every year, they wouldn't survive seven seasons. Also, devoid of sleep and full of booze, they wouldn't be able to think clearly enough to solve a complex homicide.

Now, it was Elliott's turn. Unlike those television detectives, he just needed time and few more pieces of information.

Chapter Ten

Levi had suggested they meet for a drink in Amarillo after Kat filed her story. She agreed and told him to be at Drake's by seven. Levi enjoyed the drive south from Bison Ridge more than ever. There were even more hotels along I-40, and billboards featuring the sex store were still there. The Yellow City had retained its identity as the world's largest truck stop. He exited at Georgia Street and took it north to Historic Sixth Avenue, a stretch of bars, boutiques, and other old-timey shops that had once been a part of Route 66. Drake's had been a diner back then. Now it was a dive bar.

Levi walked through a thin film of cigarette smoke at 7:47 and slipped into what had been his favorite booth in the front left corner. The tabletop was grimy as ever, but on it sat a laminated drink menu with a note about their new patio out back. *Must be where most of the smokers are.* On the list of beers were a few that didn't have "Light" in the name. Drake's had been forced to keep up with the Joneses, though the Amarillo Joneses tended to be twenty years behind the rest.

He ordered a vodka-soda from a leggy waitress and prepared to wait. Levi was pathologically early, but Kat was in the Bermuda Triangle—nobody gets out of a newsroom on time. An hour late seemed about right, and yet he'd still beat her. He had no doubt she would show eventually. His plan was working. Levi had known Kat would be angry with him initially. But, he also knew that if he got near her, got her to let her guard down for even a moment, he'd have her. And what better way than offering to help her with a story? The fact that he was able to tap into her jealousy by flirting with another woman was an unexpected advantage.

Things would get more delicate from here. RayLynn had been murdered. Brutalized. When he'd read Kat's first brief on Sunday, he had planned to take her to families around town and get them to open up about RayLynn's tragic, but very accidental, passing. He nearly scrapped the operation, but then Levi remembered RayLynn had been editing the student newspaper and called the school to arrange his surprise visit. Levi considered the cards he still held. He knew where the body had been dumped, which was where Kat could find on-scene investigators for interviews, and he knew how the girl had died.

Using this information was a morbid means to a complicated end. Levi was about to be a homewrecker. But, if people knew how much he and Kat loved each other, how obvious it was that they were meant to be together, everyone who mattered would understand.

Levi finished his drink as Kat walked into Drake's. She slipped off her blazer, revealing the shirt that put on display her proudest assets — *They're D-cups, but still perky*, she used to say. *You don't know how special that is* — and hugged her slim waist.

"Still like sitting at this booth, huh?" Kat sat and leaned in after waving over the waitress.

"You remember why, right?"

"How could I forget. You were my knight in shining armor," Kat said before ordering a shot of tequila, straight, with no lime or salt. *She's not messing around.* Levi was about to order another skinny bitch, but he decided to indulge. It would be a night of indulgences. He requested a vanilla porter.

"I remember getting my ass kicked," Levi said. "But I like your version better, so we'll go with that."

Levi and Kat had been sleeping together for about a year when they were invited to Drake's to complain about work and life. Kat had been a regular there. She and Bill lived less than a half-mile away in the San Jacinto neighborhood, so having two or three too many wasn't a problem. The group had drifted away for one reason or another, leaving Levi to guard the pool table. Kat was the first to return, giving them a chance to be alone in the crowd for the first time that night. Kat was already on her third beer. *Next one's on you*, she said. It was a joke.

They were all on him. While they were dating—or whatever guys call it when they're serious with a married woman—Levi swore he'd pay for everything. Every man he knew would do the same. They locked eyes and brushed hands, getting all the contact they could out of the moments before their co-workers returned. That's why neither of them noticed the Drunken Idiots.

Levi barely heard the rumble over Kat's left shoulder, giving him just enough time to sidestep a pair of three hundred pounders barreling down on them through a thick cloud of smoke. Kat's dulled reactions allowed them to swallow her in a sweaty mass of fists and knees. Levi dove into the flesh without thinking, knocking away one of the Drunken Idiots and flinging her to the side of the mess. His duty done, Levi tried staggering to his feet before a fist connected with his mouth like a sledgehammer. Levi felt his front teeth give way somewhere between the third and fourth punches, liquid iron filling his mouth. He endured two more blows before a bouncer pulled the Drunken Idiot off him. Another bouncer lifted Levi up by his right arm and rushed him out the front door.

Since then, Levi had always insisted they sit at the booth in the front corner, where he could see the entire bar, and there was no chance of getting ambushed.

"You know what the best part of that story is?" Kat asked.

"I know what my favorite part is. What's yours?"

"When you started singing 'All I Want for Christmas is My Two Front Teeth.' The look on those paramedics' faces was priceless." Kat smiled and shot back her tequila. "What's your favorite part?"

"When I finally said I loved you."

Kat had been the only one laughing when Levi started singing. That was the moment he knew. Just before the ambulance doors closed, Levi looked at Kat and mouthed the three words he'd been holding back for months.

"Oh," Kat said. She got the waitress' attention and motioned to her for another round. "So, I appreciate your help today. I can't believe they actually let you bring me along."

Levi tried to hide his disappointment. Kat had never told Levi she loved him. He took the hint and joined her in discussing a new subject.

"Being a celebrity has its perks."

"And yet you've remained so humble. Dick."

Though far from a household name, Levi was a public figure now, complete with a Wikipedia page that claimed he "derailed a future presidency." Levi's reporting for the *Daily Star* had exposed the sexual and criminal misdeeds of the former Texas Governor Kenneth D. Lockwood III, who was American political royalty. Less prominent politicians had overcome sex scandals—dick pics, blowjobs in the Oval Office, etcetera—but Lockwood hadn't occasionally helped himself to underage hookers and cocaine. He'd instructed a border town police department to help provide the cartel safe passage for the drugs and the girls.

Not even Lockwood could come back from those accusations. The governor claimed innocence, but public opinion shifted swiftly against him, and he resigned two weeks after Levi's first story. The lieutenant governor who'd taken over was further to the right and an even bigger friend of Big Oil, but even liberals agreed that he was not another complete waste of human life.

All the cable news networks and Sunday shows wanted to have Levi on air, and his bosses were more than happy to oblige. His stories set unfathomable records for the paper's website, and the *Star* gave him a political blog that kept it humming. Even people on the coasts, who could care less about Texas, ate it up. Levi had given them sex, power, corruption, and American history, all in one scandal. The *Star* was proud of its shiny new toy. Shortly before running the story, the bosses resurrected a position that had years ago been a victim of the organization's downsizing by attrition. After all, shouldn't all *major* newspapers have a chief investigative reporter?

Levi had gone back on the circuit when the new election cycle hit, opining about national political issues he was not qualified to discuss. But the networks liked his look and easy way of connecting with viewers, and his introduction reminded viewers of the power the press once had and could have again. He was part actor, part status symbol, with a little journalist mixed in.

"So, where do you think you're gonna start?" Levi asked.

"With the congressman. The rest are obvious. Grandmother, best friends, principal, volleyball coach. But, I did need to get some of those names. I'm counting on you getting me numbers for any that aren't in the phone book."

"You still use the phone book?"

"Yes, Levi. Us real reporters do."

"I can do better than chasing down numbers," Levi said. "Get out your phone."

Kat hesitated before digging her phone out of her purse.

"Open your maps app," he said.

Kat pecked the screen a few times and handed the phone to Levi. "What are you doing?"

"I'm dropping a pin where Shawn found the body," he said. "Or close to it, anyway. Look for a big round water tank with 'Go Stampede' spray painted on it."

Levi handed the phone back to Kat, who snatched it from his grip as though it may escape if she didn't act quickly. "How'd you get this? Your sheriff buddy?"

"You know I can't tell you that."

"Oh, fuck off."

"I'm not going to tell you. It's all on deep background, anyway."

"Exactly, so what does it matter? Do you not think you can trust me?"

Levi opened his mouth but caught his comeback before it escaped and ruined the rapport he was building. Kat's expression changed, and she slammed the rest of her liquor before excusing herself to the restroom. She knew Levi well, probably well enough to know what he'd been thinking—*I don't know, can I?*

When she rounded the corner, Levi took the time to check his phone. He'd been forced to put it in airplane mode during their presentation at the high school. The network bookers, and some political bloggers, were calling him directly. The news had gotten out quickly.

After deleting his voicemails without listening, Levi closed his eyes and took a long drink. He hoped he could get the night back on track. He tried remembering the directions to the no-tell motel he and Kat used to use, a pay-by-the-hour place on Amarillo Boulevard they started frequenting after some kids nearly caught them in the parking lot of a nearby Catholic school. It wasn't romantic, but it was close, and nobody would find them there.

Levi didn't drink dark beer much anymore because it always led to bad food choices. Drake's didn't have a kitchen, but Levi remembered a vending machine in the back that had snacks and cigarettes. It had gum, too, but chocolate would be the perfect palate cleanser after the porter. He would only need one. That would be enough.

• • • •

Kat took a long drag. Men never questioned how long women spent in the bathroom. This afforded her the opportunity to sneak a smoke on the back patio. She also bought a pack of gum, hoping the spearmint and alcohol would mask the smoky taste later that night.

Kat also needed a chance to text Bill back. Yes, she would pick up more milk on the way home. No, she didn't have their son's favorite blanket in her truck.

Kat had missed her Llama Lights that afternoon. Eliminating the smell from her last cigarette that morning was part of the reason she'd sped to Yucca and bought a new shirt and perfume before meeting Levi. Of course, her choices were shaped by how she wanted the night to go. She'd resisted the urge to smoke after filing her story, knowing that Drake's would give her cover later and allow her this opportunity to avoid a fight with Levi.

"Smoking again, I see," Levi said from over her back shoulder.

Fuck my life. "You caught me," Kat said. She turned around and held up her hands in mock surrender, burning cigarette in her right and a cheap neon pink lighter in her left.

"You could've had a cigarette before now. I'm sure it must've been tough going this long."

"And there he is. Judgy, holier-than-thou Levi. It's been a while."

"Jesus H. Christ," Levi said. "I just said I didn't care."

Kat had quit for Levi and stayed smoke-free for the pregnancy, but she started again after her son's birth. Levi wasn't there to stop her then, and he had no right to say anything now. She'd been nice trying to hide it from him, but now he'd followed her outside and was giving her shit about it. Kat's skin flushed as the anger simmered.

"Whatever," she said, trying desperately to calm herself down. Kat still had a chance to get laid tonight, she just needed to stop pushing. The frustration might make the sex even better. His eyes had gotten that golden, *I'm horny* tint at the table earlier.

"Was that text from Bill?" Levi asked.

"Yeah. So?"

"Nothing. Just wondering."

Levi's eyes were no longer golden. *Fuck it. I guess we're doing this.*

"Just go ahead and say it."

"We don't need to—"

"Fuck you, Levi," Kat screamed.

"What do you want me to say?" Levi's irises were Arctic water.

"Say something real," Kat said. "I'll start. I hate how you left without trying to work things out."

"Work things out? You chose *him* over me. Did you expect me to stick around and be happy for you two?"

Kat's hands started shaking. She took another drag off her cigarette. "It wasn't like that, and you know it."

"Really?" Levi yelled. His left hand formed a fist, and his right pointed an accusatory finger an inch from her nose. "How was it then, you slutty fucking cu—"

"Hey asshole, leave the lady alone," Kat heard from over her shoulder, almost drowning out the end of Levi's thought. It was one of the large bartenders who recognized her. Kat noticed a half-dozen people on the patio watching the scene through their cellphones.

"Things got complicated, and you ran." Kat took a step toward Levi and leaned in. "You're a shallow fucking *coward*," she whispered, "and that's worse."

CHAPTER ELEVEN

An hour outside the city, past the blinking red lights atop hundreds of wind turbines, an oil refinery bobbed as he drove over the hilly plains of the northern Panhandle, a lighthouse in some distant harbor. He still had muscle memory honed by countless hours navigating the highways and Farm-to-Market roads that crisscross the region, most of which he logged as a high school sportswriter for the *Standard*. It wasn't Levi, but his car, who was navigating the area where the Canadian River had once cut through the Great Plains, forming the north edge of the Llano Estacado.

• • •

Golf had been on Levi's Sunday morning agenda four years ago, followed by another great night's sleep, then a pre-work scouting trip with Kat in the morning. She was leaving Bill and looking for an apartment. Levi had suggested she move in with him, but Kat was still trying to fool everyone — though Levi was sure she was mostly trying to convince herself that everyone in their lives didn't already know they were together — and wanted to have an appropriate mourning period between leaving Bill and making her relationship with Levi official. Levi didn't see the point of the secrecy anymore. He and Kat were no longer the villains in this scenario.

Bill had cheated on her.

Kat had answered Bill's phone while he showered because the caller ID said *Work*. The woman said her name was Charlene, and she needed to tell Bill about a schedule change. Kat told Levi she had thought it was a strange conversation to have with a print shop that was open from eight to five. But, there were plausible scenarios. Perhaps Bill was planning some time off from work? The shop was open on Saturdays, and maybe he was trying to pick up extra shifts? Kat said she hadn't thought too much about it when she hung up, but then she noticed Bill had a missed text message from *Work*. Kat had called the print shop several times to talk to Bill when he didn't answer his cellphone — Bill never had it charged, and Kat had often thought it was on purpose so he had reasons to not answer calls or respond to texts — and it had a landline that worked just fine. So, who from his job was using their cell to talk to Bill?

Kat had sobbed on Levi's shoulder when she recounted the photo of a woman's breasts popping up on the screen. *They were so horrible,* she'd said. *Mine are so much better. This doesn't make any sense.* The photo was just below one of Bill's, his own junk as unimpressively endowed — that's how Kat described it. The text conversation went back for months. Kat said she was even more hurt by what they talked about. Bill had confided in Charlene about his *loveless* marriage to Kat. He described to her the distance that had grown between them, which combined with the lack of sex had made him depressed. Soon enough Bill and his mistress had developed a secret code that Kat said was so easy to decipher she almost felt embarrassed for them. Any mention of The Tower was a mention of sex. Ostensibly, The Tower was meant to mean The Chase Tower, the closest thing Amarillo had to a skyscraper. But, for them, it was *the world's smallest, most phallic symbol*, according to Kat. Sometimes they'd talk about needing to go to The Tower to get coffee, or about the great time she had there the day before. Sometimes she commented on how she couldn't get over how big The Tower was. Kat had told Levi she was thankful when she heard Bill turn the shower off so she had to put down the phone and stop reading.

Levi had tried to console Kat when she came to him a couple weeks before his tee time, though he'd probably sounded insincere. He was going to get everything he wanted, everything he'd dreamed about in the year since the fight at Drake's. But just as Levi was loading his clubs into the trunk of his new Optima — a thirty-eight miles-per-gallon expense he reasoned would pay for itself — his phone rang.

"Hey you," Levi said. His smile fell away when he heard Kat. "Hey hey hey. What's wrong, hon?"

"I can't," Kat said, though Levi could barely hear her through the sobbing. "I just can't do it."

"Can't do what, hon?" Levi's question was half rhetorical.

"I can't move out. I can't leave him."

"We've been through this Kat," Levi said. "Of course you can. You two don't love each other anymore. You love me."

Kat resumed her weeping. One half of Levi's heart sympathized with her. The other felt betrayed. "Listen. Just come over, and we'll talk about this again," Levi continued. "You're not leaving today, or even tomorrow. We're just looking at a place for you to stay temporarily."

"I'm pregnant, Levi. I'm pregnant."

"When did you find out?"

"Friday."

Levi had gone with Kat to the doctor on Wednesday. He told her it was stress from the recent revelations, but she insisted she'd been fighting a stomach bug. She wanted to go in and make sure it wasn't food poisoning or the flu.

"The doctor got your blood work back," Levi said.

"I swear I had no idea. I never even did an at-home test. I wasn't even a week late."

"Was the doctor able to tell how far along you are?"

Levi badly wanted her to say three weeks. That would mean the baby was his. He and Kat been so careful to use condoms the entire time they'd been together — except once, about a month ago. Levi also knew that Kat and Bill never slept together anymore. She said it had been years. Levi figured she was bullshitting him, but if Saint Bill had cheated, maybe she was telling the truth.

"About a month," Kat said.

Levi's smile returned. "Oh honey, we're going to have — "

"Were you not fucking listening earlier? I said I'm not leaving Bill. He's the father."

"Umm, that's impossible, right? I mean, we were both there a month ago. And you and Bill haven't slept together in years, right?

That's why he was cheating, right?"

Kat started sobbing again. *She's been lying to me. She's been sleeping with Bill, too.* Levi clenched his teeth. "Okay. Say you're not lying. Worst-case scenario is you don't know who the father is. When can we do a DNA test?"

"I'm not going to do that. I'm starting a family with Bill."

Throughout their time together, Kat had always told Levi she loved Bill. They had a connection that Levi had been unable to break. Kat's love for Bill remained through all the years she and Levi had slept together—including the last year when Levi told Kat he loved her nearly every day. Levi had even proposed to Kat twice. He'd never bought a ring. Levi knew she would say no, and he eventually gave up on the idea of tearing Kat away from her husband. Only Bill himself could tarnish the reputation of Saint Bill. But now that he'd done it— and she was about to have a baby with Levi—Kat was still refusing to leave him.

"Kat, listen to yourself. What are we going to do if the baby comes out looking like me? You think Bill's just going to be okay with that?"

"I'm telling you, the baby is his. But even if it's not, Bill won't see you when he looks at it. He has no idea we're sleeping together."

"Oh, wake the fuck up already. He knows. Everybody fucking knows."

"Do your parents know?"

Levi took a short pause. "That's different. I don't talk about you much when I'm with them. And I'm careful not to sit by you or touch you when we're all together."

"I'm that careful with Bill. You just don't see it. Plus, he loves me— unconditionally."

"And I don't?"

"I hope you do. I also hope you'll be here for my baby and me."

Levi's knuckles went white around his phone.

"Are you telling me that if that baby is mine—and we both know it is—you want me to keep everything the same? Just be a part of its life as Uncle Levi, mommy's special friend, who occasionally fucks her when it's convenient for her? Is that what you're telling me right now?"

"Yes. And if you're right about Bill knowing, I think there's a chance he'll be all right with us having a kind of open thing, you kn—"

Levi launched his cellphone across the apartment complex parking lot and watched as it shattered. He stared at the broken pieces. It was okay. He had a backup. It wasn't as good, but it was better than the mess he was looking at. Levi found the SIM card, went back upstairs to his apartment and found his old phone hiding in the bottom left drawer of his desk. Beside it was the old *Dallas Daily Star* badge from when he was an intern there, which seemed like a lifetime ago. Levi shoved the phone and ID into his pocket, packed some essential clothing, toiletries, anything he thought could be valuable at a pawn shop, and didn't stop driving until he hit the truck stop in Jolly.

• • •

As he crossed back into Vista County, Levi decided he and Kat were both right. What she had done was nearly unforgivable—nearly—and he had chosen to run and hide rather than face the mess in Amarillo. She'd texted him a couple years ago with a photo of the boy. He was a miniature Bill Hallaway. There was also the photo of a DNA test confirming the toddler as Bill's. Levi had been thankful for that, though never told her.

Knowing he was not a deadbeat dad had changed Levi's outlook on life. That's when he stopped drinking himself to sleep, started eating better, and began working out. He had successfully made a clean break and could reinvent himself. He had also started exchanging pleasant texts with Kat on holidays and her birthday. Levi thought perhaps he and Kat could remain long-distance friends, nothing more. But time and distance were the best healers of emotional wounds, and in the months leading up to his dismissal from the *Daily Star*, Levi had started dreaming about a life with Kat by his side—perhaps as the host of his own cable news show. Then fate, in the form of some asshole with a typewriter and a God complex who felt like toying with Levi's career, intervened and gave him a chance to make that dream come true.

Then, in five minutes at a bar in Amarillo, Levi had blown that idea to Hell. As he replayed the fight again—*I don't really think she's a … that … do I?*—Levi found himself staring straight into a pair of headlights in his lane. He jerked the steering wheel to his right and prayed his car wouldn't roll.

CHAPTER TWELVE

Levi attempted a graceful exit from his car—which had remained upright without any airbag deployment—but barbed-wire struggled to keep his driver's side door closed. He used his weight to bail out, cutting his left calf as he fell face-first into the plains. Levi stood. His neck felt fine, though straightening his back was a struggle. His calf stung from the cut, but Levi didn't think he was seriously injured. He wiped his brow and checked for blood, but it was just sweat. He assumed the warmth he felt was from the adrenaline, which had also heightened his senses because "Pretty Woman" sounded like it was blaring from his car radio despite the fact Levi hated loud music when he drove at night.

Convinced he didn't need to call 911, Levi finished brushing himself off and assessed the situation. There was plenty of paint damage from the fence, and his rear driver's side tire was flat. It was the only one, though, so driving home seemed possible. He was about to pop the trunk when Levi saw red-and-blue flashing lights behind him. He quickly counted the drinks he'd had at Drake's. Three, though the dark beer counted as two. Too many to be driving, but he didn't think it wasn't enough to have caused the wreck. An idiot wrong-way driver was to blame, but the cop would already be expecting to issue a DUI. Levi hadn't been in trouble with the law since college, but his prints and mugshot were in the system after a night spent in a downtown Amarillo drunk tank.

The SUV's headlights once again left Levi blind as he felt a trickle of blood snake its way into his left sock.

"Looks like you could use a little help."

Levi let out the air that had been unconsciously trapped in his lungs. "Man am I glad to see you."

Levi had never been so happy to see Vista County Sheriff Shawn Nichols, who helped Levi change the tire and push the car away from the fence. A few posts had been unearthed and were scattered on the ground. The damage could be quickly fixed, and he would be able to drive home if he could keep Nichols from asking too many questions and testing his blood-alcohol level. Though he was friendly with Nichols, Levi wasn't counting on him looking the other way.

"Well, I suppose it's time for me to ask the question," Nichols said.

Shit shit shit shit shit shit shit.

"I don't follow. What question?"

"Don't act dumb."

"You're going to have to help me out here," Levi said, hoping he sounded more convincing to Nichols than he sounded to himself.

"How's your investigation coming along?" Nichols asked.

"What investigation?"

Nichols chuckled. "You've been gone too long. Everyone already knows about your visit to the high school. And it sounds like you brought along your reporter friend. The one I talked to right after you."

Levi froze. He wasn't sure if his goosebumps were from the chill in the air—the temperature had dipped into the fifties, and his sweat from earlier now felt ice cold—or the thought of Nichols retaliating against him for not staying out of the investigation.

Nichols was silent as he picked up the tire iron and small hydraulic jack they'd used to change the tire.

"I'm sorry, Shawn. I know you told me to stay out of this," Levi said. "It's just that Kat and I have a long history."

Nichols stayed silent as he walked the tools to the back of his Explorer. Levi remained planted, unsure of what he could do, other than keep trying to talk his way out of this situation.

"All I did was point her in the direction of some people who knew the girl, so she can do a profile piece," Levi continued. "I mean, it's not like she's going to solve this case before you or the freaking Texas Rangers."

Nichols slammed shut the back hatch of his SUV and walked out to face Levi. He widened his stance a bit and shifted his right hand to his holster. "I think what we've got here is a failure to communicate."

Levi took a panicked step back and looked behind him to see if he was close enough to dive into the Optima. He wasn't. Levi had begun hyperventilating when he turned back, only to find Nichols doubled over in laughter.

"*Network*," Nichols said as he stood up straight. "I guess they don't show that one in journalism school."

"Jesus Christ, dude. You scared the living shit out of me."

"You don't think I would shoot you just for asking questions? Just keep that Hallaway woman out of my hair and let me know if y'all find anything that might help."

"Will do," Levi said. "So, should we put these fence posts back in the ground, or do I need to call the landowner, or what?"

"Don't worry about it. I got this. I don't know how to put this, but I'm kind of a big deal."

"*Anchorman*," Levi said. The Vista County Sheriff's strange, never-ending game was a welcome distraction as Levi tried not to think about his past or what kind of future he could cobble together.

CHAPTER THIRTEEN

Levi woke up in his childhood bed feeling hung over. It wasn't the alcohol, but the emotional bloodletting. Happiness. Fury. Fear. More real emotion than he'd felt in years, sardined into one shitty day.

In movies and on TV, the parents have always preserved their adult child's bedroom. Not in real life. In fact, Levi wasn't even in *his* room. They'd moved his queen bed into his younger brother's old room, while Levi's was now his father's fly-tying station and lure storage area. Over the years, the bed he was laying in had been used by dozens of Bison Ridge's youth. On the floor, there was a mixture of Barbies, Transformers, baseball mitts, and an Easy-Bake Oven. Levi rolled off the mattress, turned left and nearly walked into the hall closet through half-open eyes before turning around and starting toward the kitchen, ready to sit down for breakfast.

"So, he is alive," his mother said, loudly blowing out a forty-year smoker's puff. "What happened last night?"

Levi ignored the question. "Nothing much. Sorry I got in so late. I hope I didn't wake y'all up."

"Nah," his mother said. "Just wondering."

Levi knew his mother wouldn't push him. She was a patient woman, and they both knew he would talk eventually. But, for now, he sat down at the kitchen table to eat his generic marshmallow cereal. He hadn't eaten sugar by the spoonful in years. It was a potent drug, and he prayed it would help bury his guilt.

"You checked the Internet today, hon?" she asked.

"No," Levi said through a mouthful, trying to slurp back in some escaping milk. "Why?"

"Take a look. Then call Kat."

"Why?" Levi asked as he choked down his bite. His mother just repeated her line and stood to get another cup of coffee. Levi gulped the rest of his sugar milk before walking back to the room to get his phone. On the way back to the table, he stopped cold.

"Mom, I—"

"Levi, you don't have to say anything. I'm not mad."

Just disappointed. That was the one way she got Levi and his friends to behave in high school. They did dumb stuff growing up—pasture parties, house parties, firecrackers in the living room—but they tried to never do anything that would genuinely disappoint her.

The video he'd just watched had undoubtedly done that on so many levels. She now knew her son was a cheater. She might've known it anyway, but his mother had never been told about the affair explicitly—perhaps because she'd never come out and asked directly. Levi had known he would have to explain it all to his parents before he ran off to the East Coast with Kat. But he'd wanted to do it on his terms, in his own way, with Kat by his side, her hand in his.

After their fight last night, Levi had already known that difficult confrontation would never happen. But the existence of a video of their exchange—which he found quickly and without much effort—raised a new problem. Not only did Levi's parents now have confirmation of his affair with Kat, but Levi's mother would now have to defend her son to everyone. The old lady who worked at the post office. The cashiers at the AllStop convenience store. The servers at DQ. And, as if the affair weren't sleazy enough, he'd called Kat that vulgar word. That would likely be viewed as worse than the revelation of their relationship.

Levi ran back to the room, threw on some clothes—complete with a Longhorns ball cap that he could pull down low—picked up his duffel bag and wished for an invisibility cloak as he snuck out the door.

"Call Kat," his mother shouted as he tried to quietly shut the door.

Levi threw up in the street. He couldn't decide if it was from the cereal or the thought of facing Kat.

• • •

Elliott slumped in his leather chair. Loretta had done the best she could. She'd found a musty handbook that included a chapter on "Deviant Killers," which had been neatly bookmarked. He did not feel any wiser after reading the pages. He'd be better off watching horror movies or surfing the Internet. He woke up his desktop and saw an unread email from his hardworking assistant. She'd emailed him a list of links on ritualistic murders. She'd also attached the digital copy of his file on RayLynn Gutierrez. Elliott's mood perked up a bit, knowing he wasn't alone in this. He could enlist other Rangers from around the company if needed, but Loretta was his true partner and had proven over the years to be a better investigator than most other Rangers with whom Elliott had worked.

On the email was a second attachment—a scanned copy of a letter Lt. Winters had faxed earlier that morning.

Ranger Elliott Dawson,

I have reviewed your file. While this homicide is unique, we will not be pursuing any federal assistance at this time. Due to the age of the victim, we will need to keep your investigation as discreet as possible. Any requests for additional resources are to go directly through me.

Regards,

Lt. J. Henry Winters

Company C Commander

Department of Public Safety, Rangers Division

Elliott hadn't been hopeful he'd get Lt. Winters' permission to request help from the FBI, but he was still disappointed. He also noted that Lt. Winters would have to give the okay for any help, even if it was just more DPS officers. He had also not mentioned getting it solved quickly, just quietly, which meant Elliott wouldn't be asking him for departmental help, either. The more investigators that showed up in an area as small as Bison Ridge, the less *discreet* the investigation would become. The headlines would be much more to the department's liking if they could announce an arrest before the public knew the nature of the case.

Elliott started clicking Loretta's links and reading. From the material, Elliott surmised the killer was sending a message. Something about faith and sex, given that she was staged to look like Jesus on the cross and had been branded with the universal symbol for pornography. Elliott hoped the medical examiner's full autopsy report would provide some physical evidence he could use because he was getting nowhere trying to derive any meaning from how her body had been staged. So what if someone wanted folks to know she was an ungodly girl who was having too much sex? Did that make her different from any other sixteen-year-old around here? It would not be unusual for a girl that age to be having sex, perhaps with multiple partners. But, burning XXX into her chest was bold. That and the holes drilled into her hands and feet were more than the acts of a jilted boyfriend. It was not a crime of passion. The planning, the use of tools, the amount of time she'd been missing, all indicated a fair amount of premeditation. In the absence of any other evidence, Elliott ruled out the student body of Bison Ridge High School as suspects. Elliott closed his web browser and shut his eyes.

Who does that leave?

•   •   •

"Kat, I need you for a sec."

Shit.

"Rough night?" Bishop asked.

Kat just stared at her boss. She'd barely rolled out of bed in time to get to work by 9 a.m., and Kat was sure she still reeked of booze and cigarettes. After leaving Drake's, she'd stopped by a Party Barn and bought a bottle of tequila. She tried to tell Bill that she was starting a new tradition, "Margarita Monday." He had asked what was wrong. She said she was just having a tough time covering this girl's death, which Bill must've found plausible enough. He'd put Michael down and let her sit with the bottle. Bill knew when to leave her alone and let her internal cage match play out.

"I hadn't realized Levi was back in town," Bishop continued.

"Um, yeah, he is—but how did you know?"

"You haven't been online yet today, have you?"

Kat's eyes widened as she brushed away the cobwebs. One of those nosy gawkers must've posted a video. Kat took off her glasses and dropped her face into her hands.

"How bad is it?" Kat asked through her palms.

"The unedited version has a lot of F-bombs. And I don't know Levi, but I didn't realize he was like that."

Me either. "If you've seen a video of last night, it's not just on some weirdo's YouTube page, is it?"

Bishop turned to his computer and began reading as Kat stood to look over his shoulder.

"'*Scandal! Jousting journalists caught on tape.*' '*I can't believe a prominent journalist said THIS …*' And, '*C stands for more than Cole.*' Sorry you had to hear that."

"Well, you're not the one who called me a cunt, so no need to apologize."

"There's no need for you to repeat him. Especially not at work, please."

Bishop had visibly flinched at the word. He wasn't sheltered—his hair was gray, and his resume in newspapers was long—but Bishop was a gentleman. It's part of the reason he'd been hired earlier that year by the paper's new corporate overlords. Bishop was not controversial. He wouldn't rock the boat. And—most importantly to the East Coast megacorporation that had bought the *Standard*—Bishop would methodically get his staff to check all the boxes upper management required. His representation of that new mantra had turned the staff off. But his personality made up for it. The unfortunate truth was that Kat liked Bishop, despite her best efforts. And, because she liked him, Kat found herself teasing him on purpose.

"Sorry," Kat said. "How the hell did the video get picked up by *everybody* overnight?"

"Just your bad luck, I guess."

"So, all of this notwithstanding, did anything productive happen yesterday? Anything that will make a story?"

"Yeah. I need to talk to Jake about getting an interview with Ace Anderson."

Bishop looked puzzled. "I don't follow."

"The dead girl was a journalism student. She was working on a feature about Anderson for the high school and county papers. She'd interviewed him a couple times, I think. But I'll need to confirm that when I talk to him."

"All right, but tread lightly."

Kat nodded, left Bishop's office, and made her way across the bullpen to Jake Baker. Baker did not like to have other reporters work his sources. He was gruff and would tell just about anyone to fuck off, including Bishop.

Baker was Kat's favorite co-worker.

"Jake, what's up?" Kat asked.

"What do you want?"

"Good morning to you, too, friend."

"Look, I don't have time for bullshit right now, so just get to it already."

Baker was the paper's overworked senior reporter. He'd been able to focus primarily on politics earlier in his career, but now he covered just about every major story the paper printed. For the last few months, that had included a heavy load of election coverage. The House seat was up every two years, and this would be the first vote since the news industry had experienced the craziest, most controversial presidential election since anyone at the *Morning Standard* had been alive. That meant every election from now on would be the "biggest" until the political scene normalized—if it ever did.

"I need to talk to Ace Anderson," Kat said.

"No, you don't."

"Jake, I really do."

"Look, kid, I know you're hungry and need stories, but you can't come to me for help. I got my own shit to worry about over here."

"First, I'm not a kid," Kat said, trying not to sound too pissed off.

"Second, I need to talk to Anderson about a story I'm already chasing. You know that dead girl in Bison Ridge?"

"Yeah, we already got his quote in your last story. You're welcome, by the way."

"Well, she was a student reporter working on a story about Anderson for the Vista County and high school newspapers." Kat was getting bored explaining this to everyone.

"So what? You think there's another story there?"

"I don't know. But I sure as hell want to talk to him. Either way, I get to report a new piece of information. And with his name in the headline, people will click on it."

"Sounds like maybe I should be writing this story since he's—"

"Don't you try to fuck me on this, Jake," Kat said as she leaned in over his desk. "You owe me, remember?"

She and Baker stared at each other.

"Fine," he said, looking down and shuffling through his mountain of paper. "Meet me at the Coulter Church of Christ at three this afternoon. He's having a grip-and-grin there."

"See you there," she said, turning away from his desk and smiling. It had been a while since she worked this hard for something. Years had passed since she cared enough to fight for a subject she wanted to cover. As she sat down at her desk to go through emails, Kat thought about that subject. *What story am I chasing?*

CHAPTER FOURTEEN

Ace didn't *dislike* newspaper reporters. Not on principle, anyway. Hell, he'd used them to get elected the first time around. Despite his youth—even now he was only thirty-seven—Ace had known his base was curmudgeonly old white men who still got their news the old-fashioned way. They sat around coffee shops and DQs and on courthouse benches talking about what they'd read in the morning newspaper. They also loved to read the opinion page and write in with letters to the editor. During the political season, the *Courier* and the *Standard* had to print special rules every day telling letter writers not to get cross with each other or the candidate they didn't like. Matthews had said that for every letter in favor of a candidate, one or two dozen voters felt the same way, and even more would read and be influenced by the letters—and the papers' endorsements, both of which had gone Ace's way—so Matthews had factored the *Courier* and *Standard* heavily into their election strategy.

He needed reporters less this time around, if at all. Even the old men and their wives were on social media now. Plus, both newspapers had gone behind a paywall. Despite sharing their stories online, they weren't read by nearly as many voters. Subscribers could still read the stories online, but those numbers were down. Matthews had told Ace there were no hard figures for that sort of thing anymore, but his sources said both papers' circulations had dropped by double-digit percentage points. If those were election numbers, that would mean the newspapers were losing by a landslide.

The rapid deterioration of the area's newspapers had left a vacuum for Matthews and his staff to put whatever lies they wanted online.

They were paying a few interns to create websites that resembled those of real news organizations and write news-ish articles, then incorporate those fake facts, statistics, and quotes into slick-looking memes. Among those websites—which Ace had initially worried were illegal before Matthews assured him they weren't, though they were open to libel lawsuits the same as the real news media—the biggest hit was the *Panhandle Patriot-Statesman*. It looked professional, its "reporting" sounded professional, and it got dozens of comments every time a story was posted.

Though Matthews was a big believer in using these fake news sites, he held onto the idea that Ace needed the mainstream media to win again. On this, they strongly disagreed, but Ace deferred to his chief of staff. Still, allowing two reporters access after a midweek rally at a small church seemed a bit much to Ace. Ace knew Jake Baker, silver-haired and overworked, always with a dip in his mouth. Ace had gotten used to the old fart over the years. He'd even bummed a pinch of Jake's gross wintergreen long-cut a time or two. Their little secret.

Ace was not sure what to make of Jake's companion, though. A pretty girl with sexy librarian glasses, a big rack, and a scowl. His go-to with lady reporters was to flirt. It always did the trick.

"How the hell are ya, Jake?" Ace reached out his hand in fake excitement. "Who's your friend?"

"My name is Katherine," she said as they shook. "I'm working on a story about RayLynn Gutierrez, and I understand that you—"

"The congressman doesn't have time for any questions this afternoon," Matthews interrupted from over Ace's left shoulder.

That's weird. Letting these two interview Ace had been Matthews' idea. The subject matter was sensitive, but Ace knew avoiding questions about the girl would look worse.

"It's okay, Hunter," Ace said, holding up his left hand without breaking eye contact with her. "First Miss … I didn't catch your last name …"

"Hallaway," she said. "And I prefer Ms."

"My apologies, *Mizz* Hallaway. First, let me say how sorry I am for RayLynn's family and friends, and really that whole community. It's always such a tragedy when a life so young and full of promise is cut short. Yes, she was working on a story about me. We had spoken on the phone and in person a total of about three or four times." *Straight Face Straight Face Straight Face.*

"What did you talk about?"

"The issues, mostly. About living in Washington versus living in Vista County. The accident in high school, obviously."

"RayLynn's teacher said the story was supposed to come out earlier this week," Hallaway said. "When was the last time you two spoke?"

"Boy, that must've been, what, nearly two weeks ago Hunter?" Ace asked, turning around.

"I'd have to check his schedule," Matthews said. "I'll email Jake-"

"No, you'll email me," Hallaway said, handing a business card to Ace. "By five." She shot a look to Matthews. "I know you've got his schedule in your phone. Don't make me get your number from Jake and call you this afternoon on deadline."

"Sure thing, *Mizz* Hallaway," Ace said. "I'm afraid my chief of staff is right, though, I do need to get going. Thank you."

As he and Matthews made their way past the pews and out the front doors, Ace couldn't help but wonder what *Mizz* Hallaway would be like in bed. She'd be a real firecracker. *I bet she likes being tied up …*

"You're never going to stop putting yourself in bad situations for a pair of nice tits, are you?" Matthews asked.

"So, you agree—they're nice," Ace said, turning to smile at the red-faced mole man. "Relax, that went fine. Quit being such a worrywart."

Flirting always rejuvenated Ace. To him, humans were like sharks. Life was just a never-ending search for food and sex. Being a politician made getting both much easier.

• • •

"Listen, don't make a habit of this, and don't fuck up my relationship with this guy," Baker told Kat as they walked into the newsroom.

"Wouldn't dream of it."

"I'm serious. I need to get as much out of this race between him and

Billy Bob as possible."

"His name is Bobby Joe," Kat said. "And you know what? I can't promise not to piss your guy off."

"Goddamnit Kat, just stay away from him."

Kat leaned in close. "Do you want me to tell Greg your little secret? I'll go in there right now and tell him you're The Shitter."

Baker stared at her.

Bishop's first order of business had been laying off staffers. Baker was one of the elder statesmen of the paper and, along with the other *Standard* lifers, had been offered a choice rather than just getting the ax: Take a thirty-percent pay cut and stay, or swallow corporate's awful severance package. Though they'd all signed nondisclosure agreements preventing them from discussing the terms of the deal, everyone who'd been handed the manila envelopes was fine with "leaking" the information to everyone in the newsroom. It had been all the staff talked about for weeks. For every year an employee had worked, the new corporate overlords were offering just three days of their current compensation—which for the old-timers was already substantially less than their peak salaries—for up to ten years. For everyone who signed, it was half or less than the number of years they'd worked at the *Standard*.

One decade accounted for a third of Baker's time at the paper. He didn't know how to do anything else. He was also married to a career woman, which allowed them to live in the historic Plemons-Eakle neighborhood, so Baker stayed on staff and took the pay cut. But later that night, Baker snuck into Bishop's office and expressed his displeasure. Kat thought it was a bit harsh since Bishop had been at the *Standard* just a few months and was only doing what corporate told him. She knew Baker was responsible because she'd been up in The Hobbit Room hours after deadline, reading and drinking tequila. Kat went back in the newsroom to grab an energy drink from the fridge before heading home and caught Baker in the act. An old man sitting on his haunches next to the boss' computer was going to be harder to scrub from her memory than the worst murders and fatal wrecks she'd covered. The morning web editor had been at his desk when Bishop walked into his office and began cursing to high heaven. Kat still wondered if that part was accurate, but the story was too good to fact check. By the time she'd gotten there at ten that morning, there was an email reminding everyone that there were no animals allowed in the newsroom. Whether the fecal matter was human or animal had been a constant debate, though everyone later agreed it had been a disgruntled employee known only as The Shitter. Kat had promised Baker she'd keep the secret.

"You wouldn't. He wouldn't believe you, anyway," Baker said.

"Fucking try me."

She sat down at her desk and woke up her computer. Today's lede was that the dead girl was working on an Anderson profile. Kat's would be a cliché piece about an industrious young student on the verge of her first big article before her life was cut tragically short. Though it would smell worse than what Baker had left on Bishop's desk, the story would have a click-friendly headline. More importantly, the reporting had given Kat a chance to get a read on Anderson. Her conclusion? He was slimy and, worst of all, genuinely good looking. He was taller than he seemed on TV and in photos, and his blue eyes were intense. She knew what his smile could do to a teenage girl.

Though Anderson made her skin crawl, Kat had to be careful not to jump to conclusions. She needed to do more reporting. Kat pulled out her area phonebook, opened it to Bison Ridge and scanned the Js. No George Johnson. *Damnit.* The Bison Ridge High volleyball coach was too young to have a landline. She'd never had one, and she was ancient compared to a coach who'd just graduated college. Kat would've talked to Johnson during her visit to the school, but she didn't want to push her luck. Schools, like any government office, didn't trust reporters, let alone ones who wanted to talk about a dead student.

This story wasn't going to be prize-winning investigative journalism, but Kat wanted one more source. She'd already gotten the go-ahead from Dawn Whatshername to talk to exactly one of the students in her newspaper class. At least she was kind enough to give Kat the girl's cellphone number. One student, plus the teacher—who hadn't said much of anything after class that was worth reporting, but whose voice needed to be in the story—plus Anderson made three sources. Pretty shitty for a front-page story, but she'd done more with less, which for more than a decade had been the standard operating procedure for newspapers.

Kat opened her notebook and dialed the number she'd written next to *Regina Watkins, AME/close friend???*

"Umm, hello?"

"Hello, is this Regina Watkins?"

"… Yes, who is this?"

"Hi Regina, my name is Katherine Hallaway. I'm the reporter from the *Amarillo Morning Standard*. Your newspaper teacher said I could call you for a story I'm doing on RayLynn. Do you have a minute to talk?"

"Oh, Hi. Um, yeah, hold on. Let me go to my room real quick," Watkins said before putting the phone on mute. Kat thought she sounded blonde.

"You there?" Watkins asked a few seconds later.

"Yes Regina, I'm here."

"Okay, good. So, what did you want to know about RayLynn?"

"Your teacher said you were close to her. Is that right?"

"Yep. We were like peas in a pod."

Jesus, does this girl not understand clichés? Is she not in a newspaper class? What is that teacher doing all day? "I see. What kind of person was she at school?"

"Really great. She was very smart. You know she was already the editor-in-chief, right?"

"Yes, your teacher mentioned that," Kat said.

"Okay. Just making sure."

"I was thinking more along the lines of what her interests were, outside of the newspaper stuff."

"Well, she played volleyball. I'm not on the team, so I can't help you much there."

Can't help me at all, it sounds like. "That's okay, Regina. Tell me, though, did she have any hobbies or anything else interesting that I can add to my story? You know, for some color. You know what I mean, right, as a reporter?"

"I'm an editor, actually. Assistant managing editor."

Wow. What a self-absorbed bitch. "Oh, so sorry for the confusion."

"It's okay. But yes, I know what you mean. Let me think."

During the pause, Kat took the time to write *Peas in a pod* on her notebook. Unfortunately, it was the only useful thing this idiot had said so far.

"Just a couple of weeks ago, she wrote an editorial that said the pep rallies at the school were terrible," Watkins said. "About how there were no skits, just fight song, captain's speech, coach's speech, school song, fight song. No skits. No nothing. Just super boring, you know?"

"I bet that didn't go over well."

"Definitely not. The cheerleaders and the principal were very upset and wanted a retraction the next week. Instead, she wrote an editorial about the school bullying her for expressing herself. You can probably find it on our website."

"Oh right. That's Buffalo Nickel Weekly dot com, right?" Kat asked, scribbling it in her notebook.

"Yep. And last week's pep rally was back to normal. Hilarious skits, funny costumes. Then on Sunday, we found out she had passed away."

Kat took down the words verbatim. It felt strange to write the phrase "passed away." She had worked in the news business so long it sounded weird to hear and write a euphemism for *died* or *was killed.*

"Anything else you want to know?" Watkins asked.

"Well, do you want to talk off the record?" Kat asked, trying to make it sound sexy and fun.

"Sure," Watkins said, obviously excited.

"Was RayLynn into anything, you know, kinda bad?"

"What do you mean?"

"Like drugs or drinking or sex, or anything like that."

"Um, I don't know if I should be saying anything bad about her."

"It's totally off the record. You have my word, one professional newswoman to another." *Barf.*

"I mean, why would you want to know if she was into anything bad?"

"Your teacher's shown you the movie *All the President's Men,* right?"

"Duh."

"Well, maybe you can be my Deep Throat."

Kat heard Watkins giggle. "Well, okay. I guess. I do know that RayLynn smoked cigarettes and drank on the weekends. At least, that's what I've heard. I don't do any of that stuff myself."

Oh, of course not, you lying liar who lies. "Oh wow."

"Yeah. She was not as much of a goodie-two-shoes as everyone says she was. Of course, with what happened to her parents, it's almost understandable."

"What happened to her parents?"

"You don't know?" Watkins asked. "I guess you wouldn't. Go to your archives and look up stories about Ray and Clarissa Gutierrez. It would be about thirteen years ago this month."

"Okay, I'll do that. Thanks for the tip. Going back to her bad habits—was RayLynn into anything that might've gotten her killed?"

"Oh, I don't think so. You want to know who I think did it?"

Kat shifted in her seat and got her pen ready. "Who's that?"

"Those cheerleaders. Over those editorials she wrote. Now there's a bunch of mean bitches."

Kat thanked Watkins for her insight and ended the call. She was starting to like this RayLynn girl. A smoker and a drinker who stood up for her First Amendment rights. But for her story today, Kat had "peas in a pod," a mediocre anecdote about writing harsh editorials, and a series of supposedly dull interviews with her local congressman. And for murder suspects, Kat had a theory about a bunch of bitchy high school cheerleaders. Anderson—sleazy, but with no motive for murder—was in there somewhere, though she didn't know how yet.

Fuck my life. Kat pulled up the *Buffalo Nickel* website, then opened the resume she'd created eight months ago.

CHAPTER FIFTEEN

Levi felt at home. He was laying on a king-sized comforter with a half-empty bottle of Scotch just above the bedside drawer containing the Bible. Levi had driven to Yucca, across enemy lines where he could find a decent hotel to hole up in while he figured out what the hell was going on. Levi knew he would never be viewed the same again. He was now sleazy, a man who liked to carry on affairs with married women and call them terrible names. Confirmation was readily available on every major national news website. Levi had turned off the search alert he'd set up for his name.

Levi looked at his Wikipedia page. He'd been so proud to have one, but it now had a section titled **Verbal assault video** with a brief description of the video and the media's reaction to it. Anyone who read that page from now on would think, *What a terrible, sexist piece of shit who likes to emotionally abuse women.* Would they be right? Levi couldn't remember having ever actually called a woman the C-word. Not even during his inner dialogue. He'd used it to describe inanimate objects, always with a funny qualifier—his favorite was "cunt muscle," which the character Ari Gold had once used in an episode of *Entourage*—but Levi had never used it seriously. The word would now follow him. Define him. Be used in his news obituary, if one would be warranted when the time came.

Levi grabbed the bottle and took another swig. His mother was right—Levi had to say something to Kat. But, even if he finished the rest of that bottle, Levi wouldn't have the courage to call her. Levi mustered a text. *I'm sorry. I love you.* Levi polished off the bottle as he thought. Something else had been bothering him. Though his ego was prone to telling himself he was a "celebrity," the part of him trained to sift through bullshit knew he wasn't. Not in the way he liked to imagine, anyway. So how the hell did some barfly's cellphone video end up on all the major news sites overnight? The cable news networks all knew him by this point, but how did their web editors get their hands on the file so quickly?

The answer was obvious, even in his inebriated condition. Someone had to have emailed them all a link. As the alcohol-induced blackout raced closer, he drifted off thinking about his faceless enemy. Levi thought what happened in Dallas would be the end of it. But apparently he — or she, or them — still had some unknown score to settle with Levi.

• • •

Levi had tried to move swiftly to the desk in the middle of the sports and features section of the *Daily Star* newsroom. He had been in Dallas a year and was still freelance. He had eaten the meager savings from his job in Amarillo, including all the money from his old retirement account. He'd been putting his vegan food and gym membership on a nearly maxed-out credit card for the last two months. Even a paper as big as the *Daily Star* — which still had one of the twenty-five largest daily circulations in the country — could not afford to hire him full time.

Adding insult to injury was the expanded role he was playing to remain unable to pay for his groceries. Levi was covering high school sports of all kinds, which meant driving to the office three times a week and taking box scores over the phone from coaches. This was in addition to covering some sort of game or match the other days. Some were high school, though more and more often he was at college or minor-league contests. He worked under three deputy sports editors, none of whom coordinated with each other, and as a result, Levi was covering something or taking scores seven days a week. Levi and two others in his position were on a freelance retainer that was meant to keep them from writing for the competition — not that there was time. Levi was also expected to crank out a column a week for the Sports section and two twenty-inch features a week for the Life & Arts section, which had become merged under one top editor. Levi's last arts story was about fall foliage. He'd spoken with half a dozen Dallas residents who plan their year around traveling to the northeast to watch leaves fall.

Levi needed a full-time job, and he needed it fast. He'd run the numbers a couple days ago. Without more cash flow, Levi was going to be the best-looking homeless person on the streets of downtown Dallas.

"Hey buddy, what are you doing here?" Levi heard from over his right shoulder, causing him to jump.

"Robert, hey man. I was just, I mean, I wasn't—"

"You're putting together a clip file. I get it. You've been here a year working for peanuts."

"I wish. If they actually paid in peanuts, it would sure add to my diet of Ramen and hot dogs."

They both laughed, then took a momentary pause to reflect upon their dying industry. Robert was a sports copy editor/page designer who also took box scores over the phone. He used to be one of the paper's top sports columnists. This new role was his way of staying employed. One of his habits was keeping a copy of the newspaper each day and stacking it beside his desk. By the time the holidays rolled around, it had looked like the Leaning Tower of Pisa.

"Well, let me know if you need any help digging through my mess here," Robert said. "Oh, I almost forgot, I was asked to tell you when I saw you that there's some mail in the break room addressed to you."

Levi had never gotten mail at the office before. His byline still said *Special to the Daily Star*, which signaled to most readers that he was freelance and didn't have a mailbox at the paper. He walked to the table in the break room next to the fridge and saw a padded manila envelope among a lot of other junk, mostly books and DVDs sent hoping the features department would write a review. The *Star* hadn't employed a dedicated literary or TV/movie reviewer in quite some time, choosing instead to focus on locals who were published or working in Hollywood, so the unsolicited works were left for the department to pick through. So too, apparently, was mail left for freelancers.

Levi's mail had no return address but was made out to his attention. He opened it and dug out what looked like old Polaroid photos and what appeared to be a typewritten letter. *How old is this guy?*

Levi's attitude changed when he started examining the photos. They all featured Texas Governor Kenneth D. Lockwood III. Each photo featured the governor opening the door of an upscale-looking townhouse for a different scantily dressed woman. Levi had come into the office late, so nobody was there but the web department, which had one or two staffers in the newsroom 24/7. Still, Levi knew he had something of value, so he stuffed the materials back into the envelope and headed for the door.

When he got back to his apartment—which was small and in a bad neighborhood, though Levi did his best to keep it tidy and decorate it with workout equipment and calendars—Levi cleared off his desk/kitchen table and spread out the envelope's contents. After looking at the photos again, Levi moved on to the letter.

Mr. Cole,

Please find enclosed instant photographs of Governor Ken Lockwood III allowing a series of prostitutes into a suburban Dallas townhouse. The address is 4536 Maplebaum Drive, Farmers Branch, TX. You will find the property is owned by Evergreen Industries, a subsidiary of Ken Lockwood Jr.'s business, Lockwood Enterprises. The townhouses were built six years ago, which means the liaisons depicted had to have occurred during Lockwood's continuing tenure as governor.

I also invite you to log into the below email account, where you will find even more damning information.

Email: MTW28_18@securedelectronicmail.com

Password: aThE24!14

I trust you will use this information to best serve the public interest.

Cheers.

Levi re-read the letter four times before stopping to consider what to do next. He looked at the photos again. In the age of PhotoShop, this person had provided Levi Polaroids—well, not Polaroids, but a modern version—which meant the photos were almost surely genuine. The landowners of the address listed in the letter would be available on the Dallas Central Appraisal District's website. He could physically go there to verify that it was the same townhouse as the one in the photos. The man in the pictures was definitely Lockwood, and none of the women were his wife.

Levi preferred sports and features to news. But, in the end, he was a reporter with an education from one of the top J-schools in the country. He had to pursue the story, and he had to do it immediately. Levi had never chased a story of any measurable significance. The closest he came was covering athletes when they ran afoul of the law, but those were all news releases and scheduled news conferences. The only references he had for a story of this magnitude were nonfiction books and movies he'd watched that included watershed events like Watergate. And, in those instances, a story like this was usually sent to more than one newspaper.

Levi found it odd the nameless leaker had chosen a freelancer. But before he thought about it too deeply and second-guessed himself, it occurred to Levi that, as a freelancer, he had the upper hand. If somehow the *Daily Star* didn't want to run what he wrote, someone else would. And, in the digital age, there were thousands of outlets willing to pay for this kind of national exposure and traffic. Either way, Levi could use this story to get a job or a big payday. Or, to put it in a way his J-school professors would appreciate, Levi could do meaningful journalism and have a chance to get above the poverty line. *What a concept.*

Two days later, Levi couldn't believe how quickly he'd put together a cohesive story, minus the expected "no comment" quotes from the governor's office and from the Orilla, Texas, police department. He'd first given a print copy of the story to his direct supervisor, sports/features editor Melanie Frost. Her reaction was one of excitement and skepticism. She had told Levi to wait in her office while she took the pages to her boss, managing editor Tim Edwards.

Frost came back about thirty minutes later and told Levi to follow her. She led him to a section of the building he'd never seen. Inside a large, old-timey boardroom with a long, wooden table with leather seats were Edwards, a representative from legal, and the *Star's* publisher himself, Christina … er, Christopher … Applegate—much of the sports staff called him Christina behind his back—at one end. Frost sat across from Edwards and motioned for Levi to sit next to her.

"Well, we've all read your story," Applegate said. "Let's listen to these recordings."

Edwards slid a laptop over to Levi. Levi opened a browser and logged into the secured email website. In the drafts folder, there was an email with two attachments. He double-clicked the first—named *GovToCartel.mp3*—and, after a dramatic pause, hit his spacebar.

What are you doing about the police in Orilla? asked a menacing male voice with a thick Spanish accent. He sounded like he was on the other end of a telephone conversation doing a bad Pablo Escobar impression.

They know what to do. So, are we done with this? replied Governor Lockwood, his West Texas accent as identifiable as a fingerprint.

Mr. Governor, this will never be over. You should have known there would be consequences when you started sleeping with whores. But it's really a small price we're asking, isn't it? We don't tell anyone about your secret, we even let you use our services for free, and all you have to do is tell the police in Orilla to look the other way. We feel it's a very fair price, Mr. Lockwood.

The recording stopped, and everyone sat for a moment.

"We can't know this recording is authentic," the lawyer said.

"That's true," Levi said. "But we all know we just heard the governor talking to someone. Based on where Orilla is located, they have to be discussing smuggling prostitutes across the border from Mexico."

"Maybe," Applegate said. "Now play the other recording."

Levi double-clicked the second attachment, named *GovToOrilla.mp3*.

So, are we all good to go with this deal? Lockwood asked.

Yes, sir. Tonight they'll have a window from two to three in the morning. That's all I can guarantee. The man sounded American, but had the slightest accent.

All right then. Just make sure every Saturday night your officers are otherwise occupied, got it?

Long as the money keeps coming, the window will stay open.

The recording ended, and everyone looked at Applegate.

"Okay, here's how I see it. I'm sitting here looking at photos of the governor letting hookers into a townhouse owned by his daddy's company, according to what Levi here wrote," Applegate said. "And we all just heard the governor talking to folks he shouldn't've been talking to. Far as I'm concerned, all we need are quotes from the authorities, as he's outlined, and I think this is ready for print."

"I could not disagree more," the lawyer said. "This is all circumstantial. We can't prove who is on those phone calls or who those women are in those photos. We will be open to a libel suit."

"Well, what the hell do you think we pay you and your team for?" Applegate asked.

"If I may jump in, I would say that this is a good start, but it's not ready," Edwards said.

"Look, we can do follow-up reporting later," Frost said. "But we have what will be a huge headline and an amazing multimedia element with the recordings. Most importantly, we have it now, and I'm more than aware that Mr. Cole here is technically freelance and can take his story and go somewhere else."

"I know he's freelance," the lawyer said. "But if he used any company property to research or write this—"

"I didn't," Levi said.

"But if your source ever contacted you through company channels—"

"He, or she, didn't," Levi said. It was a lie, but only one other person knew he received the mail in the building, and he wasn't inclined to help the paper.

"And how did you say you know this source?" Edwards asked.

"We've been friends a long time," Levi said. "The source is in the governor's inner circle and found out I was writing for a major newspaper. Had some very damning evidence against the governor and let me have the first chance at it."

"That's very convenient," the lawyer said.

"I don't care if this source is The Ghost of Christmas Past, we're running the story," Applegate said. "We're running the story in Sunday's paper. I want a headline as big as the JFK assassination, with references telling everyone to go online to hear the recordings."

The lawyer and Edwards shook their heads. Frost didn't react one way or the other—she likely wanted to defend her staffer, but not jeopardize her relationship with the bosses. Levi kept smiling.

"I do have one request," Levi said. "And I think you will agree with this, Mr. Applegate. This story shouldn't have *Special to the Daily Star* below my name."

"He's right," Edwards said. "We'll want this to be a staff byline for awards submissions."

The lawyer shot daggers at Levi, but it didn't matter. Levi was right. A paper this size was far too vain to let a freelancer have its most significant story in decades.

"Finish this story by 3 p.m. Friday so I can take a look before the weekend, and I'll make sure HR has you full-time by then," Applegate said before checking his watch. "All right, I've got to get out of here. Everybody know what they're doing?"

They all nodded their heads and stood to leave—except Levi. He stayed seated, staring at the walls of the conference room, lined with framed front pages featuring the *Star's* biggest stories, including the aforementioned JFK assassination. Levi wondered which one they would replace with the upcoming Sunday front.

• • •

Levi vaguely remembered being happy. He almost couldn't believe how high he'd been riding until just a few days ago. How had it all changed so quickly? But, while the memories were fresh in his mind, Levi drifted into a sleep from which he secretly hoped he would never awaken.

CHAPTER SIXTEEN

Elliott slumped into his ergonomic office chair. The medical examiner's autopsy report, which had been driven up to him from Lubbock just before he was going to call it quits for the day, was about what he'd expected. He was now officially working a homicide. The cause of death was listed as blunt trauma to the head. The report listed between fifteen and thirty separate blows to the victim's face. No surprise there. The manner of death was listed as homicide, with the likely weapon being a strong right cross. The time of death was between 11 p.m. and midnight Saturday.

There was trace evidence—Elliott was convinced no killer, no matter how careful, leaves absolutely nothing—but none of it was genetic material. The most notable of the trace evidence was spermicide from a condom. The ME didn't find any substantial proof of non-consensual intercourse. It was most likely rough, rushed sex, but not rape. Whatever kind of intercourse, it appears she was abducted before cleaning herself. Did she know her killer, have sex with him, then get into an argument that led to her death? Would that explain the sadistic nature of the body? If his working theory was right, and this was the work of a man and not a boy, he was also investigating a case of statutory rape. The Vista County district attorney would likely stick to a murder charge and not concern himself with the rape, or he would argue in court that the rape was committed along with the murder. That might make it easier to pursue a capital murder indictment. Elliott was in favor of the judicious application of the death penalty. If proven beyond a reasonable doubt, this case would certainly qualify.

Other items of note in the autopsy report included the fact that the burning and removal of fingernails and toenails were done postmortem. The ligature marks were pre-mortem and were not caused by any of the usual suspects—handcuffs, zip ties, various types of wire, bailing twine, or rope—but rather what the medical examiner said were "restraints resembling leather belts fastened tightly for hours, likely similar to those used by a dominatrix or sadomasochist." Though he didn't question that analysis, he wondered how much the rest of the case had influenced the ME's decision to include that in the report. Leather restraints certainly fit in thematically with the rest of the damage done to the girl's body—except the brutal beating, which did not display any nuance or forethought—but Elliott was not a fan of such editorializing taking place in early reports.

Elliott flipped through the photos again. "How could someone hate you so much?" he asked RayLynn as he checked his watch. It was half past six, and Elliott was getting whistle-bit. One of the perks of working in a mostly rural region was getting home in time for his wife's cooking and with enough light to work on his household projects. Right now, he was digging up a section of his backyard. He would eventually install a homemade fire pit.

Elliott left the ME's report but picked up his work-issued tablet. Loretta had pulled the Vista County Probate Court records for RayLynn and emailed the file. For his nighttime reading, Elliott would find out why custody of the girl had been given to her maternal grandmother.

• • •

Kat had two unread texts: one from Bill, the other from Levi. Kat hadn't said anything to Bill when she left that morning, just absorbed his disapproving look before nearly tripping over a miniature smiling train on her way out the door. Bill hadn't seen the video at that point—he'd been too busy trying to wrangle their son and prepare breakfast while Kat held a pillow over her head. But Bill now knew Kat had been lying last night. He also knew Levi was back. Kat could tell Bill she hadn't known that when she decided to go to Bison Ridge, but he wouldn't believe her. She would spend a long time earning back Bill's trust.

As for Levi, Kat didn't give a flying fuck what he wanted. She was sure it was an apology of some kind. She was equally sure it would do nothing to dampen her anger.

To delay walking into the shitstorm waiting for her outside, Kat stayed at work after deadline and walked back to the *Morning Standard's* library, where she could get some much-needed background on RayLynn. After searching through the "Gutierrez" folders and coming up empty, Kat pulled down the book for October 2003 and started searching for news stories about Ray and Clarissa Gutierrez. Their first appearance came in a local inside brief on Tuesday, October 21.

Couple found dead near I-40 with crying toddler in backseat

Amarillo police on Sunday found a couple dead in a vehicle just south of Interstate 40 while a toddler sat crying in the backseat, the Amarillo Police Department said Monday in a news release.

APD officers found Clarissa Gutierrez, 26, and Ray Gutierrez, 30, dead in a 1989 Ford Bronco at approximately 9 a.m. Sunday, according to the release. The couple's 3-year-old daughter was in a car seat crying when officers arrived, APD said.

The bodies were discovered on the shoulder of a nearly deserted road about a mile south of a bar along east I-40, police said, adding that an autopsy was scheduled for Monday in Lubbock.

Kat cringed as she finished reading the story. RayLynn's mother and father had been discovered dead almost thirteen years to the day before their daughter was found murdered. Kat wondered if that was a coincidence or not. Television and movies had taught her that, when looking into a murder, there were no such things as coincidences. But this was real life, and Kat knew they were possible. This one could be worth a parenthetical in a future story.

She flipped through the book, which was thick and included multiple editions for each day, a practice they'd abandoned years ago.

After a few minutes, Kat stopped at Wednesday's regional A1, where the follow-up headline was above the fold. She flipped a few more pages to get to the city edition, which might include details gathered just before the final deadline.

Police: Toddler stranded in SUV nearly 40 hours after parents' drug overdose

Police on Tuesday said the couple found dead in an SUV near east Interstate 40 overdosed on heroin more than a day before their child was found alive in the backseat by officers.

An autopsy performed Monday in Lubbock revealed Clarissa Gutierrez, 26, and Ray Gutierrez, 30, died of heroin overdoses, according to Lt. Derrick McBryde of APD's Special Crimes Unit. Prescription opioids Fentanyl and Oxycodone were also found in their systems, McBryde said.

The coroner placed their times of death at approximately 2:30 a.m. Saturday, according to McBryde. The 3-year-old girl had been in the car with her dead parents for more than 37 hours when police discovered the toddler crying in the back seat of the 1989 Ford Bronco at about 9 a.m. Sunday.

Investigators have determined the couple had traveled about 70 miles south from Bison Ridge and had purchased heroin at a local bar late Friday night, according to McBryde. The Bronco was found a few miles south of the bar, and drug paraphernalia was found inside the vehicle, McBryde said.

When asked, McBryde declined to comment on whether any drugs had been found in the toddler's system.

The story continued with facts about drug use in Amarillo and other background information, but Kat had read enough. Her bond with RayLynn was growing stronger. Kat understood the kind of damage that can be suffered by victims of early-age trauma. RayLynn was probably not a well-adjusted girl and might've been involved in several things that could lead to murder. Topping the list was drugs. There was no shortage of them in the small towns around Amarillo, with methamphetamine tending to be the most available after prescription pain pills. RayLynn also liked to party, so she likely slept around and could've pissed off the wrong boy. Or the wrong man.

Kat had another itch to scratch. During her interview with Anderson, the congressman said RayLynn had talked to him about "the accident in high school." Kat vaguely recalled one of Baker's stories a couple years ago, during Anderson's first campaign, in which he'd mentioned something about a tragic football game.

Kat snaked her way through the library and found the cabinet drawer marked *Aa-Ap*. She flipped her way through and found the paper's thick file on *Anderson, Ace* near the back. Kat set the obese folder on the cabinet and found Baker's story near the top despite how old it was. The paper had fired its librarian about a year ago and hadn't given her responsibilities to anyone, so the files were outdated. The rationale was that everything had been archived online for years, so anything that wasn't in the library would be available electronically. Kat figured it made sense from a business standpoint, but not having those files was just another thing that would make the job harder.

In his story, The Shitter had spent a few graphs recounting how a member of Anderson's foe that Friday night—Levi's team, if Kat remembered right—had died on the field. Anderson was quoted as saying, "It was one of the first tragedies I'd ever seen firsthand, and it still helps me to remember how fragile life can be." *Ugh*. Political speak at its best—or worst, depending on which side of the interview you're on. Kat skipped to the back of the file. The first few headlines were just football game stories.

Anderson tosses two TDs as Diamondbacks destroy Wildcats
Anderson leads Diamondbacks to state
She found it after about seven more clips:
Player critically injured during Stampede homecoming
The byline was Jonathan Janikowski, who had been sports editor before moving to the copy desk to avoid a full layoff. He seemed to have taken the hit far better than Baker. Back then, Janikowski had just been one of the sportswriters covering the nearly sixty regional football teams that peppered the *Standard*'s coverage area—which at the time included much of eastern New Mexico, the Oklahoma Panhandle and

southern Kansas. Kat felt a bit sorry for Janikowski as she read the story. Nobody gets into covering football to write about death. During and immediately after the game, nobody would confirm the player, Jesus "Jesse" Rodriguez, had died. That fact was reported the next day, though Janikowski had to have known that night. Kat had been to the scenes of fatal wrecks and homicides. You can tell when people are looking at a dead body.

Janikowski had given the play-by-play. Bison Ridge's quarterback was attempting to throw a swing pass to Rodriguez, their star sophomore running back, but had tossed it too high and Rodriguez had been forced to jump. Anderson, Yucca's six-foot-four, 245-pound senior star quarterback/safety, laid into Rodriguez—*bulldozed him*, the story read, *the crown of his helmet hitting Rodriguez's chinstrap so hard the helmet nearly flew into the visitors' bleachers*—and stood over him, taunting the already dead player. Anderson couldn't have known he'd just killed the boy. He probably thought he'd knocked Rodriguez out cold.

Kat skimmed the rest of the stories published about the death. An autopsy revealed that the impact from Anderson's hit had broken Rodriguez's neck and he'd died almost instantly. The medical examiner's report said the neck had been severely injured within a couple months before the fatal hit. In a story a few days later, Rodriguez's coach confirmed that the sophomore had suffered a neck injury earlier in the season, but the Bison Ridge team doctor had determined he could play again after sitting out just one week. If that had happened today, Kat imagined the coach and team doctor might've faced criminal charges. But as Kat finished looking through the stories, there was no mention of anything of the sort.

Was it an accident? Absolutely. Any hit could have killed Rodriguez. But the tragic anecdote hadn't evoked sympathy in Kat like it had the voting public. She saw a cocky, violent young man who didn't yet know his own power.

Kat had decided long ago that all men are capable of terrible things. Some never act, but most do. It's all a matter of how dark their urges get. And Kat was now looking into a story about a damaged, rebellious young girl who was interviewing a handsome, arrogant man in a position of power. Within weeks, the girl is found murdered. Kat put the folder back and left the library. The newsroom was now empty except for Janikowski, who was listening to cable news while laying out the last of the night's pages. As Kat mentally prepared to face Bill and the fallout from the night before, she asked herself again: *What story am I chasing?*

CHAPTER SEVENTEEN

Levi opened his hotel room door feeling like hammered dogshit. This time the hangover *was* from the alcohol. He'd started drinking early and had passed out quickly. When he looked over and saw 7:00 on the hotel's digital clock, he'd assumed it was 7 p.m. — he had the blackout curtains drawn — but when he turned on the TV, he was greeted by a network morning news program. The balding newsman teased the headlines before making his way to the latest election coverage. Which team would win, the blue wave or the crimson tide? The segment passed without mentioning him. For television, Levi was yesterday's news.

But the newspaper, delivering all the news that happened twenty-four hours ago, would be a different story. The hotel had put Wednesday's edition of the *Standard* outside every occupied room, so he picked it up to see what Kat had written. *Jesus, this is thin.* It had gone from a hearty daily paper to something no more substantial than the *Vista County Courier*. It wouldn't be long before the corporation that had purchased the *Standard* would quit printing it every day.

Levi rubbed the sleep out of his eyes and read the top headline.

'Such a tragedy'

Rep. Anderson, First Amendment among slain student reporter's subjects

Kat had written the piece. It was soft, which had never been her forte, but it was a solid second-day story. Levi flipped through the rest of the A section. He found it buried in the national news briefs:

Popular political reporter verbally assaults local woman

It identified Kat as a staffer, though not by name, and reminded readers that Levi was a former *Standard* reporter. Both reasons are why editors had placed the story near the bottom of an inside page. Bury it in print, make it explode online. It made sense, though Levi knew the *Standard*'s new ME would catch some flak for hiding a national headline involving one of his own.

Levi turned back to Kat's story and stared at Anderson's mugshot. His smile had been mocking Levi for years. The way Anderson had used Jesse's death to humanize himself still angered Levi. *Fucking politicians.*

Levi was out of Scotch and still had at least an hour until the liquor stores started opening. He reached for the room service menu.

• • •

Ace sat on the couch in Matthews' old office reading the morning paper. The Yucca building owned by his father's firm—Anderson, Thompson & Murphy—had again been converted into campaign headquarters. The firm now had fancy corporate offices in Dallas, but it maintained a staff in Yucca. The small-town lawyers didn't get much work outside of DWI and drug cases, so they welcomed the excitement and seemed more than happy to make room for Ace's re-election bid.

"I think she likes me," Ace said as Matthews walked in with two coffee mugs.

"Speaking of the *Standard*, I spoke with their new editor yesterday, Greg Bishop," Matthews said, breezing past Ace's comment. "He said they are saving the endorsements for their election guide. It doesn't come out until the Sunday before early voting starts."

"They're endorsing me, right?"

"... I don't know yet," Matthews said.

"Really?" Endorsing Bobby Joe Carter was laughable. Ace didn't figure it would make a difference, though the thought of it bruised his ego a bit.

"This new editor, he's hard to read," Matthews said. "And he's frazzled. I think he was telling the truth when he said the paper hasn't decided yet. He said they're having a hard time looking more than a week in advance on anything."

Ace blew into his mug before taking a careful sip. "Sounds like things really are going downhill over there." Ace hadn't thought much about the *Standard* since winning his House seat, though a few months back its editor and publisher sent a letter urging him to get involved in some newsprint tariff with the Canadians. They laid out a doomsday scenario that Ace had dismissed. Maybe they weren't alarmists after all.

"Speaking of downhill, have you seen the latest polls?" Matthews asked. "Your lead's down to five points."

Ace took another sip. "I will never understand people who say they're going to vote for this clown. Should I pull out a few teeth and not shower for a few days? Try and out-redneck this guy?"

"It all flows downhill," Matthews said. "People want to get rid of all career politicians at this point."

"I'm not a career politician."

"You're in office and running for re-election. To the people around here, you're a career politician."

Ace shook his head and looked back down at the paper. Voters always had short attention spans. But this mob mentality, which seemed to ignore and retaliate against facts, was new.

"Maybe I need to grant an exclusive interview to *Mizz* Hallaway," Ace said. "Get her to *rock* the vote."

"You've got to learn to keep your dick in your pants."

"Yeah, yeah," Ace said, waving off Matthews. "But seriously, what's our next move? How do we get rid of this idiot?"

"As usual, just leave it up to me," Matthews said. He opened his leather portfolio and began shuffling through papers.

Ace smirked. Matthews thought he was so damn smart, but Ace could do things on his own.

For instance: Matthews had no idea about RayLynn.

• • •

Kat stared at her computer screen. She'd asked the web department to email her the page view total for her story. Seven to ten is morning drive-time, when people were checking the morning news before heading to work—or, like her, procrastinating with their first cup of coffee.

Kat took a deep breath when she saw an email pop in, but groaned when she saw it was from Bishop. *Subject: Election coverage.* She clicked on the email and searched for her name.

Motherfucker. Bishop had put Kat on polling center detail again. She would be out getting anecdotes from Potter and Randall County voters, conducting man-on-the-street interviews and adding to the paper's social media feed and online Election Day diary. She'd have to take videos of morons trying to articulate why they voted for one asshole over the other. During the primaries, Bishop had been a hardass about keeping the site updated. He'd justified his attitude a week later by breaking down the traffic numbers and emailing out a spreadsheet showing why their efforts had been important. He could parse the figures all he wanted, but Kat knew it was just a waste of her time. She eyed Bishop's office, where he was pounding away at his keyboard. Kat was going to give him a piece of her mind. What's the worst he could do? She might be getting laid off anyway.

"Greg, you know I'm better than doing man-on-the-street bullshit," Kat said as she slammed the door. "I've been here six goddamn years. Just let the ambulance chasers do it all. They love that crap anyway."

Bishop took off his bifocals and tossed them onto a pile of that week's editions, the pages bleeding with mistakes.

"Language, please," he said. "To your point: I didn't even want to give you that."

Kat opened her mouth and was about to lay into Bishop when he held up his hand.

"I didn't want you distracted with this circus," he said. "I need you focused on better stories. Your work lately has been the best since I've been here."

Kat shut her mouth and sat down.

"This girl deserves our best," she said. Kat knew that sounded cliché, and Bishop probably thought she was being ironic, but she had befriended RayLynn Gutierrez from beyond the grave.

"Keep on it," Bishop said. "And let me know if you have any stories I can put on the Sunday cover. Our budget looks like sh— ... Our budget is thin."

Kat fought off a smile. Instead, she nodded and walked back to her desk, where she had an email waiting.

> *From: Web Team*
> *Subject: RE: Traffic*
> *Kat,*
> *Your story's a hit! 15,000 and counting.*
> *Keep it up!*
> *-AG*

Kat took a moment to celebrate her success. But as she leaned back, Kat knew she needed to keep up the momentum. She also knew the investigation wouldn't be over in a day, and the Texas Rangers weren't going to send out any news releases until they made an arrest. If Kat wanted to keep her name at the top of that goddamn board, she couldn't be passive. And, for the first time in years, she didn't want to. Kat remembered the adrenaline that comes with tracking down sources and getting them to talk. She used to love preparing for an interview, knowing she would pry out information she wasn't supposed to hear.

Kat decided against trying to get more information from Trooper Correa, even if it was off the record. She would need to be in his good graces when the DPS released its information. Instead, Kat would have to get a little creative. She had the location where RayLynn had been found. An excellent piece of information, despite where it had come from. And, as much as she hated to do it, she'd have to return to the Levi Cole well.

She wasn't ready to talk to Levi, not even over the phone. She'd deleted their text conversation the day before without reading his latest messages. Kat had thought about deleting Levi from her address book but was now thankful she hadn't taken that step. She composed a new text.

What's Ur sheriff buddy's cellphone number? Need it ASAP.

• • •

Levi shut the door to his hotel room and set down his unopened bottle. He would get to it soon enough, but Levi's whiskey-soaked brain had come up with one last idea. He knew how to prove his Lockwood source was the same person or people who'd just blown up his life. Emily Greene was now working the evening desk down in Atlanta. She had already moved on from working for Georgia Barrett—who remained the second most popular political talking head on TV. Barrett's underlings didn't last long but usually moved up in the cable news world after an apprenticeship on her show, "The Roundup." Greene was no exception and had left Levi a voicemail from her cellphone the night before. She'd kept the same number, but now Greene was calling on behalf of a different show and had a new title—associate producer. She was high enough to know the details and liked Levi enough to provide them.

Greene picked up on the first ring.

"Hey you," she said. "Hold on, let me get everything set up to record."

"Actually, this is going to have to be off the record."

"Nope. Can't do that."

"You'll have to. I'm not commenting on anything. I actually have questions for you."

"If you don't want to talk on the record, why on Earth would I answer any of your questions?"

Levi paused. It was a good point. "Tell you what. You answer my questions, and I'll send you a statement in time for you to get something ready overnight Sunday for Monday morning. I get what I want, and you might get *another* promotion."

Greene was silent on the other end of the line, but Levi knew she'd give in. "Deal," she said. "What do you want to know?"

"It's about the video. Y'all got an email with the link late Tuesday night, didn't you?"

"Yeah," Greene said. "The night desk monkey got it and called me. Lucky for me I wasn't asleep yet. She forwarded me the email, and after I watched you call that girl … what you called her … I posted it as soon as I could. You know I didn't have a choice, right?"

"Of course not. I just hope you were first."

"Unfortunately, no. Second by less than three minutes, though. And I think I had the best headline. But I'm guessing none of that has anything to do with why you're calling me now."

"No, ma'am. I want to know how you got the link. The email address."

"You want me to reveal my sources? After all the times you said you couldn't reveal yours? No way."

"We have a deal. Plus, if I'm right, there's a bigger story for you down the road. What's the email address?"

"Hold on," Greene said after a short pause. "Here we go. It's a weird one, so I'm just going to spell it …"

Levi had never been so upset to be right. "I'm guessing the email wasn't signed?"

"Nope."

"Did the email mention me by name?"

"Yep."

"What's the timestamp."

"11:47 p.m."

That would've given the original poster of the video, UglyBittie451, just enough time to finish her drinks, stumble home and post the video before it was "leaked" to every TV news outlet in America.

"Any more questions?" she asked.

"No, ma'am."

"I'll need that statement before midnight eastern on Sunday."

"Right. And Emily, you know that I don't think women are—"

"I know," she said. "It sounds like you two had a history. No judgment here. I know you're a good guy. But that other story'd better be worth it."

"It will be. I promise."

Levi thanked Greene and hung up. He had his confirmation.

Someone had been outside Drake's, seen who all had taken cellphone video, gotten the name of one of their social media accounts, waited for her to upload it, then email blasted every major cable and network TV news organization in the country. And this same person had previously outed Levi as having made up parts of stories — nearly two years after giving Levi the greatest gift of his career.

But why? Levi thought about emailing and flat out asking. But, even if Levi figured out why someone had used him to take down Lockwood before ruining his life, what would it matter? His life was still in shambles. And, at this point, even if Levi uncovered the identity of his mystery Geppetto, who would believe him?

CHAPTER EIGHTEEN

After talking on the phone with Bison Ridge High School staff members, it had become clear to Elliott that one of the last people to see RayLynn alive was her volleyball coach, George Johnson, affectionately known as Coach J. Elliott was fine using the phone for gathering basic facts. It saved his time and the department's money. But for speaking with potential suspects, in-person interviews were essential. When possible, surprise in-person interviews were preferred.

The school wasn't modern, but it was clean. The staff obviously took pride in the way it looked. Its glass entrance was spotless and its common area spacious. There were signs of school spirit on its walls, surprisingly well done. The walls had fresh coats of light blues and greens—despite the school's depressing colors of brown and white— and there was a *WELCOME TO BRHS* sign above the hall that went from the commons to the office.

Elliott might have dressed a bit too casual. He'd chosen dress jeans over suit pants and a more traditional pair of boots to seem less intimidating. The echo from his bootheels seemed unusually loud as Elliott walked up a half-flight of steps and approached a portly woman with designer glasses sitting behind a sign that read, *All visitors must sign in with the office.* That meant him, despite the silver star over his left shirt pocket.

"Hello ma'am, my name is Elliott Dawson. I'm with the Department of Public Safety, Ranger Division. I'm investigating RayLynn Gutierrez's death."

"Good morning, Mr. Dawson. May I see some ID?"

Elliott did as he was asked and signed the sheet in front of him. A minute later a tall bald man came walking out of the office area with his right hand extended.

"Hi, I'm Principal Lance Humphries. We spoke on the phone earlier this week. How can we be of service to the Texas Rangers this morning?"

"I'd like to speak with Coach Johnson for a few minutes if that's convenient."

"I think we can make that work. Can I ask what this is regarding?"

"I just need to ask him some routine questions. We believe he was one of the last people to see RayLynn before she went missing on Friday."

"I see. Well, feel free to use my office." Humphries turned to the woman behind the glass. "Please call Coach J. Tell him to report to my office as soon as I get up there to watch over his class." He turned back to Elliott. "How long do you think this will take?"

"Hopefully only five or ten minutes."

"Very good," Humphries said as he motioned for Elliott to follow him. Humphries led Elliott into his office, then left to relieve Johnson. Elliott looked around the cramped room. Humphries had a degree from West Texas A&M, which churned out many of the area's teachers and administrators. Other than that, the walls were bare save for a couple of inspirational posters. The principal's chair wasn't as nice as Elliott's, either. Since he had another minute, Elliott inspected the chair on the other side of the wooden desk. He took his pocket knife out of its leather holster. He popped off the plastic foot on the bottom of the chair's front right leg, ensuring it would wobble enough to keep Johnson off balance.

Elliott had just sat back down when Coach J entered. He was surprisingly short—approximately five foot five—but stocky.

"Howdy," Johnson said, sitting down across the desk from Elliott and tipping forward before settling back. "So, you're with the Texas Rangers?"

"Yes, sir," Elliott said as he reached across to shake hands. "Ranger Elliott Dawson. Pleased to meet you."

"You ever meet that Chuck Norris fella?"

"No, sir. It's been quite a while since he was on that show, and I'm not sure if any actual Rangers were ever used." *Okay, this guy's no rocket scientist.* "As I'm sure Principal Humphries told you, I'm investigating RayLynn's death. Several of the staff have said that, near as they can tell, you were the last person here to see her alive."

Johnson tried shifting in his unbalanced chair. His breathing quickened, and his gaze floated to something over Elliott's left shoulder. Johnson also started cracking his knuckles. "Who told you that?"

"Like I said, other staff members here. It's not important who they are. What's important is what happened the day before she died. So, tell me, when did you see her last?"

"I, uh, I don't know. At lunch I suppose."

"At lunch? My understanding is y'all have an open campus here, and the students can leave for lunch. You want me to believe that a popular athlete like RayLynn stayed here and ate cafeteria food?"

"Uh, no sir. I mean, I saw her leaving to go to lunch with some of her friends."

"Was she walking or riding with someone?"

"She got a ride."

"Who with?"

"I don't know."

"What kind of car did she get into?"

"I, um, I don't remember."

"Make? Model? Anything."

"Um ... I guess it was a truck."

"You guess?"

"I don't know, okay?"

Elliott leaned back in his chair. This guy was dumb and a bad liar. This wasn't going anywhere. He was going to have to switch to "good cop." The trick to that is being truthful. The truth was Johnson wasn't in any trouble at the moment, though if he kept lying, he would be. Also true was that several of the volleyball girls had told their teachers they'd seen RayLynn go into Coach J's office before practice on Friday—a practice she didn't attend. Elliott put his hands behind his head and leaned back even further into the principal's uncomfortable chair.

"Look, George, you can relax. The only way you can get yourself into any trouble is to keep lying," Elliott said. "I already know most of what I need. And it's okay that you called RayLynn into your office before practice on Friday. It's okay that you let her skip practice. All I need to know is what you talked about and if you knew where she went afterward."

Johnson's shoulders fell, and he quit fidgeting. *There we go.*

"I didn't call her in," Johnson said. "She came in and wanted to talk."

Elliott took a small notepad from out of his inside jacket pocket and leaned forward as he opened it, unclipped the pen from the leather cover, and clicked it. "Good, George. Thank you for being honest. What did she want to talk with you about?"

"She thought I was playing favorites, giving someone else more playing time instead of her. The usual stuff, really."

"Were you?"

"No, sir."

The coach's heel started bouncing. But, a coach playing favorites is not a crime—except, of course, to the parent of the player on the short end—so there was no need to call him on it.

"Good to hear. Now, what was the last thing she said to you?"

Johnson took a moment to think. Elliott could tell this act was physically laborious. Elliott wondered how guys like this were put in charge of teaching kids.

"She said something like, 'I don't need this bullsnot. Eff this team and eff you.' I cleaned it up for ya just now, but that's basically it."

"Then she did what?"

"She left. I tried to get her to stop, but she walked out of my office toward the door to the parking lot."

"She went to the parking lot?"

"Yes, sir."

"Had she already changed into her practice clothes?"

"Uh … yeah, yeah she had. Why?"

"Her family was too poor to get her a car, and all of her friends were about to start practice, right?"

"I suppose so, yeah."

"So why would she go to the parking lot and not her locker to get her phone to call for a ride?"

"I suppose she was just going to walk home. She don't live but a few blocks that direction."

Elliott finished writing his notes before thanking Johnson for his honesty and telling him he could go. He gave Johnson his card and asked him to call if he thought of anything else, which Elliott knew was highly unlikely. Before leaving, Elliott thought for a minute. A teenage girl leaving without her clothes or phone? There was a chance Johnson was misremembering.

But, if Coach J was correct, RayLynn was upset about more than playing time. It may be related to George Johnson, and it may not. Elliott didn't have enough information to know. He wrote a note to himself to follow up with Johnson about the argument before closing the notepad. His next stop was RayLynn's grandmother's house. Elliott had read the statement taken by the boys in Vista County. It wasn't substantive. The sheriff and his deputies likely didn't know what information to ask for, and Sharon Smith had been unintelligible.

After speaking with her, Elliott would take a trip out to the dump site. This time he'd have fresher eyes, and he wouldn't have to contend with the sight of the girl's body.

● ● ● ●

Kat's pickup might as well have been a DeLorean as it climbed the hill to Bison Ridge. Whatever was going on in the rest of the world, life there remained constant. When someone in Russia, North Korea or Washington finally lost it and started a nuclear war—which seemed more and more possible by the day, depending on which channel was playing in the newsroom—life in Bison Ridge would continue uninterrupted.

She was driving to the spot where the Vista County deputy had found RayLynn. Sheriff Shawn Nichols had not been returning her calls to his office, even though Kat and his secretary, Beatrice, were on a first-name basis now. He was equally unresponsive to calls to his cellphone. Kat had called the school and gotten a hold of RayLynn's coach earlier that morning. He'd sung RayLynn's praises and let Kat know that Saturday's home volleyball match would include a pre-game ceremony. She'd pumped out a short story for Thursday's edition. She'd told Bishop it was ready for him to edit—even though it had just one source—but that she would drive out to Bison Ridge and let him know if she got anything that would work for the story.

Kat had passed First Baptist Church on Main Street, then continued to the one blinking stoplight flanked by the AllStop and DQ. Main dead-ended at the courthouse, forcing her to take a left on Broadway. She lit another cigarette as she passed St. Ann's Catholic, followed by Broadway Church of Christ. Kat had forgotten how many churches were shoehorned into Bison Ridge and wondered what percentage of the congregants believed their chosen preacher. Kat slowed as she approached Bison Ridge High, careful to comply with the reduced speed limit before passing the brown-and-white Vista County Sheriff's Office SUV parked dutifully at the edge of the school zone.

As Kat drove, she decided the universe was looking for opportunities to mock her. The road leading to where RayLynn's body had been discovered took her right past Levi's parents' house tucked away on the northwest corner of town. Kat noted the lack of a black Kia along the curb or under the carport. Had he skipped town and gone back to Dallas? "Stop it, stupid girl," Kat said out loud as she passed the house and approached a cattle guard.

As she made her way up a dirt road and the house disappeared from her rear-view mirror, Kat looked down at her phone. Her GPS was telling her to take a right turn in five-hundred feet—*if* she could believe Levi's pin placement—so Kat slowed down as she approached another barbed-wire fence. She used the butt of her cigarette to light another as she found a yellowing water tank with faded brown spray paint beside an opening in the fence. *This must be it.* Kat crossed the cattle guard and slowly drove along the trail leading into a nearly dead field. After a mile or so, she saw an SUV with the words *STATE TROOPER* in white against the black body next to the shape of Texas in gold. The DPS vehicle was parked beside another SUV, the same make and model, though it was unmarked and all black.

As she crawled toward the vehicles, a burly trooper emerged from the one with the DPS markings. Kat put out her cigarette in Ol' Faithful's overflowing ashtray and took the *Amarillo Morning Standard* badge out of her purse and slipped the black lanyard around her neck. It wasn't necessary with the sources she dealt with regularly, but Kat had just rolled up on a state-run investigation in a location she wasn't supposed to know about.

"Can I help you, ma'am?" the young officer asked as Kat shut Ol' Faithful's door, which she thought sounded even squeakier than usual.

"Good morning, sir," Kat said as she held up her badge. "My name is Katherine Hallaway, and I'm a reporter with the *Amarillo Morning Standard*."

"Ma'am, this is an active scene on private property. I'm going to have to ask you to leave."

"I understand that, sir. I was just hoping I could speak with someone investigating the murder of RayLynn Gutierrez. We haven't gotten an official update in days."

"I'm sorry ma'am, but you need to leave."

The young trooper took a step toward Kat. He was no longer asking. Kat contemplated how far she should push her luck.

"Sir, I'm afraid I'm going to have to insist on staying until I can speak to someone. Unless you are able to comment." Kat pulled a notebook out of her back pocket. She knew he was just the gatekeeper, but seeing the pad and a poised pen often reminded people that they were picking a fight with a place that buys ink by the barrel.

"Ma'am, please get in your truck, turn around, and leave, or I will be forced to detain you." The trooper reached his right hand behind his back, presumably to take his handcuffs out of their case.

Kat hoped he couldn't see her notebook trembling. Journalists know going to jail is a possibility. Incarceration is held up as a badge of honor, presented as proof that reporters are doing everything to protect democracy and uncover corruption. But that possibility of being restrained and confined in a concrete room had suddenly become real.

"Charlie, quit harassing this young woman." A baritone voice said from behind the trooper, followed by a meaty hand on his shoulder. "Stand down, son."

Trooper Charlie moved to the side but kept his eyes locked on Kat.

"It's nice to meet you, ma'am. I'm Elliott Dawson. Mrs. Hallaway, I presume?"

Kat nodded. "Yes, sir, nice to meet you."

"Likewise. I've been keeping up with your stories. Good stuff. So, how can I help you, Mrs. Hallaway?"

Dawson took off his felt cowboy hat—which had somehow remained a remarkably clean eggshell despite the fact he was working in the middle of a dusty field—and shook Kat's hand. She took note of his thick callouses. Perhaps Dawson was a rancher when he wasn't investigating crimes.

"Thank you, sir. And please call me Kat. I was hoping I could get an update regarding your investigation."

Dawson replaced his hat and slid his thumbs into the front pockets of his starched, creased jeans.

"For that, I'm afraid you'll have to talk to Trooper Alex Correa."

Kat suppressed an exasperated sigh. "I've spoken with him, but he won't comment until the investigation is over."

"I will, unfortunately, have to give you the same answer, Kat."

"I can't wait until then to get more information."

"I understand where you're coming from, I do. But I'm afraid I won't be able to help."

Kat weighed her options. Trooper Charlie had walked back to his SUV, and Dawson hadn't asked her to leave—yet. He may not want to give her an update on the investigation, but if she asked her questions, Dawson just might answer.

"Have you gotten back the results of the autopsy?" she asked, positioning her pen over the notebook.

Dawson grinned. "You aren't going to give up, are you?"

"No, sir."

"I can't talk to the media about an open investigation, ma'am. Not even off the record. But, when we wrap this up, I will be happy to provide a comment for you." Dawson reached past the silver badge above his left shirt pocket for a business card. "That really is the best I can do."

"That would be great, sir. Thank you so much." Kat took the card and tucked it into her back pocket. "Can I ask you another favor?"

"You can ask."

"Can I get a photo with my phone? Just of your vehicles in the field, from a distance. No license plates, nothing like that."

Dawson considered her request for a moment then nodded. "Take it and let me look before you leave."

Kat did as Dawson requested. He gave her another nod of approval.

"Thank you," she said. "I appreciate your time."

"Not a problem, ma'am. Sorry I couldn't be more helpful."

Dawson walked back to what was likely his unmarked vehicle as she turned around and started toward her pickup. She stopped short to look behind her. The wind had blown Dawson's red tie over his right shoulder. He was older and average height, but Dawson had the strut of a confident man. The ten-foot-tall and bulletproof type. She had a feeling he would find his man. After all, *Any wrong ya do, he's gonna see.* Kat cracked a smile at her corny joke, but it faded quickly. She had no new information to report, so that one-source, piece-of-shit story she'd filed earlier would have to do. Kat did have a fresh photo, though it was useless with no text to wrap around it. Then she remembered her blog. She hadn't posted anything in months, but today it would finally be useful. Surely she could come up with an opinion to pair with the picture. If the headline was good enough, she could get some clicks.

It would only be a stopgap, and she still needed to get to the heart of the investigation or risk losing momentum. But it was something.

CHAPTER NINETEEN

Ace settled into Matthews' chair with his tablet, holding it with one hand like most people hold an oversized phone. That was one secret to being a Division I quarterback that few realized. Even if he hadn't been six-and-a-half feet of solid muscle, Ace's oversized hands would've given him a significant advantage. Ace pulled up his social media feed. Though Matthews and his minions posted for Ace, it would be stupid for the congressman not to monitor links and comments with his name in them. Friday morning's post was a link to a whopper of a *Panhandle Patriot-Statesman* story with a thoroughly click-baity headline.

Patriot-Statesman uncovers BOMBSHELL about House candidate Bobby Joe Carter …

YUCCA, Texas — A Panhandle Patriot-Statesman investigation into one of the businesses owned by a candidate for the U.S. House of Representatives has revealed widespread corruption.

Bobby Joe Carter, who is trying to unseat Ace Anderson in the race for Texas' 13th District, has hired several illegal immigrants and regularly lies about the profitability of his towing company, body shop and other supposedly legitimate corporations.

According to records obtained by the Patriot-Statesman, Yucca business Joe's Towing has 36 employees. Of those workers, 17 have been confirmed as not having been born in the United States by a local business official.

"Bobby Joe Carter has been employing illegals, plain and simple," said a source in the Greater Vista County Chamber of Commerce who provided information on the condition of anonymity for fear of retaliation from the Carter camp.

In addition to the 17 undocumented workers at Carter's towing company, eight have been discovered at his other business ventures — Bobby's Body Shop in Yucca and Carter's Scrapyard near Bison Ridge.

By employing the 25 illegal immigrants — all of whom are Hispanics — the Chamber source said Carter's businesses have been able to only pay those employees minimum wage and have pocketed the taxes supposedly being taken out of their paychecks.

This has allowed Carter to post figures that make his companies seem more profitable, thus allowing him to justify higher salaries for himself and a select few managers, according to the source.

"It's really quite sickening," the source said, "that a man who holds himself up as a pillar of the Texas Panhandle community has been employing such dishonest business practices. And, worst of all, he's been taking jobs away from legal residents while providing a high demand for the supply of illegal immigration across the border with Mexico."

The source went on to say he, along with what the source called "other upstanding citizens in this area," suspect the illegal activities don't end with employing illegal immigrants.

"We've been hearing that those illegal Mexican immigrants in Bobby Joe Carter's businesses are using his warehouses to deal drugs," the source said. "They are also engaged in human trafficking, right here in the Texas Panhandle. It's disgusting."

Carter's office could not be reached for comment.

Early voting begins Oct. 22. Election Day is Nov. 6.

The post was complete with photos from various image services to which the campaign subscribed for legitimate print and TV ads. The "story" was libelous, though Carter would never sue. Even if he did, Matthews was a hell of a lawyer and had full access to the resources of Gordon Anderson's megafirm. There were already hundreds of comments on the "story." There were three times that on the social media posts that just had a meme of Bobby Joe's logo with a photoshopped image of a Hispanic mechanic, with words from the story, and a *Panhandle Patriot-Statesman* source line at the bottom.

It was dirty politics, and Ace knew it. The story read as though it were in the *Morning Standard* — until it got to the unnamed source. Then it went completely off the rails when it started talking about dealing drugs. And the kicker, human trafficking out of a local candidate's warehouses, was just too much. Ace was entertained and couldn't believe how many of the idiots had eaten it up.

But it still wasn't enough based on the latest poll numbers. Ace's lead was down to four points. He was barely winning Vista County. If Ace couldn't defend his home turf, he might as well give up. Could he get his old job back? Probably not. Maybe he would write a book and extort colleges for outrageous speaking fees.

Matthews walked in and didn't notice Ace in his chair until he was about to sit down.

"Excuse me?" Matthews said.

"I'll give you your chair back if you can explain these numbers."

Matthews took off his glasses and wiped the bags underneath his eyes. "I don't know. This isn't the same as last time."

"What's different?"

"Everything."

"That's not an answer," Ace said. "How can I almost be losing here? I'm a legend at Yucca High for Christsakes."

"It's like I said the other day, people just want to get rid of—"

"All career politicians. Yeah, I got it. Look, are we going to win this election or not?"

"Things can change quickly. And you've still got the *Morning Standard* endorsement. If we can get that, we will get a bump. Could be the difference."

"Maybe," Ace said, trying to sound open to the possibility. "What about the Internet? Why isn't that helping more?"

Matthews shrugged and took a long drink from his coffee mug.

"You should get one of those bloggers to say he killed someone. That girl's murder's still unsolved, right?"

Matthews leaned in. "Don't even joke about that. That Dawson guy—you know, the Texas Ranger—he's supposed to be here this morning."

"Wow, thanks for the fucking head's up."

"He called last night. I was going to tell you before you started in about the poll num—"

Matthews was interrupted by a knock at the door, which had been open. Dawson was leaning against the jamb.

Shit. Try a joke. "Well, your ears must be burning," Ace said.

"I always did have good timing."

"Glad to meet you, Mr. Dawson." Ace shook Dawson's hand.

"I'll make this quick, Congressman Anderson. I know you both are busy."

"Take all the time you need," Ace said. "We're happy to help in any way we can, though I'm not sure what kind of relevant information I can provide."

Dawson sat across the desk from Ace, took off his hat, and set it down carefully. Matthews remained standing on Ace's side of the desk.

"I apologize in advance for having to do this," Dawson said. Matthews shifted a bit closer to Ace, making sure he was in the Ranger's field of vision. "The autopsy on Miss Gutierrez revealed that she likely had sex within about forty-eight hours of her death. It's not totally clear whether it was consensual or not. There was no semen, but a condom left trace evidence of spermicide."

Matthews broke the silence after a few awkward moments. "I don't understand what that has to do with Congressman Anderson."

"It's my unfortunate duty to get alibis from as many of the men that she was in regular contact with the last few weeks," Dawson said. "And, based on the information Mr. Matthews gave me about the interviews she conducted with you, Congressman Anderson, you're one of those men. So, for the record, where were you Saturday night between 9 p.m. and, oh, let's say 2 a.m.?"

Matthews punched keys on his phone to search their calendar, but Ace knew precisely where he'd been.

"I was at a fundraising dinner at Yucca Country Club from eight to ten. After that, I was back here until well after midnight."

"I can provide names and contact information for donors at the dinner, and for some of the employees here who saw the congressman and me working through the night," Matthews said.

"That would be very helpful. If you could get me that info by this afternoon, I think we'll be all squared away."

When the sound of Dawson's boots had faded down the hall, Matthews turned to Ace.

"So, where were you after the fundraiser?"

*   *   *

The name Katherine Hallaway was smiling down from that bullshit fucking whiteboard. The previous day's blog post, *A lonely end to a vibrant life*, had given Kat the newsroom lead by the time the web department had updated it. The headline, coupled with the photo and a few paragraphs of Kat wishing she'd known RayLynn, gave her the bump she needed for the week.

She had a snowball's chance of keeping her job, but Kat couldn't afford to stop. Waiting until the investigation concluded to provide another update was not an option, and she'd yet to tap one major source. Kat tried unsuccessfully to swallow the lump in her throat as she flipped through the High Plains phone book. Kat had been loath to talk to RayLynn's grandmother, Sharon Smith, but that time had come. Grandma was bound to have a landline, and there would only be a couple of Smiths to call in Bison Ridge.

She flipped through the white pages and found one Sharon Smith.

"Hello, is Sharon Smith available?" Kat couldn't believe how shaky her voice was. She hadn't cared this much about upsetting a source in years.

"We aren't voting, miss," said a gruff woman on the other end of the line.

"This isn't a political call, ma'am. My name is Katherine Hallaway. I'm a reporter with the *Amarillo Morning Standard*."

"Oh, yeah. I read your story on the online yesterday. I thought it was great what you said about my RayLynn."

"Well thank you so much. First, let me say how sorry I am for your loss."

"Thank you, hon."

"I was hoping to write another story about who she was outside of school and sports. Would you be available to talk for a little bit?"

"Now's actually not a good time. Believe it or not, this old lady's still gotta go to work. Can you meet me Saturday morning?"

"Yes ma'am, I sure can," Kat said.

• • •

Levi opened his eyes and found a crime scene. He lifted his head and tried to focus. There was a bottle of Scotch on the floor by his side of the bed, and the carpet was soaked near its neck. It had fallen off a room service cart. The main plate had a half-eaten chicken-fried steak slathered in white gravy, green beans, and mashed potatoes—some of which was slopped off the plate and onto the cart and carpet below. Beside it were two dessert plates, one with the crumbs and frosting from a chocolate cake and the other with a nearly finished peach cobbler.

Levi rolled over to resume sleeping when his phone rang from under his back. He must've left it on after calling Kat twice, the liquor providing the necessary courage. She hadn't answered, and he hadn't left any messages. Levi rolled over one more time and nearly lost his balance. His feet landed with a crunch on the floor. A half-eaten bag of chips laid next to three candy bar wrappers and a bottle of Coke. He twisted around and fumbled for his phone. When Levi found it, he held it close to his eyes as they struggled to focus. *Mom cell*.

He should've ignored the call. Hell, he shouldn't have even woken up. Levi lacked the courage to kill himself—unless slowly giving himself Type 2 diabetes or cirrhosis of the liver counted—but he also didn't want to live any longer. He wanted desperately to hide in that room, buying booze and room service until his money and credit ran out.

But, as the third ring was ending, Levi answered, wondering how his father had helped raise such a mama's boy.

CHAPTER TWENTY

Kat winced at the sound of her door slamming shut. She squinted through her prescription sunglasses—amber aviators that looked good but were not keeping out nearly enough sunshine—and took a long drag off her fourth cigarette of the drive. She was hoping to have the walk to Sharon Smith's front door to finish it, but Kat tried to quickly throw down her little piece of morning heaven when she heard the door open. She cursed at herself when she saw that her source had one between her lips. Smith blew out a puff of smoke as she walked out onto the concrete steps leading to her house, which had once been painted yellow but whose weathered sides were now the same color as her dead front yard.

"Right on time," Smith said. "C'mon in. You look like you could use some coffee."

Kat thanked the gray-haired, pear-shaped woman standing in her tattered bathrobe and followed Smith inside. No reporter liked interviewing a dead kid's parent—or, in this case, the grandmother who had been the legal guardian—but there was no better way to figure out what RayLynn had done or knew that warranted such a closed-lipped investigation.

As Kat entered the messy house, the smell of burnt bacon and spilled orange juice made its way down to her liquor-soaked stomach and threatened to bring it all back up. A pounding headache similarly threatened to allow the damns, shits, and fucks to escape her mouth. But Kat knew she had to show restraint. Much of her job was reading the room and deciding how to ask her questions.

She listened to Smith—a sweet enough woman with no filter and a motor mouth—go on for nearly twenty minutes about how she'd talked to every law enforcement agency imaginable and none of them were doing a damn thing to find her granddaughter's killer. In fact, Smith said she'd just spoken with Dawson the day before. All Dawson would tell Smith was that he was still chasing down every lead. He'd asked her about the last time she'd seen RayLynn, which had been Friday afternoon when she was supposed to be at volleyball practice. Smith said RayLynn had interrupted her favorite daytime soap opera.

"And then I reported RayLynn missing when she hadn't answered her phone or come home by noon on Saturday. Her volleyball game was going to start in an hour, and she always came over for lunch before games."

"Was it unusual for her to stay out on a Friday night and not come back until it was time for lunch?"

"No. Hell, it ain't no secret that she was a wild child. Takes after her mother, even though she didn't know her."

Kat saw her chance. Smith had brought up RayLynn's proclivities.

"Sharon—may I call you Sharon?" Kat asked. Smith nodded. "Good. Sharon, why do you think someone would kill RayLynn?"

"Evil. Pure evil."

Ugh. It was an evocative quote that she'd use in her story, probably as the kicker, but *pure evil* was not a motive.

"I guess I was thinking more along the lines of something she may have done or known," Kat said. "Perhaps something she learned as a reporter."

Smith folded her hands in her lap. "Hon, what do you know about how RayLynn was killed?"

"The authorities aren't telling me anything," Kat said. "You wouldn't be willing to speak about, it would you?"

"Sure, if it'll get you to pull your head outta your ass and listen to me."

Kat clenched her teeth, nodded, and pulled out her notebook for the first time. She quickly wrote, *Evil, Pure evil* and drew a star to the left of the words.

"Oh, um, this part all needs to be … oh hell, what does your type call it …" Smith said, snapping her fingers as though it would cause the phrase to magically appear.

"Off the record," Kat said, an internal barrage of damns, shits, and fucks almost breaking through to the surface.

• • •

Kat couldn't remember where she parked. In the driveway? No. Across the street. She walked to her truck feeling overwhelmed and full of self-doubt. Her gut had been telling her Anderson was the guy. But, by all accounts, he was nothing more than a handsome doofus. A pretty boy who liked to coast through life and had basically flunked out of Yale Law School. Kat's gut had imagined a scenario during which the horny congressman and the attractive young female reporter were having kinky sex, and she accidentally died from asphyxiation. Or, at its most sinister, her gut figured RayLynn had uncovered something and Anderson had shot her—or killed her in some regular fashion—to silence her.

But was Anderson capable of that kind of brutality? Of burning Xs across the chest of a sixteen-year-old girl? Smith had seen the body when she had to identify RayLynn—which Sheriff Dipshit had her do that Sunday out where the girl was found—so Smith had seen exactly what that sick, twisted fuck had done to her granddaughter. But could Anderson be that sick, twisted fuck?

Kat opened the driver's-side door with no idea what to do next. It was all off the record, so she couldn't report any of what she'd just heard. Kat needed to get it on the record, but how? Well, there was one avenue at her disposal, but she was not desperate enough to go see Levi in person. Not yet. *No, goddamnit. Not ever.* Kat sat down in her truck and was about to turn the key when her phone rang. She pulled it out of her purse and saw *Regina Watkins, RayLynn Friend* on the screen.

• • •

Levi's mother's advice had bordered on absurdity. But, after he'd spent an hour on the phone going over every transgression since his first tour of The Hobbit Room, Levi didn't have the wherewithal to argue. *Come to the match this afternoon. Nobody will mess with you. Not with me sitting next to you.* The effect was supposed to be two-fold: Get back out into the world, and remember a time before all this mess.

He'd earned the nickname Lucky Levi in that gym, though it started as a means for the more athletic jocks to make fun of him without it sounding like they were making fun of him. Levi had played basketball his sophomore year on a dare. A husky post who could barely dribble, Levi was used more as a battering ram than a player. But in the Stampede's last home game, Levi threw up a three-pointer that seemed to miss the net on its way through—his lone bucket of the season. The crowd erupted, and someone on the team had called him Lucky Levi after the game. The moniker stuck so thoroughly, and lost its ironic meaning during the next two years, that Levi had it stitched onto the back of his letterman's jacket and etched into his class ring.

But being at a friendly venue didn't completely strip Levi of his paranoia. He tried to distract himself by eating a Frito pie and re-familiarizing himself with the Bison Ridge High School trophy wall in the foyer. The centerpiece was a tribute to Jesse, conceived and installed by their graduating class ten years after his death. It was modeled after a Baseball Hall of Fame plaque. That had been Levi's idea. Jesse was forever a sophomore, smiling at all who passed and reciting his favorite Bible verse, Philippians 4:13. "I can do all things through Christ who strengthens me." Jesse would never compete without the verse written on himself somewhere. During baseball season, it was written on the underside of his ballcap's bill. On the gridiron—on the day he was killed—it was written on the athletic tape Jesse used to wrap the outside of his cleats and ankles.

"That was a tough year," a woman said from over Levi's right shoulder, making him jump. "Sorry, didn't mean to scare you."

He turned around to see Rosemary Richards, Jesse's old girlfriend. Levi's old girlfriend. Rosemary had been Levi's greatest source of comfort after Jesse died, and it was while working through their intense grief that Levi had fallen in love for the first time. Or at least the fifteen-year-old version of love.

"How ya doing?" she said, opening her arms, her head tilted. She knew.

Levi obliged with a hug, his chin still able to rest comfortably on top of her head. Rosemary's dark red hair smelled like some faraway tropical island to which he could escape. It was the same smell he'd grown to love back then, and he remembered every moment of their time together in one deep breath.

"Been better," Levi said, surprising himself by not lying. He tried to remember what Rosemary had been up to. She posted a lot of social media updates on her job as a pharmacist and photos of her kids. She seemed to have a happy marriage with a mechanic or something.

"I heard you were in town. Glad I finally bumped into you."

"What are you doing here? I thought you lived in Yucca now?"

"I do, but my oldest goes to school here," Rosemary said. "My husband's got some friends, and they helped us get a transfer. The volleyball team was supposed to be great this year and next year, at least until their star outside hitter decided not to play. She was a lefty, which made her even better. ... Sorry, I'm going off on something I'm sure you don't even care about."

"Don't worry about it. You know I love to hear you talk," Levi said, giving Rosemary one more tight squeeze before releasing her and stuffing his hands down the front pockets of his Cinch jeans. "It's great to see you, Rosie, but it sounds like they're done out there."

"They've been done for about ten minutes now," she said, stepping back. "I was just closing up the concession stand. I better get going. It was great seeing you."

"Great seeing you too. Just so you know, I don't actually think any woman should be called—"

"If anyone knows that, it's me." Rosemary kissed Levi on the cheek and walked back toward the crowd filing out of the gym. Levi did the same and looked for his mother. She waved him over next to the net.

"C'mon kid, come help me take down the decorations in the locker room," she said.

"The volleyball locker room?" Levi asked. "That seems kind of inappropriate."

"Oh, they're all gone by now," she said. "Let's go. I need someone tall to help take down the signs."

"Where are all the rest of the parents?"

"They left. I told them I had you to help."

Levi grunted in protest. She wasn't even one of the team moms. But Levi's mother had started treating his friends' kids like the grandchildren Levi and his brother had yet to give her. His friends who'd started early already had boys and girls in high school, so she was back assuming the role.

Levi followed his mom out of the gym and into the athletics hall. They passed his old locker room—STAMPEDE painted in dark brown on the otherwise-white cinderblock wall above the matching metal door—and made their way toward the girls' door with LADY 'LOES painted above it. The nicknames for the Fighting Buffaloes hadn't always been so unconventional, but over the years they'd morphed to separate themselves from the Buffs and Lady Buffs of West Texas A&M.

Levi paused before following his mother into the girls' locker room. However foolish, he couldn't shake the feeling he was doing something wrong. He felt silly after walking in. It was an exact copy of the boys' locker room, and Levi and his mother were alone inside. They worked methodically, taking down signs saying "Go Lady 'Loes" and "Beat the Falcons" and stuffing them into a gray fifty-five-gallon trash can. They also tossed leftover snack bags into a white five-gallon bucket to be eaten throughout the week. What was left after that would be reused the next match.

"See, that wasn't so bad, was it?" Levi's mother asked as they made their way around the lockers. "It looked like you even got to say hi to Rosie Posey."

"Yeah, you were right."

"I was *what*?"

Levi laughed. "You were right," he said a few decibels louder. He had forgotten that his mother always made him say that phrase twice because he so rarely offered it up to her—or anybody.

They finished tossing the candy into the bucket and left the athletics hall. Then, as they were crossing the gym floor to leave, Levi stopped.

"Shit, I think I left my cellphone laying in there somewhere," he said. "Let me run back and get it. I'll just see you at home."

"You sure? I can wait."

"Nah. Home is what, a quarter-mile away? I'll walk. I could use the exercise anyway." Levi tossed her his keys. They'd taken his car to the volleyball match because, according to his mother, the least Levi could do is drive her around if he was going to stay with his parents.

"Okay, kid. See you in a little bit."

Levi turned back and looked around. There was a bucketful of processed sugar and caramel just sitting in the locker room, and he needed to take as much of it home as possible. It wasn't stealing, he reasoned. His mom had bought her fair share of it. As Levi backtracked through the halls, the eerie quiet was broken by noises coming from the coaches' offices across from the locker rooms. A girl's voice. Was she screaming? Crying? He stepped lightly toward the sounds and put his left ear to the door.

Chapter Twenty-One

Kat was jealous. Regina Watkins was taller than her by five or six inches. And, as Kat had guessed during their phone interview earlier in the week, Watkins was a blonde. Her eyes couldn't have been a deeper shade of blue. Then, because Bison Ridge was still getting its kicks by fucking with Kat, there was Watkins' body. Her tits were just as large and perky as Kat's, and her ass and legs were thicker below a smaller waist. Kat shouldn't have been jealous of a high school girl, but she was off balance as she sat down in an office chair next to Watkins.

"Did I hear you right when I interviewed you on the phone that you don't play volleyball?" Kat asked. "I can't remember if I printed that or not. Sorry if I got that wrong. We can print a correction if you want."

"Oh, no, I didn't play volleyball this year. I wanted to focus on school. I'm graduating early, at the end of the semester."

Oh, for fuck's sake. "Oh wow," Kat said. "Ambitious girl."

"Thanks," Watkins said. "And thanks for meeting me. I'm so glad you were already in town. I woulda felt bad if you had to make a special trip just for me."

Kat was also jealous of the *Buffalo Nickel* "newsroom," which was better than the one she walked into every day. She and Levi had been in a Bison Ridge High classroom earlier that week, and Kat assumed that's also where they wrote their stories and designed the pages. Instead, the *Nickel* had a separate computer lab with new desktops and a cork board filled with story ideas and the current semester's editions.

"I'm glad I was here, too," Kat said. "So, run this by me one more time."

"I was promoted to editor-in-chief—which I should've been *anyway* since I am the senior staff member about to graduate—so I came in today to get started on next week's issue. It has to be to the *Courier* press by noon Wednesday."

"Ouch."

"Exactly," Watkins said. "So, I was given the login to RayLynn's computer. I log in and start working. Then I see a folder called The List."

"Weird."

"Right. So, I click. There are three more folders inside. Pastor Theo Levine, Coach George Johnson, and Congressman Ace Anderson. I figure, hey, maybe there are notes for the Anderson story. I can finish it, and we can run it. With a different angle now, obviously."

"Sounds like a good idea."

"Um, yeah, of course it is. But all I see in the folder is an MP3. I think, 'Maybe she's just dictated everything into a recording to transcribe later.' Boy was I wrong."

• • •

Levi had left the school before Coach Johnson. The player, senior outside hitter Janie Franklin, had almost caught Levi listening at the door, but he'd just been able to slip into the boys' locker room while she exited. Now Levi was watching from his parents' front porch as Johnson walked into the party across the street. Longtime assistant football and head track coach Jim Franklin had been hosting Saturday night staff parties since Levi was a kid. He needed to let Johnson get a few in him first, so Levi sat and organized his thoughts, wishing he'd been able to grab some candy. It would've helped settle his nerves as he waited and planned the conversation.

After a half hour, Levi walked across the dirt road separating the houses and into the living room, which was thick with smoke and loud with Chris Ledoux's "Cadillac Ranch."

"Great match out there today, coach," Levi said, offering his right hand. "Bushland, that's a hell of a team to beat."

"Thanks. Do I know you?" Johnson asked. His hand was cold and wet from the beer can he'd been holding.

"No, sir. I'm Jim's neighbor and a former Stampede lineman. I was in town this weekend and thought I'd watch the Lady 'Loes in action. Heard they were good this year."

"Well good deal, man. Glad you could make it out."

"Must've been tough, the first match in that gym without RayLynn," Levi said. "The pre-game ceremony was real nice, though."

"Yeah, man, it sure was."

Levi leaned in close and stared at Johnson, trying to get a read. It wasn't sadness on his face. Fear? Anger? Levi wasn't sure. Either way, Johnson was about to have a strong reaction.

"So, listen, there's something I wanted to talk to you about if you have a minute," Levi said.

"Umm, okay, I guess."

"If you don't want me to tell everyone you were fucking RayLynn, you'll follow me," Levi whispered into Johnson's right ear.

"I don't know what you're talking about, buddy," Johnson said through his teeth. He tightened his grip and Levi tried unsuccessfully not to grimace. Johnson was almost hilariously short but had obviously dedicated a significant portion of his life to lifting weights—a good ol' boy who suffered from Little Man Syndrome.

"Okay, how about this one? If you don't want me to tell Jim you're fucking *his* little girl, you'll follow me."

That got Johnson's attention, and the twenty-three-year-old coach released Levi's hand. Levi led Johnson out the back door, through the Franklins' yard, across the alley, and into the vacant pasture on the northwest edge of town. Another few miles of walking and they'd have been where Levi was now sure Johnson had dumped RayLynn.

"Look, buddy, I don't know what you think you know, but—"

"I was listening outside the coaches' office tonight after the match."

Johnson stepped up to Levi, chest bowed. He was so close Levi could smell the beer and snuff on his breath.

"You didn't hear shit. And just what'n the hell were you doing back there in the first place? I oughta call—"

"The sheriff? Yeah, let's do that. I'll tell my good buddy Shawn all about how you're screwing your players on school property. About how when they threaten to tell someone about it, you rape and beat them to death."

Johnson backed off. "Whoa, buddy. What'er you talking about? RayLynn?"

"That's right, asshole. Not only did I hear you with little Janie Franklin, but I heard the pillow talk. You'd been screwing RayLynn, too, but things are going to be so much better now that she's gone."

"Jesus," Johnson said.

"I think it's about time I made that phone call."

"Wait. Just … wait. Yes, I'm with Janie. But Jim's okay with it, I swear. We're gonna get married right after she graduates. And yeah, I'd been seeing RayLynn on the side. But I didn't kill nobody."

"So, Jim's okay with you sleeping with his daughter? Bullshit."

"He doesn't know we're doing it, or at least he's never asked. But he knows we love each other. Hell, he's helping plan the wedding."

Levi took a moment to think. It sounded like a steaming pile, but Levi's gut believed Johnson. Small towns work differently.

"All right, say you're telling the truth," Levi said. "Say you're in love with Janie, and that this whole thing is more than some weird case of parent-sanctioned pedophilia. If all that's true, you were cheating on your old lady with a younger model. I bet that didn't go over real well with Janie. Sounds to me like getting rid of RayLynn would've solved a lot of problems."

"Look, I haven't been with RayLynn for weeks," Johnson said. "She'd moved on to someone else. An older, more powerful model, if you get what I mean."

Levi looked puzzled for a few seconds before it registered. Johnson told Levi the rest of the story, though there was no need.

CHAPTER TWENTY-TWO

Devil's food. That's what Levi needed. He'd already inhaled leftover chicken-fried steak for lunch, but it wasn't enough. Levi needed his old standby—snack cakes and a green sugary soft drink. The combination had gotten him through college finals and countless stories before his weight became more important than his ability as a wordsmith. Levi walked down to the AllStop to procure his future diabetes. Nichols entered as Levi rushed to the counter to buy his drugs. The ding signaling the sheriff's entrance made Levi jump.

"We gotta stop meeting like this," Nichols said.

"Yeah, we sure do."

"Everything all right? I mean, except for the whole video thing?"

What the fuck do you think? Levi wanted to stay out of everything for a while. He'd come back to town to hide from whoever was intent on ruining him, though Levi suspected enough damage had been done to meet that end and no more anonymous packages or video leaks were necessary. But he knew about Anderson's and Johnson's statutory rape of RayLynn, so Levi had to tell someone. He'd tried Kat, but she was still ignoring his calls and texts.

Levi had no proof. Just the confession of a half-idiot volleyball coach he was blackmailing. And, even if Nichols could get the same story out of Coach Jerkoff, the part about Anderson was secondhand. Still, if Levi didn't tell Nichols what he knew now, while they were standing face-to-face, he'd feel complicit. Levi took a deep breath to steady himself.

"Actually, can I talk to you outside for a minute?"

• • •

Kat popped up from her chair.

"Greg, I need you for a sec."

Bishop quit walking and turned slowly. He was wearing the navy blue jacket and a pair of fancy shoes. Kat had called Bishop's cell Saturday evening, and they'd agreed to meet in the newsroom at 1:30 p.m. the next day. He would be getting out of a meeting in the advertising building and could talk to her afterward. Bishop was working on a Sunday—after church, of course—which could only mean he and corporate were discussing the layoffs. His sour look told Kat it hadn't gone well.

"Is that the look I usually give you?" Kat joked. Bishop didn't say anything as he approached. He was pissed, but Kat couldn't waste any more time.

"I got him," Kat said. "I got Anderson."

"Got him doing what?"

"Statutory rape. Maybe even murder."

They were in the newsroom alone, but Bishop still looked around to make sure those words hadn't drawn any attention to them. "What?" he whispered.

"Listen to this."

Kat handed Bishop her white earbuds, hit the spacebar and waited a few awkward moments. When the audio started playing, Kat studied Bishop's face. She saw his soft brown eyes widen a bit when he heard the young woman's voice go from interviewer to giggly school girl. Greg's pupils dilated further when he sifted out her gasps and coos from the shuffling papers. He shut his eyelids and hit the spacebar to stop the recording when he heard the girl say, *Oh, Mr. Congressman.*

"Where did you get this," Bishop said, still whispering as though talking any louder might cause law enforcement to come storming in. "Let's go to my office."

Kat pulled out her thumb drive and followed Bishop to his desk, where she recounted her visit to Bison Ridge, trying to remember verbatim what Sharon had told her about the beating her granddaughter suffered. Then came the climax—her clandestine meeting with Watkins in the school's newsroom.

"Did this Regina Watkins say why Gutierrez had the recording? Or why she told you before letting the grandmother or investigators listen?" Bishop asked.

"She said she only trusted a fellow newswoman. Regina has watched *Spotlight* and *The Post* a time or two. She figures the authorities are covering up for the congressman. It's a great story. Too bad the facts are getting in the way."

"And just what are those facts?"

"A girl was brutally killed and dumped in a pasture in Vista County. The girl was a reporter working on a story about our local congressman, who also happens to be from Vista County. The girl recorded herself having sex with said congressman during one of their interviews."

"Assuming that is Anderson on the tape—and that's a major assumption—she baited him and set up the recorder beforehand. Why?"

"That is Anderson. And I don't know why RayLynn did it," Kat said, wanting to also point out that they no longer record things on tape. "But it doesn't matter right now. Should I send this to Sherrie to get it ready to go to the web? For drive-time tomorrow?"

"Listen, I just got out of a meeting with corporate. In addition to you-know-what, we discussed the election guide. We just finalized who we're endorsing, and guess who we're recommending for the 13th District?"

"Not anymore. And since when do they get to weigh in on our local endorsements? It's bad enough we all had to run the same presidential endorsement editorial last time around."

"Now they're dictating the endorsements of everyone in Congress. Off the record, I don't like it either. But we all have bosses. And unless we can get a second source verifying what we think we hear on that tape, we can't use it for anything, anyway. We're not cable news. Anderson could sue us if we just publish this and throw the recording online. What we need to do is turn this over to the Texas Rangers."

"Absolutely. Doing that will be part of my story."

"The guide goes to pre-press at noon Wednesday. You don't have enough time."

"Give me until noon Tuesday. If I can get the story, it'll make an epic centerpiece."

"Not a minute later."

Kat nearly jumped out of the chair and ran to her computer. She opened the email she'd gotten from Matthews.

Shit, no phone number.

Kat hit reply, praying Matthews checked his email every ten minutes, even on the weekends.

Subject: URGENT REPLY NEEDED RE: Congressman Anderson's schedule

Mr. Matthews,

I urgently need to meet with Congressman Anderson to finish up our election coverage. I am on a strict deadline. Please reply or call my cellphone absolutely ASAP.

She searched her desk and found the business card for Texas Ranger Elliott Dawson, Company C, Dumas. The automated voice informed her she'd reached the Dumas office of the Texas Department of Public Safety. She recognized the other number on the card as being an extension of the Amarillo DPS—just two digits away from Trooper Alex Correa's. *Shit.* Nobody would pick up on a Sunday afternoon, and she didn't have Dawson's cellphone number.

But Kat did have another cell number to call. He would have to do.

CHAPTER TWENTY-THREE

Ace wasn't about to let his ninny of a campaign manager keep him from seeing Hallaway again. His argument was simple and effective. The paper hadn't yet come out with their endorsements, and they must need more convincing. Ace wasn't a master political operative, but he was a hell of a salesman. Matthews lived for the power and loved being in Washington, and, for some reason, he thought the paper's endorsement would make a significant difference. So, despite his initial objections, Matthews had called Hallaway and set up a meeting between the three of them at campaign headquarters that afternoon. Ace and Matthews were waiting by the conference room window that faced the parking lot when her junker pulled up. Ace nearly jumped out of his seat when he heard the building's front door open and shut.

"*Mizz* Hallaway," Ace said, holding out his right hand. "I appreciate you coming all this way."

"Not a problem."

"Excellent. So, Hunter says this is urgent?"

"Yep. I probably shouldn't tell you this, but we've decided to make you our main story for this year's election guide. It comes out a week from today, and I just wanted to get a few more quotes for the story."

"Well, color me flattered. Fire away."

"Do you mind if I record us?" Hallaway asked, pulling out a cellphone.

"Not at all."

Hallaway fidgeted with the phone and sat it on the long wooden table that spanned the spacious conference room. But, instead of asking any questions, she sat in silence. Ace was about to speak when his ears picked up a familiar voice. *Oh God oh God oh God oh God.*

Ace lunged out of his chair and nearly had to sprawl out on the table to reach the phone. He knocked it to the hardwood and smashed it under his boot heel before looking back at Hallaway, seemingly unable to catch his breath.

"Well, that was dramatic," Hallaway said. "Good thing it was a burner."

Ace's eyes shifted from Hallaway to Matthews, who hadn't reacted. He just sat in the corner, calmly surveying the scene.

"Where'd you get that?" Ace asked.

"Does it matter? I'd ask for your official comment about the *rape*, but actions speak much louder than words," she said, pulling out her notebook, a digital recorder tucked underneath. "I do have one question, though. Did you brand RayLynn Gutierrez while she was still alive, or did you do that after beating her to death?"

Ace put his hands on top of his head and continued struggling for air. *Beating her to death?*

"Look, lady, I don't know what you're talking about. I'll admit—"

"Nothing," Matthews shouted. He stood and walked to Ace's side. "Congressman Anderson has no comment on the contents of that recording. My comment, should you decide to write anything, is that we will sue for defamation if any publication prints libelous stories about the congressman."

Ace felt Matthews' surprisingly firm grip on his elbow as the mole man ushered him out of the room's glass door and down the hallway to Matthews' office. Ace poured himself a scotch as soon as the door shut. He was more of a beer guy, but there was nothing but his father's high-end booze in the whole damn place.

"Pour me one, too," Matthews said.

"You don't drink."

"I grew up in Bison Ridge. I drink."

Ace had never seen Matthews take a sip. Ace always assumed he was a recovering alcoholic. But, if ever there was a day to fall off the wagon, this was it. Ace had been sure RayLynn would keep their secret. They'd only had sex once, in that office during their last interview.

Matthews had trusted Ace's ability to handle some airhead high school girl. Matthews had listened to their phone interviews and been at her first in-person meeting. Ace was left to his own devices for the last one. He hadn't planned on doing anything but answering more questions. As much as he liked pursuing women, Ace liked pursuing *women*. But then she started flirting. She came around the desk and sat on top, her C cups right at eye level. She was wearing a short skirt, and when he glanced down at her light brown legs, the girl re-enacted Sharon Stone's famous scene from "Basic Instinct."

But now Ace recalled a few other details. How RayLynn had "put her phone on vibrate" and dropped it into her purse. How she put the purse in the middle of the desk. How she stopped her digital recorder as she stood, trying to make it obvious that they were no longer being recorded.

That little bitch.

Ace had gotten anxious when he learned of RayLynn's death a week later. He'd damn near panicked when he read in the paper that her death was being investigated as a homicide. But the anxiety was short-lived. Given where RayLynn was found, he'd thought it was one of her classmates. Pasture parties were known to get wild, and someone must've taken it too far. Ace knew firsthand that she was an adventurous girl. Anything could've gone down out there.

"What do we do now?" Ace asked, sitting one of the tumblers on the coffee table and flopping down on a chair opposite Matthews. "You got a guy here in town, right? You used him when I slept with dad's secretary during the first campaign."

Matthews picked up the glass and downed the drink in one gulp.

"I can't use him."

"We don't have a choice."

"I said we can't use him."

"Goddamnit, Hunter—"

"Ace, look at me. Hear me." Matthews' hands were shaking. "We. Can't. Use. Him."

Ace stared at Matthews for a moment, then closed his eyes and slumped back into the chair. Ace had been walking around relieved at the wonderful coincidence he'd stumbled into. RayLynn's death had eternally sealed his latest indiscretion, one that could land him in prison. But Ace should've known there was no room for coincidence in a campaign run by Hunter Matthews.

"He was only supposed to scare her," Matthews said. "I sure as hell didn't tell him to kill her. And I had no idea he'd done … that other stuff."

"How'd you even know I slept with her? Did RayLynn tell you? Was she trying to blackmail us with that recording?"

"No. I had a recording of my own." Matthews pointed above his own head. There it was. Ace was staring into a camera, one of those discreet ones that blend in with crown molding.

"Fuck me."

"I checked the footage that night, just to make sure everything had gone all right while I was out. I deleted the video, but I didn't want to take any chances, so I called my guy and gave him the same instructions as before. I'd already worked up a dossier on her before granting her access to you. It was supposed to be clean and quick."

Was Ace born a screw-up? The night after his fundraising dinner, Ace was with yet another woman, the wife of a wealthy local business owner. They'd carried on a relationship—approved by Matthews—since the first campaign. She was his Vista County wife. Ace's real wife never left Washington.

But Ace's problem with women started long before he ran for office. After graduating from Texas A&M, where he'd played backup quarterback for five years behind a rotation of blue-chip freshmen and star transfers, Gordon Anderson had gotten his son into Yale Law School. Ace tried at first. But without football to help occupy his time, partying and getting laid became more important than graduating. Gordon cut Ace off after he dropped out, which led to a sales job that Ace liked. He might've been happy doing that the rest of his life, but his father was mortified. So Gordon Anderson created the opportunity for Ace to be powerful. It was too good to pass up—even if his father was once again pulling the strings.

Ace poured them three fingers each and walked the drinks over to

Matthews.

"Looks like I really screwed us this time."

"Maybe not," Matthews said, downing his drink again before opening the liquor cabinet and grabbing an unopened bottle.

"I've got a plan."

Chapter Twenty-Four

Elliott hated that he was working on a Sunday, but he couldn't quit thinking about the case. His wife had suggested he take a few hours and organize his thoughts, then return and get back to work on his fire pit. Now that he'd set up a timeline, Elliott had a decent idea of what RayLynn Gutierrez had done in the eight hours or so before she went missing.

Though his office didn't have a whiteboard or big glass wall for him to compose a timeline, he did have a large cork board that took up most of one wall. It was usually decorated by college football posters. There were several featuring his alma mater, Texas Tech. Elliott's son went to school at WT in Canyon, so there was usually a Buffs poster or two. There were also posters with the Big 12 and Lone Star Conference football schedules. They were now in a pile on one of the chairs in his office, replaced by printouts and photos that created a visual representation of RayLynn Gutierrez's final days.

Her grandmother, Sharon Smith, said RayLynn left her house around 7:15 a.m. that Friday for school. Several teachers confirmed she was in her classes that day. Nobody would tell Elliott where she went for lunch. Sharon said RayLynn hadn't come home to eat, which was normal. She had her newspaper class next. The teacher didn't know where RayLynn had gone either, but she remembered smelling marijuana on RayLynn when she returned from the lunch period. The teacher told Elliott it wasn't out of the ordinary and that she excused such actions for creative types like RayLynn, so long as the work didn't suffer. Elliott disagreed. He was a third-generation lawman and second-generation Ranger. Between his experience and stories from his father and grandfather, Elliott knew drugs almost always lead down a dangerous road. That had probably been the case for RayLynn.

After classes, she had gone to volleyball practice and confronted coach George Johnson. Elliott had written a note on the printout that denoted the time and event. *Possible sexual partner.* Coach Johnson had continued with practice. His roommate—another member of the coaching staff—and the roommate's girlfriend had provided a reasonable alibi for Johnson. Elliott also knew Johnson was not smart enough to have planned and executed the murder. He hadn't killed RayLynn, but Elliott would circle back with the sheriff's office and Texas Education Agency to help open an investigation into Johnson for having an inappropriate relationship between an educator and a student.

After she stormed out of the Bison Ridge High School field house, RayLynn had walked to her grandmother's house. Smith confirmed that her granddaughter was in Lady 'Loes workout gear and without her cellphone, just as Johnson had said. RayLynn had taken a pack of cigarettes and lighter from her grandmother. She was too young to legally buy tobacco products, but Sharon said she was okay with her granddaughter smoking. She figured that RayLynn had drawn a bad hand in life, and if she needed to smoke to get through it, Sharon wasn't going to stop her. As far as Elliott could tell, RayLynn was surrounded by enablers. No matter who had taken her life, Elliott would view them as partially responsible for her death.

RayLynn had left her grandmother's house en route to the field house to get her things, according to Sharon. That was at about 3:45 p.m. During his trip to Bison Ridge, Elliott had spoken to Vista County Sheriff Shawn Nichols and had seen the contents of RayLynn's athletics locker. It still had her cellphone and street clothes, as well as other miscellaneous personal items. She hadn't made it back to her locker, which meant there was a giant gap from 3:45 p.m. Friday until 7:15 a.m. Sunday, when Nichols said her body had been found on the pasture near Bison Ridge.

Somewhere in that vast expanse of cork, RayLynn had experienced the worst humanity has to offer.

"You know, something's missing from your board," Loretta said as she walked into the office holding another printout, causing Elliott to jump.

"Jesus, you scared the hell outta me," Elliott said. "You can't be here on the weekend, you know that. How'd you even know I was here?"

"Your wife called. She told me she'd sent you in and wanted me to make sure you had what you needed."

"You two need to quit scheming behind my back."

Loretta just waved Elliott off.

"Well, since you're here, I guess you should tell me what I've missed."

Loretta pushed past Elliott and pinned a sheet of paper in the middle of the gap in the timeline. When she stepped back, Elliott read what she'd printed in the largest type that would fit.

WHERE WAS SHE KILLED?

"A damn fine question," Elliott said.

"Any ideas?"

"Well, when I went out to the dump site, I drove around the back roads for a few miles in each direction. There was one little shack out there, but nothing was disturbed, and the door was wide open. I bet it hadn't been used in decades."

"So, she wasn't killed close by," Loretta said, crossing her arms and contemplating. Elliott was grateful for her help. There was a lot of wisdom underneath that silver hair.

"Right. So, assuming that's true, I went to the courthouse and looked at the maps and property records for all of Vista County. While I was trying to pinpoint where her body was found, guess what I saw?"

Loretta looked up at Elliott over her bifocals. "Just spit it out. I'm old and tired and am not getting paid to be here."

"Oh, come on. You know what I'm talking about. In the middle of all those private ranches and oil leases, there is a small patch of county-owned property ... right along the Canadian River ..."

When the answer registered with Loretta, she snapped her fingers then pointed up at Elliott in excitement. "Oh, you're right. That would be a perfect place. I bet if you drove out there you'd find a hundred places to hold someone for a day and a half and nobody would find you."

"I thought the same thing, which is why I hauled ass out of the courthouse and drove there, ready to break this thing wide open."

"Wait, so you went out there and didn't find anything?"

"Not exactly. The road in has been blocked by a gate."

"So? Why didn't you just get some bolt cutters or drive through it or something?"

"I could have. Or I could have driven down into the riverbed and found a way out there that way. But, just in case the property records were out of date and someone does own that land now, I didn't want to risk any illegal search and seizure issues coming up later if I had found the crime scene. Instead, I called Sheriff Nichols and arranged to go out there first thing tomorrow morning."

"I'd've gone in there anyways. What if those extra days give this guy the time he needs to get away?"

"He's not going anywhere. If he wanted to flee, he wouldn't have staged the body for us to find. He'd've just buried the girl out in the middle of all that land where nobody would ever go. Instead, he made this big production of mutilating her body and putting it where everyone knows to look for a Bison Ridge high schooler on a weekend. He wanted her to be found. He's getting off on reading about her every day and us not having a clue who he is."

"So, he's hiding in plain sight, just hoping we don't ever catch him so he can live out the rest of his life knowing he got away with it?"

Elliott frowned. "No. My bet is he's out there looking for someone else to kill."

• • •

Levi thought about reneging on his deal with Emily Greene. She had no real leverage against him. In fact, Levi had even more reason to hide now that the news was out about his "resignation" from the *Daily Star*. The networks had reached out to his old bosses for comment, and after a day they'd released a statement saying Levi had left the paper before the night at Drake's and that they had no further comment. Most media suspected Levi was in rehab, though some said they'd heard he was working out a deal with a network or national cable news organization. As they gossiped about Levi's future, they also speculated that Levi's outburst meant he was a domestic abuser. According to social media, someone capable of an outburst like his was likely to have physically assaulted women in the past. Pundits said accusers would come forward soon. If the roles were reversed and Levi was asked his opinion on live TV, he'd probably agree.

Despite the myriad reasons to maintain his silence, Levi decided to honor his agreement. He'd removed all email accounts from his phone days ago, and he wasn't in the mood to talk directly to Greene, so Levi sat in his old bed in Bison Ridge on Sunday evening, feeding his sugar addiction and crafting a text.

Emily, my statement is as follows: I sincerely apologize to the woman in the video for my actions last week. There is no excuse for the way I behaved, and my language reflects neither my feelings toward her nor my views toward women in general. Regarding the departure from my former employer, I left of my own volition for personal reasons. - Levi Cole

Not perfect, but it didn't matter. He was now the semi-public figure who had called an innocent woman a cunt. There would be no coming back from that. Levi read over his statement one last time with a few minutes to go before their agreed-upon deadline. Just after Levi hit send, the name *Bill Hallaway* popped up on the phone's screen. Levi closed his eyes and prepared for his comeuppance.

"Bill, I—"

"Is Kat with you?"

"God no. Bill, I—"

"Look, we'll talk about all that later. Right now, I just need to find Kat."

"What do you mean?"

"I mean I haven't seen her since she left for work this afternoon and every time I call I get sent to her voicemail."

"She was working on a Sunday? Have you called the newsroom?"

"I'm not a freaking idiot. Of course I called the newsroom. I know she's been chasing that story about the girl who got murdered out there. And I know if anyone knows where she is, it's you."

Levi's heart sped up.

"Let me call someone. The sheriff out here is a friend of mine. She was trying to use him as a source. Maybe he knows something."

Nichols didn't pick up after two calls and a voicemail, so Levi drove to the courthouse to see if he was burning the midnight oil. If not, Levi would have to wake up his mom to see if she knew where he lived, or if she knew someone who did. Levi felt relieved when he saw the sheriff's SUV in the building's back parking lot. He walked up to the rear door and pulled down on the handle. No dice. Levi walked around to a side door. It was also locked. Levi picked up his pace as he made his way to the next door. His speed walking turned into a jog, and Levi found himself sprinting by the time he had circled back to the back door. He tried it one more time, then pounded on the metal before yelling Nichols' name while trying to catch his breath.

Levi walked over to the SUV and looked in the windows as he leaned against the driver's-side door. *What the hell? Doesn't he drive this home at night?* He pulled out his phone and used its flashlight to look around the poorly lit parking lot. Levi saw a pack of cigarettes about ten feet away and stepped closer. Llama Lights. He picked up the pack, looked inside, and saw a neon pink lighter.

Levi's phone buzzed, nearly causing him to drop it on the asphalt.

"Hey Bill, it looks like she did visit with the sheriff, but they're not at his office anymore."

"I think I know where she was headed. Kind of. Right after I hung up with you, I remembered we have this find-your-phone app. It showed her like thirteen miles northwest of Bison Ridge, just out in the middle of nowhere, not even on a road. Then it showed nothing."

Levi thought for a few seconds. There was only one destination out that direction, but he had no idea why Kat would be driving there.

CHAPTER TWENTY-FIVE

Shawn made a mental note: Thank Lucky Levi before killing him later. Without running into him at the AllStop, Shawn wouldn't have been able to adequately set up. And proper preparation is the key. It's what separated Shawn from all those idiots in TV documentaries and true crime books who get caught.

Lucky Levi had told Shawn about sneaking around the high school after Saturday's match and eavesdropping on that pervy Coach J. *I bet he got hard while he was listening.* He'd also told Shawn about giving that lady reporter his cellphone number. Lucky Levi had asked if she'd called. Shawn had been truthful and said no. Shawn had been ignoring the calls and voicemails. He usually didn't deal with the media.

But, less than two minutes after Lucky Levi left the AllStop parking lot, she called again. Shawn answered, apologized for not picking up all week, and asked if she was available to come tonight. It was the only time he could meet, what with this big investigation and all. It turned out she was already on her way to ambush Shawn, dogged newswoman that she is. If Lucky Levi knew about Fuckface Anderson and The Gutierrez Girl, Shawn would bet his bottom dollar that she knew, too.

That's why Kitty Kat was now down in The Hole.

Shawn had packed some supplies before her arrival. In the Vista County Sheriff's SUV he had hidden a duffel bag containing the essentials—duct tape, a blue bandana, extra handcuffs, zip ties, rubber gloves, a hairnet, bleach, and a clean pistol—but made sure it was easily accessible in the back. He had soaked a handkerchief in chloroform and stuffed it in his back pocket as he saw her driving down

Main Street.

"It was perfect, Kitty Kat," Shawn told her unconscious body. "You had no idea what was coming."

Shawn had changed into street clothes to put her at ease and made sure he was typing an email on his phone as she parked her truck, looking hard at work after hours. It wasn't all for show. Shawn had been sending an email telling his staff he had urgent personal business and wouldn't be in on Monday, perhaps even Tuesday, but that he'd left the SUV and the spare keys on Beatrice's desk.

Her "interview" in Shawn's office had been cordial. Friendly, even. She'd given him a copy of the recording The Gutierrez Girl had made. She assured him it was the only one. After walking her back out to the truck, Shawn shook Kitty Kat's hand and didn't let go. She put up a hell of a fight, but the chloroform always wins. Shawn shoved Kitty Kat into the back seat of her rusted-out extended cab, then grabbed the bag from out of his SUV, got her keys from out of her purse, and calmly drove out of the parking lot.

"And it was all thanks to Lucky Levi," Shawn said.

The only downer was Shawn's cellphone, which would not stop ringing. He'd already broken Kitty Kat's phone—which had four missed calls from Husband Bill—and tossed it out onto the lease that leads to Lucy's Bridge. Now Lucky Levi was calling Shawn. Husband Bill must've finally called looking for his whore of a wife. Shawn would have to proceed much quicker than he'd hoped. Not ideal, but Shawn chose to see it as an unexpected opportunity to prove his plan's efficiency.

"I love it when a plan comes together," Shawn said, then paused expectantly. "Come on. That's an easy one. *The A-Team*."

Kitty Kat was still unconscious, but Shawn's excited voice caused her to stir. He smiled.

The fun was about to begin.

• • •

Kat heard breathing. Or was that the wind? Either way, it was aggravating her headache. She was freezing. She could smell dirt. She could taste ... *What the fuck is in my mouth?*

She tried to scream through the gag—which, near as she could tell, was a bandana—and her sore throat. She then tried to pull the bandana out, only to find that her arms were strapped down. When she looked to see what was around her wrists, Kat realized her shirt and bra were missing, and her forearms were held down by medieval-looking leather straps. Kat's next instinct was to stand up. That's when she found out her lower half was also bare, and her ankles similarly restrained.

Kat tried again to scream through the gag as she craned her neck looking for Nichols. He'd been standing to her right but moved in front of her. Nichols stared at her with dark brown eyes, which seemed to be almost all pupil thanks to the low light in whatever fucking hellhole she was in. Her own eyes darted around, piecing together her surroundings. It looked and felt like a cellar, though not like any she'd seen before. Off to one side, she could see a blowtorch. The room was encircled by a molded concrete bench, books of varying ages and sizes stacked in piles all around, except where there were hand tools arranged in neat lines.

"All that screaming won't do any good," Nichols said, wiping a tear from Kat's cheek. "Nobody's gonna hear you down here."

CHAPTER TWENTY-SIX

Hunter cursed under his breath as he drove down the hill toward Lucy's Bridge. By the time he reached the cutout just to the side of the bridge's entrance, he was nearly screaming. Hunter had planned on getting to The Hole the easy way, by heading down Dickson's Crossing Road, which would almost lead him straight there. He just had to remember to turn left at the outhouse with a pentagram painted on it. Instead, Hunter slammed on his brakes and flung open the Suburban's driver's-side door so hard it came back at him, slamming on his shin.

"Goddamnit," Hunter yelled as he pushed the door open more slowly and hopped down out of the Suburban.

Dickson's Crossing Road was now blocked by a gate. *Why would they do that but leave access to this creepy fucking bridge?* He walked up to the blockade and confirmed it was locked with a thick padlock and shiny stainless-steel chain. The whole setup looked new. He cursed again and kicked the gate.

Hunter was usually calm. Calculated. But since he'd been back in Vista County trying to save Anderson's dying campaign, things had been spiraling downhill quickly. He'd planned on being in Yucca for two weeks at most, popping between the campaign offices and Anderson's unused house, which the congressman needed to represent the district. And Hunter had never planned to get within ten miles of Bison Ridge. But when the lead had slipped to five points, Hunter knew they needed to launch a real campaign. The whole damn world was devolving into that movie *Idiocracy*, and he was going to have to fight tooth-and-nail to out-dumb Bobby Joe Carter. Then, in the middle of staving off defeat, Hunter's stupid-but-necessary show dog let his pink thing hang out in front of an underage girl. Hunter didn't have time to deal with the situation, so he called in His Guy—a colossal fucking mistake that had led to Hunter standing in the middle of nowhere trying to get into a ghost town and save Anderson from going to prison. If Hunter couldn't get to The Hole, he was sure Anderson would either go down for the murder he didn't commit or the statutory rape he did.

Hunter had been vague with Anderson when describing his plan. Go get evidence against His Guy, just in case the reporter ended up writing anything about the affair or accused Anderson of killing the girl. Hunter could discreetly give his evidence to the Texas Ranger, Elliott Dawson, who could then investigate and catch the real killer. Once that was set into motion, Hunter could release a statement saying Anderson's office was cooperating with authorities in their investigation. As for the underage sex, Hunter still had enough cash to bribe one of Gordon Anderson's cyber forensics guys to say the recording was doctored, casting enough doubt to avoid charges.

Hunter had left out a few details when talking to Anderson—The Hole, and the fact that His Guy is Vista County Sheriff Shawn Nichols. Hunter needed Anderson to have plausible deniability for whichever investigation was headed their way. But there was now something physically keeping him from executing his plan. Hunter didn't have any bolt cutters. Could he use his tire iron to break the lock or chain? Hunter knew he wasn't strong enough. But he also wasn't going to give up. Hunter hoped he could remember the back way into Dickson's Crossing. It'd been almost a decade since he'd used that way.

Hunter turned around and took a few steps toward the Suburban when his heart stopped. Headlights were bobbing and weaving on the road. They were coming fast. Hunter knew the gate on the other end of Lucy's Bridge was closed, so he couldn't jump in the Suburban and drive away unnoticed. If Hunter headed toward the oncoming vehicle, and Nichols was behind the wheel, Hunter would be in a high-speed chase with a trained law enforcement officer. No good. Lacking better ideas, Hunter ran toward the riverbed to hide. He peeked around the sagebrush and prayed he was wrong.

• • • • •

Levi could hear his heart beating over Tim McGraw's "Just to See You Smile." Lucy's Bridge wasn't exactly a Vista County secret. On the drive out there, he couldn't remember ever discussing it with Kat, but she still could've known about it. Hell, as many years as she'd been in the area now, it was probable she knew about it. But what could she be doing out there, especially when it was too dark to see anything?

"What's this bullshit?" Levi asked himself as he began easing down the final hill. There was a vehicle parked near the front of the bridge—a one-lane steel structure that had been abandoned since the fifties—but it wasn't Ol' Faithful. It was a generic black SUV. Probably some kids making out. That's what the spot had been good for when Levi was in high school. He stopped to ask them if they'd seen an old pickup drive by.

Levi knocked on the tinted back window. He didn't see anything moving inside, so he walked around to the front and put his hand on the hood—a move he'd seen on detective movies and TV shows—and sure enough, it was warm. Levi was deciding whether to venture out onto the bridge when he felt a hand grab his shoulder. He spun around with his fist cocked, though Levi hadn't thrown a punch in so many years it probably wouldn't have made a difference.

"Don't hit me," the man said. Levi could tell the dark figure was short and round. He didn't recognize it, but the voice was ringing a bell. "Levi, it's me. It's Hunter. Hunter Matthews."

Levi took a moment to think, which was becoming more difficult by the minute. Everyone in Bison Ridge always expected him to remember them. It was exhausting.

"Look, dude, I don't care who you are," Levi said. "Sneaking up on me like that was a dick move."

"You don't remember me?"

"Should I?"

"Well, for starters, I was in your grade at Bison Ridge High. I was the football team's manager. We were both in debate class our senior year."

That last clue made it click. Hunter Matthews had been shy, but he had been a psychological terrorist in that debate class. He was

150

awkward, but he enjoyed outthinking everyone and making them feel inferior. Levi had done well in the class, too, but only because he loved research and was discovering his knack for public speaking.

"Oh yeah, I remember now," Levi said. "What are you doing out here?"

"I was going to ask you the same thing."

Oh shit — Kat. The adrenaline flooding Levi's brain was making it hard to focus. "I'm actually looking for someone who I think came out here. She's sorta missing. Have you seen an old brown truck driving around out here?"

"Can't say that I have. I was actually just leaving."

Levi nodded. He'd called Bill on the way out and asked if there was any signal on his find-your-phone app, but he hadn't seen anything since they last spoke. Levi couldn't call Bill and tell him he hadn't found Kat. Not yet. "All right man. I think I'm going to stay and take a look around."

"Good luck," Matthews said. "If I see that pickup, I'll come back and let you know."

Matthews headed for the Suburban. Levi turned toward the bridge, flicked on his phone's flashlight, and started looking along the ground as he heard gravel crunching. The adrenaline began subsiding. Levi wondered what Hunter had been doing out there in the middle of the night. *Damn. Too late to ask him now.*

There wasn't anything helpful on the ground. Broken beer bottles. Cigarette butts that were too old to be Kat's. A syringe — *People come out here to shoot up now?* — and a giant Styrofoam cup with a faded AllStop logo on the side. This quick search was not going as well as the last one. Levi got goosebumps as he formulated his next move. He would have to confront Lucy's Bridge. Maybe he could get a view into Dickson's Crossing. Maybe he could see her headlights. Or, unlikely as it was, maybe Kat was on the bridge, her truck far enough down that Levi couldn't see it. There's a chance she would've driven down Lucy's Bridge. She didn't know what Levi knew, that a gate blocked the other side of the bridge, which was too narrow for turning around. A person could drive down there, but then they'd have to reverse the half mile back.

Or, the person could walk.

CHAPTER TWENTY-SEVEN

Shawn walked over to Kitty Kat and softly stroked the pink spot on her left cheek. Soon enough it would start to bruise. He enjoyed watching the color change. A slow, painful darkening.

"I'm sorry I had to hit you so early in our process," he said.

Shawn had tried taking the handkerchief out of Kitty Kat's mouth. He'd been careless, and she'd bitten his finger. Not to worry. He was wearing the rubber gloves. Preparation.

"You know, The Gutierrez Girl had given up, almost willed me to continue hitting her," Shawn said. "She asked me for permission to die."

That might be why he had lost control so early. Shawn could've worked on The Gutierrez Girl until Sunday night, but she'd baited him into killing her long before that. "But, before I got started with the physical stuff, I asked The Gutierrez Girl how she'd ended up so rotten. She must've talked to me for hours, hoping it would help get her out of here. She was very different from you. This time, I think *I'm* going to have to talk to *you*. Who knows, it might be nice to have someone know about my work, even if it's only for a little while."

Shawn sat back down and relaxed. "I suppose all this began on September 11th. I was in my fourth year of college, my second at UT-Abilene after playing baseball at Yucca Community College for two years. But, rather than finish my kinesiology degree and try to be a high school coach, I joined the Army."

Shawn had lied. This all started long before he walked into that recruitment office. About the time Shawn hit puberty, he started to have impulses. Needs that weren't being met. He would sneak out to the door to his parents' room at night and wait until they started having sex so he could masturbate. Later came the desire to strangle the family pets. Not to torture them, but to let them know he had the power to take their life. The desire to go through with it came a bit later.

Shawn had been smart enough to realize he wasn't normal. So, rather than talk about these impulses with his parents or his friends, he started borrowing most of the words he spoke. Shawn was a genius, so memorizing just about every movie, TV show, and song he heard was easy. Shawn mostly parroted movies and television, though any pop culture reference would do. Everyone else turned it into a game. He never stopped playing.

Shawn removed his filter in only two places. Iraq had been one. The Hole was the other.

Shawn lowered his gaze to Kitty Kat's breasts. They were large and shapely with small nipples. That wasn't important to him sexually—long legs were his thing—but Kitty Kat's chest would be useful later. He had a much broader canvas this time. Another difference between Kitty Kat and The Gutierrez Girl.

"Where was I?" Shawn asked, taking off his gloves. His mind wandered a lot, a sign of his high intelligence. "Oh yeah, my time in the Army. About three years in, I was stationed in Iraq, at a prison we'd overtaken. You've heard of Abu Ghraib? It wasn't there, but you get the idea. We weren't stupid enough to take pictures, though. I was an MP—that stands for military police—so it was my job to 'soften up' the prisoners for interrogation. Stripping them naked. Beating them. Cuffing them in 'stress positions.' That's where ... well, you'll find out. I never did see what those spooks in the CIA did during the interrogations, but a few of them described their techniques to me in detail. Pretty nice guys, actually. We didn't have any lady spies where I was."

Shawn stood, picked up a pair of needle nose pliers and started toward Kitty Kat. Her muted pleas once again filled the cellar. He thought he could make out *stop* and *please*.

"Later, the Army gave me a medal for pulling two of the guys in my unit to safety after an IED—that stands for improvised explosive device—hit our convoy. That's what people know about my time over there. I preferred the earlier stuff, myself."

• • •

Kat knew she had to stall. She didn't want to talk to this maniac, but that's what helped get him off. She was going to survive long enough to watch this asshole get the death penalty. Nichols leaned over Kat, making a show of holding his pliers in front of her face before dropping them down to her left hand.

"The fingernails are one of the best places to start when you want to inflict maximum pain with minimal damage," he said, isolating her index finger with his left hand. "You have short nails. I just can't stop spotting the differences between you two."

Breathe. Don't panic. That's what he wants.

Nichols held the pliers still and looked at Kat. "Ready to talk?"

Kat nodded.

Shawn slowly slipped two fingers between her left cheek and the bandana, moved them around her head, through her hair and to the knot in the back. He then used both hands to loosen the knot and let it drop to her neck.

"Oh, I almost forgot. I know you smoke. I don't have any on me, but I do have some nicotine gum if you want a piece. I've been trying to quit for years. I was smoking two packs a day overseas. It was the one bad habit I picked up over there."

"No thank you," Kat said, trying to decide if he was joking or not. "So, what do you want to talk about?"

"I want to talk about you. Don't worry, this is a safe space. I know there's not a whole lot in the way of decoration, but I've been working on this place for a lot of years, and I have it just how I like it."

Kat's working theory was that if she could somehow get him talking, she would find a chink in his armor. Something that might get him to think twice about taking this any further. She could bargain, tell him that she was willing to forget all of this happened. It never seemed to work out in the movies, but she had to try something.

"Did you come to this place often while you were growing up?"

"I didn't take that gag out of your mouth to have you ask me questions," Nichols said. He sat down, leaned his back against the concrete wall, and folded his right leg over his left. "I'm asking the fucking questions here, private. Do you understand?"

Nichols smiled, but it disappeared when Kat didn't say anything. "*Full Metal Jacket*," he yelled. "Nobody's any good at this anymore."

This guy's a fucking Looney Toon.

It was time for Kat to get on Nichols' side. Make herself relatable to him. It sounded like he hated women and he loved movies. Kat was a trained extractor of information, too.

"Darn, it was right on the tip of my tongue," she said. "So, what do you want to know about me?"

"Why did you cheat on your husband?" he asked, leaning forward. She had his attention. Good.

"I fell in love with another man."

"Wrong answer. See, if you'd done that, you'd've left him. But you didn't. The way I heard it, the way *everybody* heard it, you decided to stay with Husband Bill rather than leave him for Lucky Levi."

How does he know Bill's name? Kat struggled to keep her composure. This freak apparently knew more about her than she thought. And he was using that information to ask her real questions. Questions aimed at getting into her head. Kat knew she could not let that happen. Not if she wanted to make it out alive.

"You see, this place is about finding out who you truly are," Nichols continued. "We all behave one way on the outside. Everyone wears that mask out there. But not down here. Down here is where we tell ourselves the truth."

Kat shut her eyes and dropped her head.

"I can put the gag back in if you don't want to talk anymore—"

"You want answers?" Kat shouted as she raised her head.

Nichols stared at her. Kat lifted her eyebrows and tried her best to convey the message.

His eyes widened. "I want the truth," he yelled.

"You can't handle the truth," Kat screamed, as though the louder and more convincingly she gave the line the more likely Nichols would release her.

Nichols stood and clapped. "Very good. Thank you for that. But, I know you're just stalling, and I don't have enough time for that."

Goddamnit. Kat's mind started racing. She needed a different approach, and she didn't want him to pick up the pliers again.

"We're still going to have to figure out why you cheated," Nichols said, sitting back down. "Let's start with Husband Bill. Why did you marry him?"

"I fell in love with him. That's the truth."

"Okay. We'll go with that for now. What made you fall in love with him?"

"He was there for me."

"There for you how? Kitty Kat, this isn't going to work if you keep yourself shut off like this. The devil is in the details."

"Look, the why doesn't matter—"

"You don't get to decide that," Nichols said. "I do, and I say the why is important. What happened that he was so 'there for you' that you fell in love?"

There were only a handful of people who knew the answer to that question, and she loved them. Kat tried to think of a lie to tell Nichols. Anything believable that would keep him at bay.

Nichols got up from his seat, shaking his head. He walked past the pliers but headed toward the blowtorch instead.

"All right, I'll tell you," Kat yelled. She couldn't tell if her tears were from fear of her tormentor or fear of saying the words out loud again. "I was raped."

Nichols closed his eyes and nodded. "Now we're getting somewhere. Tell me more about that."

"Jesus Christ. You want the play-by-play so you can jerk off to it, you sick fuck?"

Nichols' coal eyes snapped open. His nostrils flared as he took two angry steps toward Kat.

"That's not what this is about," he yelled, pointing at her. "Not

156

everything's about sex. At least not for me, you dirty fucking whore."

Kat wasn't sure which she disliked more, *slutty fucking cunt* or *dirty fucking whore*.

Nichols retreated, and a look of peace seemed to wash over him.

"Sorry about that," he said after taking in a meditative breath. "I'm still learning to control my temper down here. Last time didn't work out so well."

Chapter Twenty-Eight

Levi felt increasingly uneasy as he turned around and started walking back toward his car, which was parked more than a half-mile away at the other end of Lucy's Bridge. He didn't believe in ghosts, but he couldn't help but remember how Dickson's Bridge—its official name, according to the Texas Historical Handbook—got its nickname. A group of Devil worshipers in the eighties was known for hanging goats and calves over its sides. After this had gone on for some time, one of the Satanists happened upon the young daughter of one of Bison Ridge's local preachers. She had been walking home from Bison Ridge Elementary School by herself. Though it was a short walk, the high schooler was in a car and offered her a ride, which she accepted.

It was the afternoon before the group's weekly sacrifice, so they were primed and ready. The group's leader took the girl into a nearby shed and comforted her. He talked her into taking off her clothes. He convinced the girl they were playing a game, and that if she played along, she would be home soon. Lucy was a Christian, so, in a way, the teen was telling her the truth. He walked her out in front of the crowd and slipped the noose over her head before two of his lieutenants pulled her up. But, rather than let her hang to death, the leader sliced Lucy's throat just below the rope. As the blood started dripping off her extremities, the group took turns letting it flow into their mouths like an evil sacrament. After she had been completely drained, Lucy was lowered to the ground.

The group leader was then ceremoniously presented a Bowie knife that was used to skin Lucy. First came her face, which was later turned into a mask. As more of the flesh was pulled from Lucy's body, it was passed around to the Satanists, each piece to be used in whatever capacity the member pleased. The final act of the ceremony was cutting out Lucy's heart. The leader took the first bite, then passed it down the line until the group had eaten the entire thing.

That's how the story went, anyway.

The evil fairy tale was usually used to scare girls into submission. For years, guys had taken their dates to the bridge and told the story of Lucy's demise. Their adrenaline would spike, and they would crave protection. Some even said they saw the girl's ghost. Telling the story of Lucy's Bridge was one of the easiest ways for a teenage boy to get laid in Vista County.

Levi reminded himself of the bridge's given name, derived from the same historical figure as the nearby town built along the Canadian River. He might've been able to forget the horror story were it not for the phrases spray painted all along the bottom and sides of the bridge, mostly in red. Levi couldn't help but read them as he walked. The words assaulted him, like forgotten, sinful scripture trying to sink their hooks into all who passed over them. They were the Bizarro Dead Sea Scrolls of Vista County.

"What a waste of time," Levi said to no one as he picked up his pace. He hadn't seen any sign of Kat. The only thing he'd found was *the path to the dark lair of enlightenment.* Levi shivered and wondered where those eighties freaks had gotten all that shit. As he started reading another one of the bridge's wicked phrases, the light went out, and he nearly fell into the darkness below.

• • •

Hunter smiled as he remembered how much his fellow outcasts had loved coming out to Lucy's Bridge. They were from a different decade than those who'd decorated it with spray paint, but the concept was the same. All the Normals went to one of the dozen churches in town at least once a week, and most also went on Wednesdays. So, while they were in one of Bison Ridge's many houses of God, Hunter and his group went to their temple. Instead of reading scripture and singing hymns, they spent their time crossing Lucy's Bridge, reading and reciting their favorite spray-painted phrases.

Hunter eventually tired of the routine and started researching their Anti-church. The rest were so focused on what was written on the bridge, they never thought to learn more about it. They thought they already knew why it was called Lucy's Bridge. According to Bison Ridge lore, a local preacher's daughter had been kidnapped and killed as part of a blood sacrifice in the eighties.

Debunking the myth couldn't have been easier. The news articles were easily accessible at the county library. A young girl had indeed been kidnapped. She was a preacher's niece, not his daughter, though the police said even that relationship had been purely coincidental. Her name was Elizabeth, not Lucy. She was taken early enough in the day that the evening edition of the *Vista County Courier* had run a short story about the incident. The sheriff's deputies caught the teenager at the bridge soon after the abduction. The high schooler was alone and perhaps thinking of doing something terrible to the girl at the bridge. But, as the *Courier*'s follow-up stories detailed, law enforcement found Elizabeth unharmed and playing a card game with the boy, who was charged and sent to juvie.

Deputies did find evidence of animal cruelty and what appeared to be a functional noose hanging from the side of Dickson's Bridge, along with the satanic passages. After the *Courier* printed the details, adults in Bison Ridge took to calling it Lucifer's Bridge. Lucifer was eventually shortened to Lucy.

With such a pitiful origin story, Hunter lost interest in attending meetings there. He recruited a few of his ballsier friends to take their rituals into Dickson's Crossing. There was a cemetery there, though that was about all anyone knew of the place. There was no physical barrier keeping kids out of the town, but few had dared cross its threshold.

As it turned out, there was no reason to be afraid of the ghost town, which had started as a small settlement in the late 1800s named after "Buffalo" Bill Dickson. The town was an unincorporated outpost at one of the most natural places to cross the Canadian River. Dickson had been a buffalo hunter and Army officer. He became a hero during several skirmishes with local Native Americans, including the Quahadi Comanches and their last chief, Quanah Parker. When the settlement got caught up in the region's oil boom of the early 1900s, a town was quickly formed and named after its hero, who became sheriff of Vista County.

But, as with all oil booms, there was a bust. Vista County fared better than many areas—it still had two large refineries and several carbon black plants—but Dickson's Crossing was one of the bust's casualties. The town folded in 1953 and many of the residents left everything. Whatever they owned could be purchased again during the next Black Gold Rush that never came.

Hunter and his braver compadres drove around and did their own spray painting on the buildings that were left standing nearly fifty years later. Curse words. Skulls and crossbones. Pentagrams. They desecrated the church. The cemetery became the new hang for the three or four of them. It was a site for weekly Ouija board sessions and seances. Hunter eventually started going to Dickson's Crossing on his own. He was more interested in exploring the town. Now that he knew there were no actual ghosts or crazy hill people out there, he spent hours walking around, inspecting the ruins of a lost civilization.

It was during one of those solo sessions that Hunter opened an old storm cellar door. It was a time capsule, musty and caked with decades of settled dust. He spent weeks methodically cleaning it out. The owners had stocked it mostly with canned goods but had mixed in other, more interesting items. A globe. A box of Cuban cigars in what had once been a beautiful humidor. A pile of books. He kept those and added to the collection.

Hunter also found a back way into Dickson's Crossing, a section of barbed-wire between two fenceposts big enough to drive through. It blended in well, though it wasn't hard to spot the somewhat shoddy workmanship if you knew where to look.

As he approached the storm cellar—which would later come to be known as The Hole—Hunter was impressed with how quickly he had recalled the location of the entrance to Dickson's Crossing. Then, when he was about thirty yards from reaching his destination, Hunter gripped the Suburban's steering wheel and slammed on the brakes. He didn't curse this time. He froze, his face and knuckles turning white as he tried to figure out if he was having a panic attack or a legitimate cardiac episode.

CHAPTER TWENTY-NINE

Levi looked down at his cellphone. He could still see the glow from where the screen had been alive—likely trying to warn him his battery was almost out, but not buzzing because the damn thing was still on airplane mode. It slowly faded into a piece of obsidian and became just as useful. He frantically tapped on the screen and pressed all the buttons, willing them to bring back his lifeline.

He gave up and slid his right foot forward and to his right. He stuck out his hand and prayed he would reach a railing of some kind. When Levi's hand touched metal, he pulled it back. The bridge was freezing. Hadn't the temperature been in the sixties when he'd parked his car? Levi reached out again, grabbed the bridge's icy edge and began following it back toward his headlights. Thank God he'd left them on, though now he hoped his car wouldn't suffer the same fate as his phone.

With his sense of sight all but gone, Levi's other four came alive. In addition to feeling all the rust and welds along the railing, he could smell the formation of a distant rainstorm and taste the dirt blowing across the bridge from the riverbed. Levi could hear animals moving among the brush where the river had once flowed. Levi stopped walking when he thought he heard a car door slam. He looked toward the headlights, which were about fifty yards away. They remained still. Nobody had jumped in his car trying to take it for a joy ride. Levi listened harder. Was that a person's voice? Another door slamming?

Levi took off in a dead sprint and only fell once before diving into the driver's seat and plugging his phone into the car charger. He didn't have time to wait for it to awaken. He had to start driving. Getting into town via the riverbed wasn't an option in Levi's car. He knew about a back way into Dickson's Crossing, but it had been a lifetime since he'd been there.

Levi had gotten his driver's license about a year after Jesse's funeral, and Rosemary had suggested she and Levi drive out to Lucy's Bridge that afternoon. They walked up to the edge and read as much of the sadistic drivel as possible without putting the soles of their shoes on the metal. As they started driving back to town, Rosemary showed Levi the opening in the roadside fence her sister had helped create. Beyond the barbed wire was a trail leading into Dickson's Crossing. They drove toward the church steeple—the only thing they could see on the horizon—and parked near the cemetery.

Levi and Rosemary had been consoling each other for a year. He had grown attracted to her but hadn't dared to do anything about it. When they parked, Rosemary looked over at Levi and leaned in. Levi backed away. Rosemary cried. He moved in to give her a platonic hug, but Rosemary took advantage, pressing her lips to his and holding his head in place. They ended the night making love in the bed of his father's cherry red pickup.

●   ●   ●   ●

Hunter recognized the truck. It was the clunker Katherine Hallaway had driven out of the offices in Yucca a few hours ago. But, just to make sure, Hunter had snuck over to get a closer look. After coming to terms with what was happening, he had run back to the relative safety of his Suburban—cursing *Fuck Me Fuck Me Fuck Me* the whole way—and slammed the door shut.

Now back to the perceived safety of the Suburban, Hunter opened the liquor bottle. He wasn't an alcoholic. He'd chosen sobriety not because he had a problem stopping, but because he liked having a clear head. The liquor was supposed to be for afterward, when the thinking would be over. He was there to see the true depravity of his best friend. He'd want a few drinks after that.

He and Nichols had been nearly inseparable in elementary school and through seventh grade. That's when their paths split. Nichols was more genetically gifted and was invited into the middle school "in" crowd through athletics and band.

Hunter was a different story.

After Columbine, Hunter liked to imagine most of the students and teachers in Bison Ridge were glad he hadn't struck first. *Thank God*, they probably said before making a derogatory joke about his wardrobe. Hunter hadn't worn a trench coat, but black T-shirts and jeans with a wallet chain sent the same message. He doubted anyone made jokes and comparisons like that anymore. Teenage Hunter would've been put on a watch list of some kind before being sent to an alternative school.

Hunter and Nichols went a few years without talking. But, when Nichols needed help in math to stay on the football team, the jock reached out to his old friend. Hunter initially told Nichols to go fuck himself. But it was nice to have his friend back, even if it was limited to one-on-one interactions. Despite their long history, it had been a hard decision their junior year to let Nichols into his clubhouse. What would he think of the books on Satanism stacked on the bench? How about the homemade poster of Charles Manson—Hunter's psychedelic colored-pencil illustration based on the iconic 1960 LIFE Magazine cover—hanging above them? To Hunter's surprise and relief, Nichols had been fine with the decor. They sat down there on weekends reading and discussing. Nichols was like a different person and started bringing his own material. Mostly philosophy and psychology texts, along with classic literature. Nietzsche, Freud, Hawthorne, and dozens of other authors Hunter couldn't remember.

They vowed this would always be their spot, where they could talk about and do whatever they wanted. Fuck society. Fuck its contracts. Its obligations. *No matter how old we get, we will always be able to come back here and be ourselves.* They had their own society down there, and nobody else was invited.

CHAPTER THIRTY

"Where were we?" Shawn asked. He had done it again, embarking on a long tangent about what had happened "last time." But it was an experience worth sharing. He would eventually involve Hunter. For now, though, Shawn wanted his buddy to have plausible deniability until Fuckface Anderson was re-elected.

Shawn's time with The Gutierrez Girl had been nice and long. She was also a little whore, and getting her into his SUV had been as easy as catching her smoking alone outside the high school gym while the rest of the volleyball team practiced inside. *Smoking on school property — especially for a minor — is strictly prohibited, little missy.* It helped that they knew each other's reputations. The Gutierrez Girl was as loose as they come, and all the high school girls knew Shawn would exchange a blowjob for tearing up a ticket or not reporting infractions like hers to the school administration. She hadn't needed much convincing. What he had to offer interested her more than volleyball, anyway.

It almost wasn't her fault she'd turned out so slutty. Clarissa Lynn Smith had also been a little whore. Shawn had slept with Classy Clarissa about eight months before her daughter's birth, the result of a drunken night during which she was also on Oxy. Shawn had been a bit worried the baby was his, but when it came out looking Mexican it was obvious he wasn't the father. That distinction — she claimed — belonged to Ray Gutierrez, a twenty-something who was couch-surfing around town and working odd jobs. He'd been a nice enough guy, but Classy Clarissa had turned him into her cash machine and drug buddy. They both vowed to stop using when the baby was born. Instead, they went further down the rabbit hole, killing themselves and, in a way, their little girl.

When Shawn had gotten the call a couple weeks ago from his old pal asking him to take care of another one of Fuckface Anderson's conquests, he knew it was his chance. Years ago, Shawn had handled The Slutty Secretary according to plan: Intimidate her and use the dirt Hunter had gathered for blackmail. This time Shawn already knew the dirt. He also knew The Gutierrez Girl did *not* give a shit about being blackmailed. As Shawn would find out during their time in The Hole, she was an expert.

They fucked by the bridge first. Afterward, Shawn asked if she wanted to see his "secret spot." She was game. They entered through the gate into town—which he'd erected years ago after convincing the county judge it needed protection from local hooligans—and she walked right into the cellar. After he'd put The Gutierrez Girl into the chair, Shawn commenced with the psychoanalysis. She was, to his surprise, a willing patient. First, they discussed why she wanted to be a reporter. She said she liked to learn about people's secrets. Her goal was to get to interview the worst of the worst—rapists, serial killers, etcetera. Anyone with pasts more fucked up than her own. Shawn said he would be happy to help her live that dream before she died. She was a thoughtful girl who asked pointed questions, even in her last days.

Shawn eventually shifted back to interrogator. He asked The Gutierrez Girl how her parents' death had impacted her. She was smart like Shawn and knew their deaths were why she had turned into a little whore. They discussed her first time—at eleven years old with a local man of faith—and myriad other sexual topics. Shawn had to take periodic breaks to make sure he wasn't missed in town, but he always left the light on and blasted the sounds of people and animals screaming from a boom box behind the chair.

After only a day in The Hole, The Gutierrez Girl gave up. Shawn was infuriated. He was not done. Who was she to deny him?

"What about raping her?" Kitty Kat asked, interrupting his train of thought.

"I didn't rape her. You need to stop projecting. And don't worry, I'm not going to rape you, either. I know it's hard to believe, but none of this is about sexual gratification. Sex with The Gutierrez Girl had been about disarming her. Sex was how she communicated with men. To get what I wanted, I gave her what she wanted."

Kitty Kat thought she was smart. But she didn't know Shawn had an associate's in psychology from Yuca CC, which he'd earned while beginning his career as a Vista County Sheriff's Office deputy. Law enforcement was the smart play, considering his military background and the stagnant economy when he got back. The degree came in handy during his campaign to replace the retiring Sheriff Brumley. Between that and Shawn's documented history as a war hero, it was a landslide. But the degree was not about furthering his law enforcement or political careers. Shawn had become infatuated with learning people's secrets and fears after his stint at the Iraqi prison—a connection with The Gutierrez Girl he'd missed during her session but had discovered while going back through his notes—and Shawn was determined to continue the practice stateside. Studying psychology became a steadying force in his life. It allowed him to explore his urges safely and without judgment.

But Shawn didn't have time to be sheriff and get a bachelor's in psychology, so he continued studying on his own time. His book collection had become quite expansive. Much of it was in his office, but the better reads were lying in The Hole next to Hunter's Satanism propaganda. Shawn kept that crap around for sentimental value—and because the titles were thematically appropriate. The most crucial fact Shawn learned during his studies was that he was a psychopath.

Soon he would be a serial killer, too.

"But enough about The Gutierrez Girl. That's all in the past. We need to get back to you," Shawn said. "Now, regarding your rape, I need the rest of your precious Ws: Who, where, when, why, and how."

• • •

The ranting had given Kat a chance to think. She had to do as Nichols asked. He was going to hurt her. Then he was going to kill her. But, if she kept talking, kept him happy enough, he may keep her alive long enough for someone to find her. Surely Bill had organized a search party by now.

"One of my cousins. My room, mostly. Many, many, times, from when I was about nine until I was twelve. I have no idea why. I think you can figure out the how."

Kat was working hard to keep her shit together, but she was mildly hyperventilating, and her jaw started quivering. Only one other person knew even those sparse details.

"So, it was incest and rape. Not an uncommon combination, unfortunately. And, it was not one traumatic event, but a systematic string of assaults," Nichols said, stroking his beard.

This asshole thinks he's fucking Freud.

"But, did he start with sex, or did it begin more innocently and escalate over time?" Nichols asked.

Kat had tried so fucking hard to never think about any of this. Not since she'd first told Bill. "Why do you need to know that?"

"It matters. We don't have time to go into why. Just answer the question."

Kat closed her eyes. Her cousin, Cooper, flashed into view. He was about eleven when it started. They were outside on a swing set at their grandmother's house, each in their own seat. Cooper told Kat she looked beautiful and leaned in. She knew she wasn't supposed to kiss her cousins. But Kat liked Cooper. He had always been kind to her when he visited. He was the one older cousin who was still okay with playing with her. They must've watched *The Lion King* and *The Rescuers* together a dozen times over the years, back when they were still on VHS tapes.

Then they were in their aunt's house—their parents were part of a trio of siblings—with her and Cooper sitting on a couch in her basement. They'd been sneaking kisses for a year or so, and she'd been introduced to his tongue. But this time Cooper had been deemed old enough to babysit his younger cousin. Alone together for the first time, he laid her down on the couch. The kissing was more forceful, and now he was touching her with his hands below her waist, down the front of her pants. Kat should've told him to stop, especially when it started to hurt. But she didn't want to disappoint him. Cooper rolled Kat on top of him and unzipped his fly. He asked her to touch it. To grab it and put it in her mouth, to squeeze it and treat it like one of those popsicles that come in plastic tubes. She had no idea why he would want that, but she did it because he liked it and she liked him.

Kat's mind skipped forward to their last encounter, just before her twelfth birthday. She was still using her mouth. It was gross, but she also liked having a secret just between them. She had started throwing up afterward, though she didn't know why. Cooper said all big girls did it, and it meant she was old enough for more. He was fourteen and had discovered pornography at least a year earlier. Cooper was once again charged with babysitting Kat, and this time he moved it to his mother's room. The bed was large. She remembered being comfortable, except for the edge of the towel digging into the small of her back. She hadn't realized what it was for until he entered her. She yelled out in pain and tried to get away, but Cooper was developing into a strapping young man. He held her down with one arm until he finished a minute later.

Nichols snapped his fingers rapid-fire in front of Kat's face, causing her to suck in a lungful of damp air and open her eyes again.

"Hey, hey, hey," Nichols said. "I love introspection as much as anyone, but this isn't hypnosis. You need to talk for this to work."

"It escalated. Kissing, French kissing, oral sex, then vaginal sex when I was almost twelve."

"A very clinical way to put it," Nichols said. "That's okay. I know this is hard."

Kat tried not to allow his soothing tone to comfort her. Feeling the leather restraints helped.

"How old were you when you had your first consensual sex?" Nichols asked.

"Eighteen."

"With Husband Bill?"

"Fuck you." Kat started sobbing. She couldn't believe she'd resigned herself to telling this lunatic the truth.

"That wasn't very nice. Plus, you can't keep stalling like this,"

Nichols said. "That was a very basic question."

"Yes, goddamnit," Kat said. "It was with Bill."

"You had to tell him about the rape first, didn't you?"

"Yes."

"What about Husband Bill made you trust him enough to talk about it?"

"He was my best friend in middle school. As we got older and I developed, he was the only boy who wasn't trying to get into my pants. Or he was really good at hiding it. He had always been so caring. So tender. We decided to go to the same college, and he proposed during our high school graduation."

Nichols stood up and started pacing. "Good. You're finally starting to open up now. Please, continue."

"On our wedding night, I had to tell him. I loved Bill, and I wanted to give myself to him. I was so upset I couldn't give him my virginity, but I could give him everything else."

Nichols moved back around to his seat. "Very touching. You do have a way with words, even if that last part was a little sappy for my taste."

"I guess I'm just a little emotional right now, you sick piece of shit."

Nichols smirked. "Okay, time for your diagnosis. Rape Trauma Syndrome. R-T-S. It also explains your alcoholism, but I'm sure your shrink has told you all of that already."

"I never needed a shrink."

"You needed one. Yours was just nice enough to give you a diamond ring."

Was he right? Without Bill, there's a good chance she'd have died without telling another soul. Bill made her life tolerable for many years. Without him, she might not have been able to go to Cooper's funeral seven years ago. He had gotten heavily into meth. Kat started to move on after seeing him in a coffin.

"How do you know what kind of *syndrome* I have?" Kat asked, her fingers just loose enough to make faint air quotes.

"Call it a hobby of mine. So, you two get married and have sad sex on your wedding night, but you have sexual issues. There's virtually no lovemaking. When you are successful, Husband Bill is so damn gentle you can't even finish."

Kat looked down and squeezed her burning eyes shut. She hated that Nichols knew so much about her.

"When was your first orgasm?" he asked.

"Fuck you."

"Oh, come on Kitty Kat. You're so close. Why hold back now?"

You're so close. He was getting antsy. She had to keep him talking.

"About six years ago."

"That's when you started screwing Lucky Levi, isn't it? You were okay with a mostly sexless marriage with Husband Bill until you met someone who got you moist. With those two, you had the perfect relationship. Loving husband and terrific father at home, perfect lover at work."

Kat nodded, causing two tears to fall on the dusty cellar floor. Bill had treated her like a broken thing for him to fix. Kat loved him for it, but he would never—*could* never—do for her what Levi did with ease. It was chemical. It had been since the first time she'd set foot in the newsroom. Being with Levi had even helped her connect with Bill. She could finish with Bill now—if she thought about Levi while Bill was inside of her.

"That brings us to this infamous video," Nichols said. "In it, Lucky Levi said you chose Husband Bill over him. Tell me about that."

Kat shook her head. She was prepared to take that story to her grave.

Levi had taken her by surprise, sliding in without one of his SkinSoft XL condoms. She had been concerned for a fleeting moment. By the time he was fully inside, she didn't care. He offered to pull out— told her three times he was close—but she made sure it didn't happen. At that moment, with that connection they had never shared, Kat realized she did love Levi. She told him to shut the hell up and wrapped her legs around his waist, pulling him deeper inside as they finished together.

The ecstasy of that moment didn't last long. When she got in her truck to leave, Kat thought about getting the Plan B pill at a nearby pharmacy. But she wanted to get pregnant. She'd started sleeping with Bill more regularly, and the logical half of Kat's brain used that as an explanation for what had just happened. She wanted Levi's baby. But Kat could not lose Bill. She needed them both. The solution hit her on the drive to work, and Kat had talked herself into it by the time she got home that night. She had unprotected sex with Bill, doubling her chances and establishing an incontrovertible pregnancy timeline.

But Nichols—this fucking maniac who had her tied up and crying in a fucking cellar in the middle of fucking nowhere—would never know any of that.

"Did you hear me?" he asked. "I asked you to tell me about why you 'chose' Husband Bill over Lucky Levi."

"Go get your blowtorch."

• • •

A question kept swirling around Hunter's lubricated brain. Which is worse: The bloodthirsty animal, or the keeper who lets the beast off its leash? Nichols had relished his job as Hunter's intimidator, which was a red flag.

So was the afternoon before their high school graduation. Nichols had walked down the concrete stairs into The Hole holding an animal carrier. Inside was a feral cat he'd caught earlier that day. When Hunter asked what he was doing, Nichols said it was time to kill something. Hunter was confused. Both had hunted their fair share of prairie dogs growing up.

Nichols went on to explain that, while he'd ended the life of those animals, he needed to feel the soul leave another living thing. He needed to hear its death rattle and watch the soul fade from its eyes. Hunter figured all would be fine, never expecting Nichols to follow through.

When Nichols put on a pair of welding gloves, reached in and removed the cat, Hunter feigned excitement, hoping he'd get to talk shit about his friend when he pussed out. Nichols got the animal in what he called the "kitty clutch." The feline's neck was nestled in the V formed by Nichols' right index and middle fingers. Its right arm was held out by the L of Nichols' index finger and thumb, and the cat's left arm was secured by the V made by Nichols' middle finger and ring finger. It took a few seconds for Nichols to grab the tabby's flailing hind legs with his left hand.

Once the cat realized it couldn't escape, it went stiff and began howling. That's when Nichols stared the cat down and, with a forceful jerk, snapped the animal's back legs. Hunter threw up. Nichols kept eye contact with his victim and laid it down on the concrete bench that encircled The Hole. He knelt and moved his face closer as he transitioned his right hand from the "kitty clutch" to a death grip around the cat's throat while his left hand kept the animal's front legs at bay. The cat started jerking as hard as it could. After it was over a few moments later, Nichols looked at Hunter, satisfied. They never talked about it again.

Hunter now faced the truth he'd buried in The Hole. Nichols was crazy. Actually, literally, clinically crazy. And Hunter had given him an opportunity to graduate from animals to people. When Hunter agreed to run Anderson's first campaign, he knew he would need a Vista County law enforcement ally. Enlisting Nichols was a no-brainer. It never crossed Hunter's mind that the same kid was now wearing a sheriff's uniform. Hunter assumed the military had straightened Nichols out.

When Hunter used Nichols to intimidate that secretary Anderson had banged two years ago, he never thought twice about it. He gave Nichols the information for blackmail and got back a signed non-disclosure agreement. When Hunter watched the video of Anderson screwing RayLynn Gutierrez on his desk, calling Nichols was once again a no-brainer.

Hunter knew he shared the blame for the girl's death. Could he sit idly as another one was being slowly executed? Hunter swigged his liquid courage. He was a master problem solver. This situation had a solution, and Hunter knew what it was. He just didn't like it.

All right then. Time to do this. Hunter took one last deep breath before screwing the cap back onto the bottle. He lifted the Suburban's center console and pulled out a black case, which he sat on the passenger seat. Hunter paused one last time, then pulled out his pistol.

Chapter Thirty-One

"It's interesting, the differences I keep finding between you and The Gutierrez Girl," Shawn said, more *at* Kitty Kat than to her. She was done talking back. "You should have had more similarities. You were both reporters. Both reporting on the same person, in fact. Both whores."

Shawn had hoped this would be another useful session. He'd spent a long time turning his dark urges into socially acceptable activities. This process is the foundation of high school sports, which is how most boys and young men put their negative energy to good use. The military is an extension of that. Being in law enforcement had helped, too, as had formally studying psychology. But the longer Shawn went being a Podunk sheriff, the less stable he was. He started helping people outside his official capacity. He helped rebuild fences for local ranchers. He helped old ladies cross the street in town. He kept studying on his own time.

Shawn was not afraid to admit his quick fixes had stopped working. But he found an answer in The Gutierrez Girl. The world would not miss her. Even her grandmother would move on quickly. Her schoolmates were all either jealous or disapproved of her behavior, and the teachers wouldn't remember her by next semester.

Unless, of course, her death served a higher purpose.

Shawn had turned her body into a warning against the loose morals and sexual deviancy that plagued the world today. People wouldn't remember her life, but they would remember her death. That's why he'd told Lucky Levi about the torture and had shown him the photos. Shawn could've just buried The Gutierrez Girl in the riverbed or under the foundation of one of Dickson's Crossing's abandoned houses. But with the precautions he'd taken, Shawn knew he'd never get caught. He could treat her body like a billboard, a public service announcement of sorts. A celebrity reporter would be the perfect way to get the message out since Shawn knew the Texas Rangers would never divulge the full scope of her death. Lucky Levi had apparently chosen Kitty Kat as a surrogate, which would've been fine if she hadn't also found out about the affair with Fuckface Anderson. That would lead to Hunter, which would lead to Shawn, and he couldn't allow that to happen.

"As much as I'm enjoying this, we're gonna have to move this along," Shawn said. "Husband Bill and Lucky Levi won't let you stay missing for much longer."

One thing Shawn had learned from CIA torture was that people break before the unbearable pain begins. The threat of that pain—and the hope of preventing it—is what causes people to give up their secrets. Getting people to confess is easy. It's the same recipe Mother Nature uses to create diamonds—apply pressure over time. Shawn knew how to apply the pressure. But he was out of time.

Shawn had also learned that if someone is mentally prepared to take the pain, they will never tell you the truth. Anything that comes out of their mouth will be a lie. Torture, therefore, is nothing but gratuitous punishment.

The threat of denailing her had gotten Kitty Kat talking, but the pain wouldn't start there. He would instead begin with the burning. Then, like he'd done with The Gutierrez Girl, Shawn would bleach Kitty Kat's entire body before burying her and parking her truck in an old abandoned junkyard on the outskirts of Bison Ridge. Her piece-of-shit pickup would fit right in. If Shawn weren't so smart, that would mean walking back to town. But Shawn had already stashed his own truck out there that he could drive back.

Preparation.

Shawn walked over to his tools, put his rubber gloves back on, and picked up the self-igniting blowtorch.

"Finally," Kitty Kat said.

"You ever been burned?" Shawn asked as he walked toward her. "By the way you're acting right now, I'm guessing not."

She hocked a loogie and spit it toward Shawn.

"That's okay," he said as he turned the orange knob on the back of the blowtorch, letting out a sinister hiss. "The human brain is a magnificent thing. The pain will be intense but brief. It won't take long for the area to go numb."

Shawn pressed the knob. Kitty Kat's face glowed blue.

•   •   •

Shawn had nearly completed the A when someone knocked loudly on The Hole's tin door. Five booms in a familiar cadence. *Hunter?* When he was still playing sheriff, Kitty Kat had told Shawn about the confrontation in Yucca. Hunter must've figured out what was going on. Did he want in on the fun? Or was he trying to be a hero?

Shawn went to his duffel bag and pulled out the pistol. He jacked a round into the chamber and stuck it behind his back as he walked up the concrete steps. Shawn paused before opening the door.

"Hunter, how the hell you been, buddy?" Shawn asked the barrel of Hunter's gun. "It looks like we've got some catching up to do."

CHAPTER THIRTY-TWO

Levi turned on the heater, but it didn't help as he drove through Dickson's Crossing. He crept around each turn, passing the overgrown remains of long-crumbled homes and toppled windmills. The dirt road was barely visible as Levi dodged the occasional outhouse and concrete foundation. He rolled past the old church, its steeple still standing tall among the ruins. It was covered in a hodgepodge of cliché satanic symbols. Levi parked with the lights illuminating the church, which would serve as his lighthouse in the darkness of Dickson's Crossing. Levi was barely out of the car when he heard it. Yelling. A man? Yes. An angry man. The voice was coming from deeper inside the town, toward the riverbed. Levi started jogging and regretted wearing sweats and sneakers as he brushed past the sage and prickly pear. After a minute, he stopped to listen again, making sure he was still heading in the right direction.

Nothing. *Shit.* Levi did a 360 to make sure he could still make out the church. Then he closed his eyes, hoping once again for heightened hearing.

Another shout. Levi wasn't close enough to make out the words. He needed to get closer. Levi took off again and nearly ran into Matthews' Suburban. Then he spotted Ol' Faithful. Levi's mind raced faster than his feet. *What did this guy have to do with Kat? Wasn't he a lawyer or something? Why the hell were they meeting out here? Why was he yelling at her?* Levi was almost to the pickup when he dropped to a knee behind the rotting corpse of a house. The wall listed so hard Levi hoped his breathing wouldn't topple it. He peeked out to study the scene. Matthews was pointing a gun at another man standing at the opening of an underground cellar. *Shawn's out here, too?* Levi listened but still couldn't make out the conversation. It didn't matter. Levi had already pieced it together. Matthews, the weirdo who could never fit in and was awkward with girls, had taken Kat out here to do something terrible. But Shawn, by the grace of God, had found her. Now they were in a showdown.

Levi tried to move swiftly toward them while staying low to the ground. When he got within five yards, Levi charged at Matthews, lowered his shoulder and tackled him from behind, sending his gun flying.

• • •

Shawn hadn't prepared for any of this. Hunter said he'd come to get evidence to prove Shawn had killed The Gutierrez Girl. *Traitor.* Then, as Shawn was formulating a new plan, Lucky Levi had taken down Hunter the Traitor. Shawn had only prepared to kill one person. Now, he had to figure out what to do with three bodies.

"Thank God you're here," Lucky Levi said, driving a knee deeper into The Traitor's shoulder blades. "What was he doing to Kat when you found him? Did you get here in time?"

"Got here *just* in time," Shawn said. "So did you. You saved my ass. Keep him down, and I'll run down and untie your friend."

"He had her tied up? Jesus."

"You don't want to see what he had going on down there." Shawn moved his right hand behind his back. He thought about pulling the pistol. Lucky Levi and The Traitor were just a few yards away. Kitty Kat was tied up downstairs and posed no threat. Shawn could end it all right here. Two bullets. Simple.

But Shawn was in control and had time to figure out a better plan. The person searching for Kitty Kat was here and looking for a reason to kill the only other man who knew about The Hole. The play that was least likely to come back on Shawn was to get Lucky Levi to kill The Traitor. Or, if he could swing it, get them to kill each other. He could then make it look like The Traitor had killed the girls. Anyone in Bison

Ridge who remembered The Traitor's high school days wouldn't think twice.

"Never leave home without them," Shawn said as he tossed a set of handcuffs in the dirt. "Book 'em, Danno."

"Hawaii Five-0."

Shawn turned around and laughed as he descended the stairs toward Kitty Kat's muffled screams.

• • •

Levi had a lot of questions, and he was going to get them answered.

"Why did you take her?"

"I didn't," Matthews pleaded. "Shawn is the psycho here, not me."

"Shut up," Levi said as he handcuffed Matthews. It wasn't as easy as it looked on TV. "Did you have RayLynn down there? Is that where you raped and killed her?"

"It wasn't me, goddamnit. It was Shawn."

Levi elbowed Matthews in the back of the head. He was surprised at how much he enjoyed it. He'd spent so much of his life as a pacifist. Even during the fight where he lost his teeth, Levi hadn't thrown any punches or defended himself. That wasn't an option now. Levi was about to hit Matthews again, but looked up when he heard Nichols coming back up the stairs.

"You always were a dumb sonofabitch," Nichols said from the cellar door. "Looks like I'm going to have to change the nickname I gave you. Lucky Levi just doesn't fit anymore."

CHAPTER THIRTY-THREE

Kat hated the smell of her burning flesh. It had taken about thirteen seconds for the area to go numb, but now her wrists hurt as she struggled against the zip ties. It was nice to be standing again, though. She also appreciated breathing fresh air and feeling a sprinkle of rain against her face. And people had arrived to help her, including Levi.

On the other hand, there was now a gun to her head.

"What the hell are you doing, Shawn?" Levi asked.

He looked confused. Kat was also confused. What the hell were Levi and Anderson's henchman doing there? But it was now three against one if she included herself. Much better odds.

"You should listen to our friend here," Nichols said. "He's the smart one, after all."

Kat could feel Nichols' hot breath in her ear. She wanted to puke.

Levi lifted Matthews by his arms, which were handcuffed behind him. Kat badly wanted to tell Levi to stop working against Matthews. To tell him they could overpower Nichols if they worked together. But she needed to wait until the barrel wasn't against her temple before talking or moving.

"I tried to tell you," Matthews said. "Shawn's a goddamn psychopath. He killed that girl, and he was about to kill your friend, too."

· · ·

Hunter's buzz was starting to wear off, and panic was taking its place. With nothing to lose, he decided to play to one of his strengths: bargaining.

"Look, Shawn, there's a way out of this that works out for everybody," Hunter said. "We can all forget we know each other and go back to living our lives. We can all keep one secret, right everyone?"

Hunter looked around. Hallaway would agree with whatever got her the hell out of here. Cole looked confused and angry. Hunter knew better than anyone that the man was in a dark place, but he probably wasn't suicidal. Nichols, however, was the wild card. If he were a true psychopath, there would be no reasoning with him.

"And ruin all the good work we've done? I wouldn't dream of it," Nichols said. "And friends shouldn't keep secrets. In fact, I think we'll all feel much better if we get some off our chests. Hunter, why don't you start. Let's begin with you and Levi."

Fuck me. Hunter silently debated what to say. Nichols had a gun, and Hunter's was useless sitting out there in the dark. Giving Nichols what he wanted was the logical choice. But if Cole and Hallaway knew the truth, and either of them survived, Hunter and Anderson would be screwed.

• • •

"Hunter, what in the Sam Hell is he talking about?" Levi asked, tightening his grip on Matthews' arm.

"I'm the reason you're here," Matthews said.

"What does that mean?"

"I'm Ace Anderson's chief of staff."

"Wait, what?"

"That's why I'm back in Bison Ridge. I'm running his re-election campaign."

"So, you do know Kat," Levi said, stepping in front of Matthews to face him. "You want her to stop looking into your boss' affair with

RayLynn."

Levi turned around to look at Nichols. He was still holding Kat—who was naked and had a massive burn on her right breast—at gunpoint. If Matthews had the motive to hurt Kat, why was Nichols the one torturing her?

"You're half right," Nichols said. "Now, ask yourself: Do you think the man you have handcuffed could intimidate anyone, let alone a girl with a snake tattooed down her leg, or your feisty ex-girlfriend here?"

Levi thought. *No, not a chance.*

"Now, me, on the other hand," Nichols continued, "I know how to handle a woman."

"You're working as a fixer for Anderson."

"There you go," Nichols said. "But you're burying the lede, newsboy. Think bigger. Hunter said he was the reason *you* are here. So, here's the next question: What does any of this have to do with *you*?"

Matthews and Nichols were working together. If they were trying to keep Anderson's secrets, Nichols would've called Matthews after Kat conducted her first interview and visited the high school with Levi. Matthews had been in Bison Ridge that day and could have followed Kat after she left. Hunter would've been at Drake's. ...

"The video," Levi said, turning back to Matthews. "That was you."

"You're almost there," Nichols said. "It's right on the tip of your tongue."

Levi knew from Emily Greene that the person who emailed the video link was ...

"You gave me the story on the governor," Levi said. "Then you got me fired."

"Bravo," Nichols said. "It took you long enough."

"Why?" Levi asked. He jerked Matthews' arm so hard the slippery handcuffs moved halfway down his left hand, ripping the skin as it reached the thumb and pinkie.

"The video was about protecting Ace," Matthews said. "I knew spreading the video would discredit any work you did with her."

"Okay," Levi said. "But what did exposing Lockwood and then getting me fired have to do with your boss?"

Levi shook Matthews when he didn't answer and nearly lost his footing in the mud. "Answer me goddamnit. You owe me a fucking explanation before we all die."

"We don't have to die, you idiot," Matthews said. "It's two against one if you let me go."

Levi didn't want to stop questioning Matthews, but he was right. Levi let go of Matthews' arms and charged Nichols.

CHAPTER THIRTY-FOUR

Kat was done with this shit. When Nichols swung his gun at Levi, Kat did an alligator roll and broke free from his grip, which had gotten slippery in the rain. She started to run toward the riverbed. *Should've tied up my legs too, asshole.*

Kat felt the burning in her left side before she heard the gunshot. She then felt her ribs splinter and the oxygen escape her lungs just before falling onto her back. She nearly passed out from the pain, but kept her eyes open long enough to see Nichols hovering over her.

"It wasn't supposed to go down this way," he said. "But, you know what they say. Curiosity killed the Kitty Kat."

Nichols disappeared when Levi tackled him. Kat looked back toward the cellar and saw Matthews running toward the fight. He jerked his left hand from behind his back and yelled in pain. Kat felt herself drifting, but she had to flag down Matthews. Kat had landed on what she thought was a gun, which was now digging into her shoulder blade. If she was right, and she could get the gun into Matthews' hands, they had a chance of getting out alive. Kat tried to scream and kicked her right leg up and down furiously.

Matthews stumbled down to her.

"Under my back," Kat said, the words barely escaping her throat. "There's a gun under my back."

Matthews lifted Kat and groped the mud below. She heard him say "Got it," then allowed the darkness to take her.

• • •

Hunter immediately fired a round into the air. He turned around and watched Cole and Nichols stop struggling to cover their ears. Hunter got to his feet, the gun shaking in his right hand. He and Nichols locked dueling black pistols on each other as Cole scurried away.

•   •   •

Levi cursed out loud when he saw where Kat had been shot. He pulled his white T-shirt over his head and ripped off one sleeve. He tried to pack it into the hole in Kat's side. He wrapped the rest of the rain-soaked shirt around her bare torso.

"Kat … Kat … wake up," Levi said as he slapped her face lightly. He slapped her face harder when she didn't respond.

Her eyes opened a moment later.

"Hey, there you are," Levi said. "I need you to stay awake, okay?"

"Levi," Kat said, her voice barely audible over what had become a downpour. "I'm sorry I never told you I loved you. I did. I do."

"Don't worry about any of that right now. Let's try to stand up. Those two can shoot each other, but we're getting the fuck out of here."

Levi tried picking up Kat, which was nearly impossible in the slick mud.

"Whoa now, what do you two think you're doing?" Nichols said. "You stay right there."

Nichols turned his attention back to Matthews. "We got ourselves a real Mexican standoff here, don't we? You know, I was a good friend to you. The only one you had, for all those years. Since you and I go way back, I'll give you a fighting chance. I'll count to three, and we'll each pull our triggers. See who's the quicker, better shot. But you gotta ask yourself a question: Do I feel lucky? Well do ya, punk?"

Nichols paused, then arched his eyebrows at Matthews. After a few seconds of silence, he rolled his eyes and turned to Levi and Kat.

"Really? Nobody?"

"Jesus Christ, you're insane," Matthews said. "Just let us all go, and we'll move on with our lives."

"One."

"For fuck's sake, Shawn. Let's just put down our guns."

"You can if you want, though I wouldn't advise it. Two."

"Hunter," Levi said. "Just shoot this motherfucker right now before he gets to—"

Levi wasn't positive, but he thought he heard Nichols say "three" just before the simultaneous gunshots. Levi opened his eyes. He couldn't get the ringing to stop, but he saw both bodies lying on the ground. Nichols was screaming in pain and holding his right shoulder.

"Hold on Kat," Levi said. "I'll be right back."

Levi nearly lost his balance between the mud and the disorientation caused by the deafening gunshots, but he made it over to Nichols and pried the gun out of his right hand before sloshing over to Matthews. Levi didn't have to bend down to take a pulse. Nichols, the Army vet and longtime law enforcement officer, had hit Matthews dead between the eyes. The blood pooled out from behind his head and flowed with the floodwater past his mangled left hand.

Levi walked back over to Nichols and kicked him in the ribs.

"You sorry sack of shit," Levi said. "Why would you do all of this? What happened in your life that was so bad?"

Nichols laughed. "Hunter needed to keep some people quiet. That's the why. As for my life? That's a complicated topic. It took me years of studying to come up with an answer."

"It was the war, wasn't it?"

"No, it wasn't the war. I was born this way. Just like you were born a lazy liar. Levi the Lazy Liar."

"You realize I'm the one with the gun now, right?"

"Like that matters. You don't have it in you to pull the tri—"

CHAPTER THIRTY-FIVE

Levi stared at the hole he'd just put into Nichols' forehead, expecting to feel guilt. There was none. He was amazed at how easy it had been to kill Nichols. The trigger was easy to pull, though the kickback was harder than he'd expected. Levi looked down at the pistol and realized he had committed a crime. He was no doctor, but it didn't take one to know that Nichols could have survived his wound with timely medical treatment.

But dealing with that would have to wait. Levi dropped the gun and sprinted over to Kat. His shirt looked black from the blood, and her eyes were still closed. Levi leaned in. He could still feel her breath. He shook her violently and screamed her name. After a few more seconds with no response, Levi grabbed Kat under her armpits and stood her up until they were face-to-face before hoisting her onto his shoulders. It would've been a textbook fireman's carry if he hadn't slipped onto his knees in the mud.

Levi got to his feet and fought the water that was rushing down the hill toward the riverbed. He had half a football field to go, and Levi could feel her blood running down his back and legs. When he got to his car, Levi opened the back door and rolled her onto the seat. Levi tried to run around to the driver's side but slipped and fell on his ass. When he got into the car, Levi stepped on the gas and went nowhere. His four-cylinder was winding up as the back of the car sank into the mud.

"God-fucking-damnit," Levi yelled. He looked back at Kat. Her chest wasn't moving.

CHAPTER THIRTY-SIX

Elliott hated coffee. But, after getting called out to High Plains Memorial Hospital, he was grateful the nurses were allowing him to partake. He was waiting to talk to a Levi Cole, who he'd been told was a well-known news reporter, though the name didn't mean anything to Elliott. Cole had brought in another reporter, the Katherine Hallaway he had met earlier that week, after what a Vista County Sheriff's Office deputy had called a "clusterfuck" out at Dickson's Crossing. Elliott now wished he'd been more like Loretta and just gone there without waiting for the sheriff. A cold thought passed through his mind. If this night hadn't happened, and Sheriff Nichols had led Elliott into Dickson's Crossing, he might never have made it out.

Elliott shook off the vision and distracted himself by reviewing what he knew about the night's events: Three people had died. Cole had arrived at the hospital shirtless, carrying Hallaway into the ER. Both were covered in blood, and the doctors said she was dead before they got to her. Hospital officials had called the Yucca Police Department, per standard protocol whenever they get a victim with a gunshot wound. YPD officers called the Vista County Sheriff's Office and got dispatch to radio a deputy, who then tried several cellphone numbers until he reached Elliott.

Elliott looked back at the nurse's station. Cole, who was wearing a hospital gown, was sitting up straighter now and nursing his own cup of coffee, so it was time to hear his version of events.

"Mr. Cole, I'm Elliott Dawson with the Texas Rangers. Can we go out into the waiting room and discuss what happened tonight?"

"Do we have to? I already talked to the sheriff's deputy."

"Unfortunately, yes, you do," Elliott said as he turned his shoulders and motioned to a set of double doors. "We're assisting in the investigation since you're claiming corruption by an elected state official."

"Corruption? You need to call it what it is: murder."

Elliott tried not to get upset and reminded himself that Cole had suffered a considerable loss. "Yes, it is. I hate to ask this of you, but I need to get your statement while it's still fresh in your mind so we can get this squared away as soon as possible. In that respect, I imagine we have the same goal."

Cole nodded and stood. As they walked, Elliott took note of the amount of dried blood on Cole's hands and arms. He must've known Hallaway was dead well before he got to the hospital. If the nurses' accounts were accurate, Elliott had no doubt that Cole loved the woman, even though she was married. That fact alone was enough to cause Elliott to question Cole's version of events.

"Thank you, Mr. Cole," Elliott said as he sat down and pulled out his notepad. "Now, I've been told that Mrs. Hallaway was killed out at Dickson's Crossing, along with Vista County Sheriff Shawn Nichols and a man named Hunter Matthews, who worked with Congressman Ace Anderson. Does all of that sound correct?"

Cole nodded. "Yes. Matthews is … was … Anderson's chief of staff."

Elliott nodded and wrote *KNEW MATTHEWS* in his notepad, followed by a note to look deeper into Cole's background.

"What were you doing at Dickson's Crossing tonight?" Elliott asked. As he looked at Cole, Elliott noticed his eyes were blue. The nurses had given Elliott a photocopy of Cole's driver's license, which they had gotten for insurance purposes before offering him medical attention. It listed his eye color as green.

"I went there looking for Kat. Her husband, Bill, had called me asking if I knew where she was. As we were talking, he said he'd used a phone app to track her, and he described an area that I knew led to Lucy's Bridge."

"Why did her husband call you?"

"Because Kat and I were working on a story about the RayLynn Gutierrez murder."

"I'm also investigating Gutierrez's murder, and we had spoken about it. She didn't mention she was working with anyone else."

"I was helping her with background information since I'm from Bison Ridge."

Elliott finished scribbling in his pad then looked back up at Cole. "Okay, so, you drive out to the bridge. Then what?"

"I saw Matthews there."

"At the bridge? Before you drove into Dickson's Crossing?" Cole nodded, and Elliott made a note to have a forensics team process the bridge. "Why was he out there?"

"I was so busy trying to find Kat I didn't ask. But I found out later he was trying to confront Shawn."

"When did you find that out?"

"After I got out to where they were arguing in Dickson's Crossing. They had guns pointed at each other. Shawn was holding Kat hostage in an old storm cellar in town, just like he had done to RayLynn."

"How did you find them?"

"Like I said, they were arguing. I followed their voices."

"Okay, so you walk up on this scene. Then what?"

"I asked Shawn what the hell was going on, which distracted him. That gave Kat a chance to break away from Shawn, who shot her as she ran. I went over to her, and the next thing I know I hear two gunshots and see them on the ground. I checked, saw they were dead, then got Kat into my car and drove her here."

Elliott knew there had to be some fabrication in Cole's story. It was too clean, too rehearsed. The man writes for a living, after all. Elliott was forming his next question when he heard a booming voice from somewhere near the ER entrance. He and Cole turned around to see a tall, lanky man pointing their direction and cursing loudly.

Elliott jumped up to head off the man he assumed was Bill Hallaway.

"Sir, I'm with the Texas Rangers, and I'm going to need you to calm down."

"Oh really, you're with the Texas Rangers? Why haven't you handcuffed that sonofabitch yet? He killed my wife."

"Mr. Hallaway, first let me say that my thoughts and prayers are with you and your family. We are early in the investigation. I know you're in a lot of pain right now, but I need you to allow me to do my job. We'll find out exactly what happened and those responsible will be prosecuted."

"Bullshit," Mr. Hallaway said as he tried to run past Elliott. Elliott quickly wrestled him to the ground and put him in handcuffs. The scene had summoned the Yucca police officers into the ER, and they helped get Mr. Hallaway to his feet.

"Officers, can you please put Mr. Hallaway in holding until I come around to talk to him?"

They nodded and took him outside. Elliott looked over at Cole, who hadn't gotten out of his seat.

"Where are you staying tonight?" Elliott asked Cole.

Cole provided an address in Bison Ridge and said it was his parents' house. Elliott wrote it down and got Cole's cellphone number.

•   •   •

Elliott inhaled the pleasant scent of the High Plains after a heavy rain. The phenomenon became rarer every year, so Elliott had to enjoy it when he could, even if he did so at a murder scene.

The DPS forensics team had Dickson's Crossing lit up like Candy Cane Lane at Christmas, complete with a parade of vehicles. Part of him wanted to believe Cole so he could tell everyone to go home and get some sleep knowing they'd closed the Gutierrez case. But Elliott knew Cole had lied. Elliott also needed to see for himself where that girl had been killed. As he approached the bodies of Matthews and Nichols, Elliott was intercepted by a DPS tech he'd worked with a time or two. A younger kid named Jarrod.

"Welcome to the horror show," Jarrod said as he shook Elliott's hand.

They walked over to Matthews. "Looks like this one was pretty easy for you," Elliott said.

"Yep, cause of death is a single GSW to the head. There was also serious perimortem damage to his left hand, likely caused by the handcuffs."

Elliott took notes as the two made their way over to Nichols, who wasn't wearing his Vista County Sheriff's uniform. *Good. He didn't deserve to die while wearing it.*

"This one's not so neat," Jarrod said. "He has two GSWs, one to the right shoulder and another to the head. I won't know until I get him to the lab, but my initial read is that he was shot in the shoulder, incapacitating him. He was then shot in the head."

"We can assume the second shot didn't come from Matthews since this looks like an old-fashioned duel that Nichols won. That leaves Levi Cole and Katherine Hallaway, who was shot once in the side and showed up at the hospital with her hands zip-tied together. How many guns have you found?"

"Just the two. Which leads me to the other thing I found interesting: Nichols' gun isn't where it should be. There's a chance he would've dropped the gun when he was shot in the shoulder. But it wouldn't have traveled that far from his hand, and the angle isn't consistent with that scenario."

Elliott knelt and inspected the gun. "I see what you're saying. So, you think the gun was picked up, used to shoot our sheriff in the head, and was staged afterward."

"Exactly."

Elliott went back to his notes. Cole had gone over to Nichols and made sure he was dead. He didn't blame Cole for that. However, Cole had committed homicide. And, if Cole hadn't lied, he might've convinced Elliott and everyone else it was self-defense.

"All right," Elliott said. "Take me down to the storm cellar."

As they made their way down the stairs, the smell of burnt flesh mixed with the dampness of the cellar smacked Elliott in the face. Jarrod looked back and handed Elliott a paper mask.

"Sorry, I should've warned you," Jarrod said. "So, this is where Nichols was holding the woman, and where he tortured and killed

RayLynn Gutierrez."

Bolted into the middle of the cement floor was a metal chair with leather restraints on the legs and arms. Dark stains surrounded the chair, which Elliott assumed were from the blood of Gutierrez and Hallaway. On the concrete bench that encircled the room were stacks of books and tools, including a butane torch with an evidence number next to it.

"This guy had a personal torture chamber down here," Jarrod said. "Hopefully we only find the blood of two women. Otherwise, we'll have to start looking for more bodies."

Chapter Thirty-Seven

Ace stared at his father, who was rambling on about something. That Texas Ranger had asked to look through Matthews' office as part of the investigation, and Gordon Anderson wanted to be present during the search. Ranger Dawson was in Matthews' office across the hall, and Ace was doing his best to stay out of the way.

"What are we supposed to do now?" Gordon asked. "With Hunter gone—may he and that lady reporter rest in peace—we might as well just tell everyone you're resigning. We could say you're too upset over what happened. People will believe it."

"I know I haven't always acted like I wanted all of this, but I don't want to quit, either. I think—"

"Don't do that. We both know thinking ain't your strong suit. That was always Hunter's job."

"Yeah, yeah, I know. He was the son you never had. Blah blah blah."

"Have some respect, you insolent prick. You have no idea what he—what *we*—have been doing for you."

"Hunter kept me in the loop on everything."

Gordon snorted. "Oh really? Did he tell you that before all of this, we were going to make you governor?"

Ace looked around to make sure the Ranger wasn't around. "We shouldn't be talking about this kind of stuff," he whispered.

"Quit being such a pussy. He's down the hall spinning his wheels."

"Whatever. So, how the hell were you two going to *make* me governor?"

"The hardest part was already done," Gordon said. "We already got one governor out of office, and his replacement's a goddamn nutjob who will be easy to knock out when the time comes."

"What do you mean *we* got one governor out of office? You're talking about Lockwood, right? That idiot resigned."

"Jesus you're slow. Did you notice the name of the other person there when Hunter was shot? Levi Cole. Ring any bells?"

Ace thought for a moment. It did sound familiar, but not familiar enough.

"Look, Dad, just get to it already."

"Levi Cole is the reporter who broke the scandal on Governor McFucksalot. He and Hunter were both from Bison Ridge. Hunter anonymously gave him the story on a silver platter."

Ace started to remember the details about the scandal. He nodded at his father to keep going.

• • •

Matthews' office had been stripped bare. Elliott knew Gordon Anderson had done some cleaning, though Elliott got the feeling there hadn't been much to take out. Matthews had done most of his work in Washington. His desk had one neat pile of campaign-related documents and a couple of files in one drawer. Gordon had given Elliott permission to send Matthews' tablet to the DPS lab in Austin, but nothing noteworthy would be on the device—not if he'd been given access so easily.

Elliott was almost mindlessly sifting through the last drawer when the bottom slid slightly. This piqued his interest. The desk was well-made, the kind you'd expect to see in the offices of a successful law firm. It wasn't mass-produced, but handcrafted, and there was no wiggle anywhere else.

Elliott pulled out a pocketknife from its belt holster and began prying on the wobbly slat. He eventually worked open the false bottom and uncovered a green stenographer's pad. He looked around to make sure he was alone in the office—Gordon Anderson must've been very confident he'd found everything he wanted to hide—then picked up the pad. There was no heading written at the top. Instead, it started with a Bible quote:

Then Jesus came to them and said, All authority in Heaven and on earth has been given to me. — Matthew, Ch28, V18

Another Bible quote followed:

And this gospel of the kingdom will be preached in the whole world as a testimony to all nations, and then the end will come. — Ch24, V14

Below the Bible quotes were an email address and password:

Email: MTW28_18@securedelectronicmail.com
Password: aThE24!14

Reading all the writing on one page helped Elliott see that the email address and password were a combination of the Bible verses. He had no idea what it meant, but he thought logging into the email may provide some clarity. He didn't have a computer, and his tablet was in his service vehicle. Rather than trying to sneak the notepad out without drawing attention to himself, Elliott tried his phone. In his effort to be cooperative, Gordon had allowed Elliott to log on to the firm's wireless internet. Elliott opened a web browser and typed in *securedelectronicmail.com* hoping he wouldn't be denied access. After thinking for a minute, he was taken to a login screen.

He typed in the information, and after another minute of thought, Elliott was in. There was nothing in the inbox, but an email sat in the drafts folder. He opened it. Nothing. He was about to close out when he realized there were two attachments. *Music files?* He opened the first and, after a few seconds, realized he was listening to what was now a famous piece of audio from the scandal involving the former governor a few years ago. He opened the other attachment and listened.

Levi Cole had broken the Lockwood scandal. Matthews held the keys to those stories, or at least two of them. Elliott assumed that the leak had gone from Matthews to Cole—the reporter had obviously been the beneficiary of the information. Elliott turned his attention back to the notepad and flipped to the next page. Matthews had written a woman's name and a YouTube web address, followed by emails that appeared to belong to the major news networks. A couple started with names, others just said "news" or "tips." Each had a check mark next to them. Elliott typed in the web address, which took him to a video that was still being played on cable news.

Matthews and Cole had deep ties – though it was not clear whether they were friends. Elliott looked back at the first page of the pad and studied the Bible verses again. He decided they couldn't have been very close.

•   •   •

"Hunter always was poetic," Ace said. "How did you two settle on which reporter to give all of this to?"

"We needed someone we could squeeze if needed. Then one morning Hunter saw an old classmate's byline in the Dallas paper. It was divine intervention."

"Sounds like it," Ace said. The name Levi Cole was starting to come back to him. He'd seen it on TV screens. Cole was a regular on the Sunday shows and cable news.

Gordon got up and walked to the liquor cabinet. He poured himself a Scotch and pointed at a second glass. Ace shook his head. Day drinking was at least partially responsible for his father's obesity. "Problem was, he got too much exposure. When he was asked back onto the news networks this election cycle, Hunter and I knew we couldn't have him hanging around on the national political scene. Not with the plans we had for you."

"Why's that?"

"Use your head, son. If ever there was a reporter who would want to take you out, it would be a guy from Bison Ridge. The way Hunter tells it, Levi was the best friend of that player you killed."

Ace cringed. He hated that phrase. *You killed*. Whenever the player's death was mentioned, Ace would see the helmet flying. He would never forget Jesse's eyes. Even as he started whooping and hollering, Ace watched as the last flicker of life evaporated from them. Nobody seemed to remember how Ace had been the first to bend down and check to see if he was breathing. How he'd waved his own team trainer over, screaming like a madman. Ace hadn't spoken about that night in detail since the first campaign. Since then, he just mentioned it vaguely as *the incident* or *what happened in high school.*

"Are you listening to me, son?" Gordon asked.

"Yeah, sorry," Ace said. "So, what did you and Hunter do?"

Gordon sat down with his drink and popped one of his pills, probably something for his blood pressure. The old man already had one heart attack on his medical chart. He also took insulin for Type 2 diabetes and a host of other medications for his various maladies.

"Hunter knew that this Levi guy was a bullshitter by nature," Gordon said. "So, we used the firm's resources and tracked down some of his old sources. Got them to admit that he'd misquoted them and gotten some facts wrong. Got them to say it on video. Then there was that 'cunt' video Hunter sent to the cable news channels. That kid was something else."

Oh shit, Levi is that *guy. They screwed him over hard.*

"Wait, let me get this straight," Ace said. "You didn't want him around for when you wanted me to run for governor, right?"

Gordon nodded.

"Then why did I run for Congress last time?" Ace asked. "Hell, why am I still trying to get re-elected to the House after you already put another guy in Austin?"

Gordon downed the rest of his drink. "Without that degree from Yale that you pissed away, we knew you'd need plenty of experience in Washington to be taken seriously as a candidate for governor."

Ace resented being a puppet for his father. Worse, he didn't even know why his father was playing Gepetto.

"Why would you even want me to be governor?" Ace asked.

"I didn't want *you* to be governor. I wanted Hunter to be your chief of staff. Believe me, I wish Hunter could've done it on his own. But with no looks and no social skills, I needed you to be his face."

Ace let out an exasperated sigh and poured himself a drink. "Damnit, you know what I meant. Why did you want Hunter in Austin?"

"Do you know how this firm makes money?"

"Not really. Just a bunch of lawyers screwing people."

"We are diversified, but most of our clients are energy companies. I hope I'm not going out on a limb to assume you know what fracking is."

Ace nodded yes as he slid his father another Scotch.

"Well that process, when done as cheaply and quickly as most companies like to do it, can really do a number on the groundwater," Gordon said. "It can make the water flammable. People sue. When they do, we step in and get them to settle for next to nothing. Or, when those people are stupid, we defend our clients in court and win. And those clients pay us a small fortune for our services."

"Sounds like you should be up for Humanitarian of the Year. But, again, what the hell does any of this have to do with me?"

"Lockwood had been meeting with our CEOs and letting them know about his plans to 'help' them become more environmentally friendly. He said he would work with scientists to make fracking less toxic, and work with the Legislature to pass anti-business laws. As you can imagine, our clients weren't too happy about that expected rise in costs."

"So, you get rid of him, get Hunter and me into the office and push the energy companies' agenda through Hunter?"

"Now you're getting it."

No wonder everyone hates lawyers and politicians.

Ace and Gordon were interrupted by a knock at the door. Gordon yelled at Ranger Dawson to come in.

"Mr. Anderson, Congressman Anderson," Dawson said as he tipped his cowboy hat at Ace and his father. "I just wanted to let you know I'm done and headed out."

"Very good," Gordon said. "Do you need anything more from us?"

"No sir, I don't think so. But I'll call if that changes."

Gordon took out his wallet and pulled out a business card. "Ace, hand this to Mr. Dawson." Ace did as he was told and traded cards with Dawson.

"If you think of anything else I should know, please give me a call," Dawson said. "My cell number is written on the back."

"Will do," Ace said, hoping they would never see each other again.

CHAPTER THIRTY-EIGHT

Levi sat cross-legged on the bed of his parents' RV, staring at the black case in front of him. He'd been sitting like that so long his knees were starting to hurt. Levi had talked his folks into letting him move out to the Coachman, which was situated under a custom carport in their side yard, for a few days to mourn. People were always buzzing in and out of their house, and it was worse now that two of his classmates were dead.

It hadn't registered until his second day out there that Levi's father, who was not a hunter but a firm believer in his Second Amendment rights, kept a pistol in the bedside cabinet. It was for protection when he and Mom took trips. They sometimes snuck off on their own, and even a small Texas or Oklahoma Panhandle lakeside campground had its risks. Levi knew the combination to the pistol's case. It was four numbers, and every member of his family used the same code. The real puzzle was much harder to solve. Did he want to open the case? Levi put off that question for a few more minutes. He still needed to get dressed for the funeral.

He would wear the same black button-up shirt from Kat's services a few days ago. Levi's mother had also bought him black dress pants, a black jacket, some black shoes and a reversible faux leather belt. The pants and belt were far too big—his mother was still working on old information—so he'd cut a new notch. But Levi had lost the strength to watch what he ate and already needed a slightly looser belt.

Levi walked over to the RV's kitchen area and pulled a steak knife out of the drawer. He stood for a moment in his gray boxer briefs, contemplating the blade. There was a way to make the pain stop. Levi had thought seriously about suicide once in high school when he was about to get his first B, in English of all classes. The straight-A student who was supposed to be the next great writer—who had gotten the school to start a newspaper so he could put it on his college applications—couldn't decode the meaning of *To be, or not to be*. It was a goddamn Shakespearean tragedy. Or was it a comedy?

Levi was sure he could do it this time. He could take the knife and cut his wrists—longways on his arm, with the vein, not crossways like those attention-seeking pussies—and bleed out in his parents' RV the way Kat had bled out in the back of his car.

But Levi didn't want to kill himself. He wasn't sad. Instead, he needed to take back his life and make someone pay for Kat's death.

Since that semester in English class—he ended up getting an A— Levi had felt in control of his life. Things didn't always go his way, but there's a reason Nichols' nickname, Lucky Levi, had stuck. But what was perceived as luck had been, in Levi's mind, a product of his decision-making skills.

But that hadn't been true for years. Levi had become a pawn in a political game and done precisely what they wanted. They had seized control of his life. Levi's autonomy had been taken from him, as evidenced by everything that had happened in the last couple of weeks.

But he was about to get it back.

Levi knew he may lose his freedom, but that's not the same as control. He would gladly sacrifice the former to get the latter. Matthews' funeral was scheduled to begin in half an hour at the Bison Ridge cemetery, about a quarter-mile out of town. Levi's mother would be at the RV door soon, telling him it was time to go. He punched in the code—5-3-9-0, the last four digits of his late maternal grandmother's old landline—and took out the handgun. Levi realized he didn't have anywhere to put it. It was too big for the inside jacket pocket and too heavy to go unnoticed in its outside pouches.

As he heard the knock, Levi put the gun between the belt and the small of his back, the way they did in the movies.

• • •

Ace was confused by Levi Cole's blue stare. It's not like he had anything to do with what happened to Cole's lady friend. Matthews had gone rogue and used a maniac to keep himself in office. Ace's role, if any, was screwing the wrong girl. Ace was no Boy Scout, but he damn sure wasn't a murderer.

He had tried to ignore Cole during the ceremony and had looked around for him after the preacher finished up. Ace gave up when a horde of people lined up to give him their condolences. He was so used to shaking hands that he didn't see faces anymore, which was how he let Cole sneak up on him.

• • •

Levi grabbed Fuckface Anderson's hand and jerked him in close.

"Hunter told me everything out there at Dickson's Crossing, asshole."

"Okay," Anderson said. "So, what do we do now?"

"What do you mean *we*?"

"I mean, *we* are both victims in this thing."

Levi squeezed Fuckface Anderson's hand tighter. Matthews had worked for this prick, the same prick who just happened to have killed his best friend. The same prick who had told everyone that Jesse's death was an accident. Now he was saying essentially the same thing about killing Kat.

Levi wasn't going to let this motherfucker get away with any of it. He reached behind his coattail and fumbled for his father's semi-automatic. But before he could find the gun, Levi felt a meaty right hand on his. Fuckface Anderson had enough wingspan and strength to keep Levi's right arm secured behind him. He leaned into Levi and wrapped his left arm around Levi's back before releasing the right hand. As far as the crowd was concerned, Fuckface Anderson was now giving Levi a giant, teary bear hug.

Levi tried to jerk away but hardly budged an inch. *This guy is bigger than I remember. A lot bigger.* The rage Levi felt a moment earlier was subsiding.

"Look, Levi, you don't want to use that thing."

• • •

Elliott felt his instincts kick in. He'd seen Cole reach back as though he had a gun. Elliott should've disarmed Cole, a grieving man who'd already killed at least one person. Plus, it would've been a convenient time to arrest them both.

But after taking half a step, Elliott decided to let it go. It was apparent Cole couldn't pull a gun, if he had indeed brought one, and Elliott didn't have enough evidence on either of them to make the arrests stick. Not yet, anyway. Instead, Elliott would keep monitoring Cole and Anderson, hoping one of them would do something incriminating. Elliott needed solid evidence since he wasn't getting any help from his superiors.

Elliott had suggested to Lt. Winters that Anderson might have ordered RayLynn Gutierrez's murder, but his boss told him to let it go. Even if Anderson was guilty of something, Lt. Winters correctly pointed out that it would be the FBI's jurisdiction since he was an elected official in the *federal* government. Elliott thought about slipping information to the feds, but he knew there wasn't enough there to warrant an FBI investigation.

He'd also told Lt. Winters about the discrepancies between the scene at Dickson's Crossing and Cole's statement at the hospital. Elliott wanted to get a search warrant for Cole's vehicle and the house he was staying at, but Lt. Winters said there wasn't enough probable cause to go to a judge. As far as Lt. Winters was concerned, all the cases were closed. Elliott had not-so-respectfully disagreed.

CHAPTER THIRTY-NINE

Levi was surprised by how much he missed his old newsroom. The floors had another layer or two of grime, and the walls were dingier—the *Morning Standard* hadn't had a regular maintenance crew since long before he left—but he still knew his way around. There was just one thing missing: people. In addition to the staff that would never come back to the news business, such as those that used to operate the Linotype, there were dozens of non-reporter positions that had been cut since his days there just over a decade ago. A lounge had been fashioned where a newsroom secretary used to operate. Levi forgot her name, but she would book his travel to away tournaments and perform myriad other functions that were eventually absorbed by reporters and editors.

There was also a time when all the desks were full, and the photo studio was inhabited by shooters and editors. As Levi walked through the bullpen in the late afternoon, a lone reporter sat in front of a laptop listening to a scanner with white earbuds. No more than two other desks showed signs of regular use. A white dry-erase board on the back wall caught Levi's eye, and he counted six names, the size of the sports staff alone when he left the *Standard*. Marker had recently been erased between the first and third names, leaving only the ghost of Katherine Hallaway. Levi steadied himself. If he was ever going to move on, these next few steps were crucial.

Levi waved to the newsroom's lone copy editor, Jonathan Janikowski, as he made his way into the office of the new managing editor, a longtime newsman named Greg Bishop whom Levi had studied before driving to Amarillo.

"Just the man I needed to see," Levi said, holding out his hand. "I appreciate you taking the time to meet."

"No problem at all," Bishop said as he halfheartedly shook Levi's hand. "On behalf of the staff, please accept our sincerest condolences. Have a seat."

"And my condolences to you and your staff, obviously," Levi said.

"Congratulations on the new job," Bishop said. "You said you're Ace Anderson's new chief of staff, right?"

"Yes, that's right," Levi said. "Like I said on the phone, during the tragic events that led to Kat's death, some negative information was discussed concerning Congressman Anderson."

Bishop remained silent. He'd probably played this game a lot. And, despite the fact Levi had been an award-winning journalist in his previous life, Bishop saw Levi for what he was: a guy with an agenda in direct opposition to those of the *Morning Standard*.

"Kat, Hunter Matthews, Sheriff Nichols and I discussed a recording that Kat had gotten ahold of," Levi continued. "She claimed it contained audio of Congressman Anderson having sex with RayLynn Gutierrez."

Levi paused. Bishop again gave him nothing, so Levi kept talking. "As I'm sure you know, Ms. Gutierrez was only sixteen. Allegations like these would be very damaging to the congressman."

Bishop was a block of granite.

"Are you aware of any such recording?" Levi finally asked.

Bishop took off his glasses and leaned across his desk, closing the gap with Levi. "You're talking pretty coldly about a girl you supposedly loved."

"I did love her. But I have a new job to do, and she would've understood that."

"You think so?"

"I know so," Levi said. "I knew her a helluva lot longer than you did."

"Fair enough," Bishop said, leaning back in his chair. "I interrupted you. My apologies."

"Actually, I'm still waiting on you to answer my question. Did you know about the recording Kat claimed to have had of Congressman Anderson?"

"I was aware," Bishop said. "I listened to it before her death."

Now we're getting somewhere. "Were you able to draw any conclusions?" Levi asked.

"No."

"What did you tell Kat to do with the recording?"

"I suggested she interview Mr. Anderson and then turn the recording over to the proper authorities."

"Sounds like good advice," Levi said. "Now for the part you didn't hear. Before he died, Shawn Nichols claimed that it was his voice on the recording. That he and RayLynn had been having sex for some time, and that they had taped one of their role-playing sessions, during which he was playing a congressman. Because he was psychotic, Nichols thought it was funny that Kat was going to die chasing a false story."

Pause for effect.

"Congressman Anderson and I have regrettably been unable to listen to this recording, though not for lack of trying," Levi continued. "Congressman Anderson watched Hunter break one copy of the recording in our campaign offices in Yucca. Another copy was possibly on her cellphone, which Nichols broke during the kidnapping. The authorities have been unable to find a copy of the recording on Kat's cloud drive. A flash drive was found in the storm cellar where he was keeping Kat, but it had been drilled through by Sheriff Nichols." That last sentence was the only piece of truth Levi had told Bishop.

"That's quite an extensive list of places you haven't found it," Bishop said.

"Yes, it is. So, my question to you is this: Do you have a copy that Congressman Anderson and I could listen to?"

Bishop pulled his statue routine again. Levi couldn't tell if he was trying to decide what to do, or if the editor was still playing a game.

"No," he finally said.

"That's unfortunate. Do you know if anyone has a copy?"

"No."

"What a shame," Levi said. "One last question and I'll get out of your hair. Do you think Congressman Anderson was on that tape having sex with RayLynn Gutierrez?"

"I do. But, I don't think we could prove the authenticity of the recording I heard, even if another copy existed."

Finally, a little truth in journalism.

• • •

Elliott watched Cole leave the paper's employee entrance and walk to his car. Cole was sending an email or text and didn't notice Elliott, though he was a block away in his personal vehicle and likely would've gone unnoticed anyway. He hadn't been following Cole. Elliott had an appointment with the *Standard*'s editor. As far as Elliott was concerned, Cole was still a homicide suspect. And now he was Anderson's henchman, which meant that if Elliott didn't get enough to satisfy Lt. Winters, Cole might end up in Washington and out of Elliott's reach.

Elliott couldn't live with that. He pulled out his phone and dialed Greg Bishop's office number.

"Good afternoon, Mr. Bishop, I'm downstairs at your employee entrance," Elliott said as he exited his pickup. He was almost to the glass door when Bishop opened it and waved him in. No handshake.

When they got to his office, Bishop motioned for Elliott to sit and lumbered across the room to get back behind his desk.

"Thank you for taking the time to meet with me," Elliott said. "As I said in my email, I want to have an off-the-record conversation about my investigation."

"I usually don't conduct off-the-record interviews, Mr. Dawson. But, from what I hear, Texas Rangers don't usually talk to the press at all, on or off the record."

"You're right. But, in this case, I need your help."

"We never want to impede a law enforcement investigation, but I'm not interested in keeping secrets for the government, either," Bishop said.

Elliott thought for a moment. Bishop didn't trust him. More likely, he didn't trust the center of power Elliott represented. Bishop was used to being treated as the enemy, especially by the government, especially now. But he and Elliott had at least one common interest.

"It looks like you just had a meeting with Levi Cole. How did that go?" Elliott asked.

"That, unfortunately, was also an off-the-record conversation."

Elliott could tell Bishop was irritated. *Good.*

"I have reason to believe he lied to me about what happened in Dickson's Crossing and how Sheriff Nichols, Hunter Matthews, and Katherine Hallaway died. I don't trust him. Do you?"

Bishop stared at Elliott for a moment before answering. "No, Mr. Dawson, I don't."

"I'm glad we agree. I need to find a way to keep my eye on him, and Congressman Anderson. Unofficially."

"Why unofficially? If they're dirty, can't you investigate them?"

The unfortunate answer to Bishop's question was no. Forensics had found a thumb drive in the storm cellar. Elliott had initially hoped they could pull some information from it, but the hole drilled in the middle had rendered it useless.

"Not presently," Elliott said. "I'll get to that point, I just need some time and help."

"I have no doubt. But how do you think I can help?"

"I've been ordered not to push my investigation any further. But you and your staff can investigate whoever you want. And I assume this is the kind of story that you would want to break. Think of this conversation as a news tip, and a promise that you will get information from me when I am able to launch an official investigation. Strictly on deep background, of course."

Bishop motioned out to the mostly empty newsroom. "Look out there. I have no resources to dedicate to an investigation like that. I can hardly cover city council meetings half the time. I'm about to start using a stringer to ..." Bishop looked back at Elliott with the spark of a much younger journalist chasing his first big story. "Actually, I think I might be able to help you after all. Let me make a few calls."

Ace re-read the text from Levi, hoping he could find a different interpretation.

Talked with AMS editor. We're good. You still in?

Ace wasn't sure. He had liked Matthews well enough, and they had grown close by necessity. He even thought of them as friends. Ace, therefore, was genuinely grieving over Matthews' death, and he'd shed some tears. But the loss Ace was feeling could not compare to that of Levi Cole. But could that amount of grief send a man over the edge?

They had a good cry together a week ago after the funeral, then went back to campaign headquarters in Yucca. Ace was already a little drunk when he agreed to let Levi take over for Matthews. Ace didn't see the harm in it. Levi was a smart enough guy and had an impressive list of media contacts. They drank some more to celebrate and brainstormed for the campaign's homestretch. They drank even more and began planning for the Anderson-Cole presidential ticket in 2020. What a great time that would be. A pair of good ol' boys from Vista County, Texas, without Ivy League educations, running the world. The conversation devolved into a laughable high-stakes game of truth-or-dare. The first few chapters of a political thriller.

They woke the next morning with hangovers, each having taken a couch in the campaign offices. Ace told Levi to go take a shower, then come back. He would honor his commitment and make Levi his new right-hand man. The campaign was probably dead anyway, so if it turned out to be a mistake, it would be short-lived.

Ace had no idea Levi would be good at the job. Or that the *Morning Standard* would endorse Ace. Or that the polls would continue to move in his favor after Matthews' death. Now they were right there, a day away from pulling this thing out.

Ace had all but forgotten about that drunken night and figured starting a new career in Washington, D.C., would be enough for Levi.

His text suggested otherwise.

• • •

Levi double-checked the number he'd dialed, then tapped the green receiver on his cellphone. He knew he wouldn't get an immediate answer from Ace, who was still on the edge. He needed Levi's push, which meant having the pieces in motion before they spoke again.

"Hello?"

"Rosie, it's Levi Cole."

"Levi, it's good to hear your voice," Rosemary said. "I'm so sorry for your loss."

Levi couldn't wait until people stopped saying that. "Thank you."

"How did you get my number?"

"I know a guy."

Rosemary laughed. "Glad you've still got your sense of humor. What's up?"

"I need a favor."

CHAPTER FORTY

Ace stood to pour his father a nightcap as they finished dinner. Campaign headquarters in Yucca was still buzzing after the race had been called in Ace's favor several hours ago. Ace and Levi had capitalized on the sympathy bump from Matthews' death and trounced Bobby Joe Carter.

Ace walked the Scotches over to his father, who was sitting at his desk reading the *Morning Standard* sports section.

"I can't wait to be back in Dallas," Gordon said. "The NFL coverage is terrible in this rag."

"They don't have room to cover local sports, let alone the pros," Ace said as he put down the drinks. "Cut 'em some slack."

"That's always been your problem, son," Gordon said. "You think everybody deserves some slack. Everything's always good enough. You can't go for the jugular."

"I did okay as a salesman," Ace said. "I was making a living."

"There it is again," Gordon said, finishing his drink in one gulp. "'Did okay.' 'Making a living.' Surviving, not thriving. Haven't you ever wanted something more? Don't you have any ambitions?"

It took a few gulps, but Ace finished his drink.

"I sure do, Dad," Ace said, standing up to get the expensive bottle of celebratory single-malt. "I want to eat, drink, and be merry. Wouldn't that be the life."

"It would. But you know who gets to do that? Nobody."

"Say you're right," Ace said as he finished pouring fresh drinks, a little fuller than the last round. "If nobody gets to be happy, why try to be such a big shot? What's the point?"

Gordon looked stumped as Ace sat down his drink.

"I know why you wanted Hunter to be the shadow governor," Ace said. "You needed him to further the interests of the big oil barons."

"So, you were listening," Gordon said as he sat his empty glass down on the table.

"I listen more than you think," Ace said before choking down his drink and picking up the bottle.

"One more round?" Ace asked.

"Why not? We're celebrating, right?"

"Absolutely," Ace said. "So, back to my point. The big oil barons are going to continue to fill their vaults and keep swimming in them like Scrooge McDuck. Were you going to make more money?"

"You bet your ass I was getting kickbacks. Big ones."

"So, the super-rich oil guys are making their piles of cash, and you're making a slightly smaller pile of cash. You know who we haven't talked about yet?"

Gordon took a sip. "Who?"

"Me," Ace said. "The future governor of the great state of Texas. Where's my money? Or how about something for Hunter, if he were still with us?"

"But you'd've had all the power, son," Gordon said. His words were starting to slur, but he still took another sip.

"Okay," Ace said, his own buzz kicking in. "Here's a curveball. If I'd've gotten to be governor, and, by some miracle, you were given the chance to swap places with me, would you do it?"

Ace shot back the last of his drink. They were starting to go down smoothly as he prepared for what was coming.

"Well, son, I'm not a young man anymore," Gordon said, finishing off his drink to keep pace.

"No, you're sure not. I think I've finally figured you out, old man. You don't even want power. You just want money. Hunter and I were your meal ticket."

Gordon shrugged. "So?"

"One more?" Ace asked as he picked up the bottle. "I mean, we still haven't properly toasted to my victory?"

Gordon looked a little green, but Ace knew he wouldn't say no.

"Didn't we?" Gordon asked. "No, I suppose not. Alright, one more."

This time the tumblers were full. Gordon took his reluctantly.

"To my victory," Ace said. "And everything else that's about to happen for me."

Ace gulped his entire drink. He stared at Gordon, daring him to do the same.

"All right, it's getting late," Gordon said through a cough as he sat down the empty glass

"Just one more question Dad, I promise," Ace said. "Then I'll let you go."

"Fine," Gordon said, his breathing more labored. "What is it?"

"What are you going to do with me now?" Ace asked.

Gordon looked at his son, his eyes sloshing. "What do you mean?"

"I mean, now you have a puppet in the U.S. House of Representatives, but you've got no puppet-master," Ace said. "Hunter's gone."

Gordon closed his eyes and opened them, trying to focus. "Son, you can do whatever the hell you want. I don't give a shit if you stay in Congress for fifty years or if you resign tomorrow."

Ace nodded. Levi was right. "Hey Dad, don't you need to take your medicine and insulin shot?"

Gordon nodded and clumsily reached into a desk drawer and pulled out his pills. He popped two with no chaser then dug around in the drawer for his insulin kit.

"Here, let me," Ace said, slipping past his mammoth father to the drawer. "It's not like you can reach your ass, anyway."

"I usually make a cute secretary do it," Gordon said with a laugh that developed into a gross hacking sound.

"Well today you'll have to settle for me," Ace said, a syringe in his right hand. "Don't worry. It'll be over in a minute."

CHAPTER FORTY-ONE

Elliott shut his eyes. He hadn't slept the night before, or the night before that. He hated lying, and Elliott's brain would not allow his body to rest while he was running an off-the-books investigation into a United States congressman and his chief of staff. The expensive bottles of wine he and his wife had collected from old dinner parties were providing no help. On the other hand, Elliott would be just as sleepless if he allowed Anderson to get away with being complicit in, if not actively participating in, the brutal slaying of RayLynn Gutierrez.

Elliott was contemplating how long he would be going without rest when he smelled Loretta's coffee brewing in the break room. He usually didn't partake, but it would likely become a necessity. Elliott found Loretta reading the *Morning Standard*. She looked up suspiciously when he reached for the pot of classic roast.

"Something wrong?" she asked.

"No. Just getting some coffee," he said as he looked for a mug. Loretta saw him struggling and directed him to the correct cupboard.

"What's wrong?"

"Nothing. Just didn't sleep well last night."

Elliott was sure he'd eventually tell her, hopefully after he had enough proof to arrest Cole and take his case on Anderson to the FBI. Until then, he wanted to preserve Loretta's plausible deniability.

Elliott picked up the paper. "What's new in the world?"

"Oh my gosh, have you heard about Gordon Anderson?"

Elliott looked at the front page and found the headline, **'A life well lived'**, and scanned the story for information, which he had to separate from the obligatory obituary fluff. Ace Anderson's father had died of what a family statement said was "likely a heart attack" the night his son was re-elected. An autopsy was scheduled for today in Lubbock. The Yucca Police Department released a statement saying no foul play was suspected.

Elliott didn't buy it for a second. Cole now had two bodies to account for. Or perhaps Ace Anderson had caused his father's death, meaning he'd graduated from ordering hits to killing people himself.

"Tragic, isn't it?" Loretta asked. "As if that poor young man hadn't been through enough."

"Yep." Elliott felt a headache coming on. He was about to ask Loretta if she had any ibuprofen when he glanced back at the front page and noticed the story's byline.

Elliott smiled. Bishop was holding up his end. Things were going to be rough for a while, but the good guys had the upper hand.

• • • •

Levi chuckled to himself. He never thought he'd enjoy his face being covered in makeup.

"You ready?" asked a voice in his earpiece. It was Georgia Barrett.

"Yes ma'am," Levi said, nodding into the camera in front of him. Beside it was a TV that showed Georgia sitting behind her desk. She was live in Atlanta, and Levi was about to be interviewed remotely for her show. He sat up straight in the leather chair as he heard the back-from-commercial music and slapped on a fake smile.

"Welcome back to 'The Roundup.' I'm joined remotely by our friend Levi Cole all the way from tiny Yucca, Texas. Thank you for coming on the show, Levi."

"Thanks for having me, Georgia."

"Many of my viewers will remember Levi as the reporter who broke the scandal that led to the resignation of former Texas governor Kenneth Lockwood, whom I and many other Washington insiders thought would be elected president two years from now. Others may know Levi from the viral video he was featured in."

She wasn't supposed to bring that up. What a cunt.

"Levi is now the chief of staff for Republican Congressman Ace Anderson, who just got re-elected to represent Texas' 13th District, which consists of Amarillo and the rest of the Texas Panhandle, including Yucca," she continued. "I know most of my viewers are used to me exposing corrupt politicians, but I'm going to give everyone a break from that for just a few minutes tonight to share a story of the *good* guys overcoming long odds."

"Well that's mighty kind of you to say," Levi said, laying on the drawl as thick as possible. Yankees love that.

"For my viewers who don't know, you were literally taken hostage by a madman not long ago, correct?"

"Actually, I wasn't taken hostage. I was looking for a friend of mine who'd been taken hostage, Katherine Hallaway."

"Ah, right, the woman you called a very vulgar term on that video."

"The woman I carried up a hill in torrential rain while she was dying in my arms."

"Oh, um … my apologies. That wasn't in the news stories I read. You must've cared for her deeply."

"Yes ma'am," Levi said, allowing his head to drop. He raised it a moment later with watery eyes. "But, back to your point: yes, I was one of the victims that night. I was the only one lucky enough to survive."

"Not only did Vista County Sheriff Shawn Nichols shoot and kill your friend, but he also shot and killed Hunter Matthews, Congressman Anderson's former chief of staff," Barrett said.

"Yes. He and Hunter shot each other. Hunter was a hero that night."

"And then, out of your mutual grief, you and Congressman Anderson teamed up to finish his re-election campaign."

"Yes, Georgia. We both lost someone important in our lives. It's amazing the strong bonds forged through intense grief."

"Beautiful words, Levi, as always."

Levi fought off a smile, amazed at what pass for "beautiful words" on cable TV.

"Thank you," he said.

"But the story didn't end there, did it?"

"Unfortunately, no."

"After losing Matthews—who, by all accounts, was a true Washington power player—the Anderson family suffered another tragic loss when the congressman's father, successful Dallas attorney Gordon Anderson, died at campaign headquarters the night his son was re-elected in a landslide."

"That's right, Georgia. Less than a hundred feet from where I'm sitting."

"Our viewers should know that we originally planned on having both Levi and Anderson with us today, but the congressman is still mourning the loss of his father."

"Yes, ma'am," Levi said. "His father's death hit Ace real hard."

"I know it's still very early, but do you know yet what happened?"

"You know, the old journalist in me doesn't want to speculate," Levi said. "But, there's no doubt Gordon had been drinking. We all were. It was a night of celebration. Gordon also had blood pressure problems and Type 2 diabetes."

"I see."

"Congressman Anderson was actually the one who found his father," Ace said. "Between his description and other factors, we are expecting the cause of death to be a heart attack or some other catastrophic symptom of his chronic cardiovascular disease."

"Thank you for being so frank with us, Levi," Georgia said. "Since you're being so honest, I have one more question to ask."

"Go ahead, Georgia, fire away."

"Will Congressman Ace Anderson continue his political career, or will he resign after these terrible losses."

"You know, Georgia, these tragedies might've devastated a lesser man. But, by the grace of God, Congressman Anderson has found the strength to persevere. We are so thankful to have the confidence of our amazing constituents. They voted overwhelmingly for Ace Anderson, and we will make sure that's who goes to Washington and fights for them."

"Wow, Levi. What an amazing story. Thank you for taking the time to come on the show with us. Now go pack your bags."

"Thank you for having me on. It was a pleasure as always."

"Up next, we've got our panel to break down the latest social media scandal in Washington. Stay tuned. You're watching 'The Roundup.'"

Levi took out his earpiece and shot a text to Emily Greene, who—despite the fact she no longer worked for Georgia—had arranged the interview. *Thanks for getting me on Georgia's show. Owe you one.* Levi chuckled to himself. Here he was, literally spreading fake news. What a country.

CHAPTER FORTY-TWO

Levi loosened his tie as he sat down on a couch next to Ace and twisted off a bottle cap.

"How's the mourning coming?" Levi asked.

"Just getting started," Ace said, picking up the remote to turn off the sixty-inch TV hanging on the wall. "You did good on the show. Especially when she brought up the video."

Levi lifted his bottle, and they toasted. It'd been more than two weeks since Ace had told him about Gordon's master plan. Ace had been right—they were both pawns in a political chess match. Ace told Levi about Gordon's far-flung ambitions for Matthews. Told him about how Matthews chose Levi because they thought he could be easily manipulated.

At first, Levi laughed at the possibility of Ace Anderson as governor. But, after polishing off the rest of the Scotch in Matthews' old office, Levi realized he and Ace weren't that different. A couple of good guys getting screwed by the same people.

What Ace hadn't understood, and probably still didn't, is that having control is much more important than the power or the women he was chasing. Despite taking away Kat—and generally being one of the worst human beings he'd ever come across—Levi had to thank the late Shawn Nichols for one thing. With his actions that night in Dickson's Crossing, Shawn had taught Levi about control. About how control over one's self is the key to control over others. It takes so much energy for a person to suppress his or her baser instincts. That's why most people go nowhere in life. They're too busy fighting with themselves. But the people who rise above, the people who make a real impact, are not. They take control of their own lives and do what's necessary to make that impact.

That's why Gordon Anderson had to go. Levi had decided to take over for Matthews, to hitch his wagon to Ace. Then Levi told Ace that, so long as Gordon was alive, he would never have control of his own life. And for Gordon's death to have maximum effect, Ace would have to do the killing.

Levi did his part by getting Rosemary to steal the injectable potassium chloride from her pharmacy, which mimicked a heart attack and left no trace in Gordon Anderson's system. Levi had been surprised at how little convincing Rosemary required. She was rebellious by nature and would've done anything for Levi after what he'd been through. By now, Rosemary might've put together what the chemical had been used for. But she couldn't go to the authorities without implicating herself. And her husband, Bobby Joe Carter, was a public figure. Even if Rosemary wanted to turn on Levi, she wouldn't want to shame her recently humiliated hubby.

"Has the medical examiner said anything yet?" Levi asked.

"Yep. Heart attack."

"Good. Funeral?"

"In two days," Ace said. "And you're sure about your visit with the *Morning Standard* editor?"

"Absolutely."

"How can you be sure?"

"He bought it, hook, line, and sinker." Lying to the congressman is often necessary. "And, if not, he wants no part in putting Kat in the middle of some political scandal from beyond the grave. Plus, he said there are no more copies of the tape, and I believe him."

"So, no story about me having sex with that girl?"

"No story about you having sex with that girl."

"No other loose ends?"

"No other loose ends." That was mostly true. Levi would have to kill Rosemary. But he hadn't yet worked out how to do that, and Levi was confident she would stay silent for now.

Ace nodded and took another drink from his longneck. "I have to be here for my dad's funeral, but you don't. You should go ahead and get settled in Washington."

As Levi stood to gather his luggage, which was neatly stacked in the corner, a girl walked in. She was tall and blonde, the bright shade of red on her lips matching her tight shirt and short skirt.

"Hi there," Levi said. "What's your name?"

"Regina," she said, holding out her left hand. "Regina Watkins."

"Regina, so glad you could make it," Ace said, popping up to greet their guest. "You two talked on the phone the other day. She wrote the story on my father's death for the paper."

"Oh, right. Hi," Levi said, struggling with an awkward left-handed shake. "Are you writing a follow-up story?"

"No," Ace answered for her, unable to contain his enthusiasm. "Regina here is going to be our new intern as soon as she graduates at the end of this semester."

"Oh yeah?" Levi asked. "Which college?"

"High school, actually," Watkins said.

"Oh, my apologies. You're graduating a semester early?" Levi asked, still awkwardly holding her hand.

"Yes, sir," she said. "I can't wait to get out of Bison Ridge."

"You're from Bison Ridge?" Levi asked.

"Yep," Watkins said. "And I know all about you."

"Regina called our offices a few days ago saying she really wants to intern with us this spring and summer before going to college in the fall," Ace said, unable to contain his excitement at the prospect of one day sleeping with his new intern. "She practically begged me. Then I got glowing recommendations from her editors. And when I read that beautiful story she wrote about my dad, I just couldn't say no. I told her to come and meet us before you left."

"Sounds like fate," Levi said. "Where are you going to college?"

"I'll start at UT next fall," she said. "Just like you."

"Well, how about that? A girl after my own heart."

Watkins kept smiling and gripped Levi's left hand tighter.

"Something like that."

ACKNOWLEDGMENTS

Though this is not the first piece of fiction I've started, it is the first one I've finished, which would not have been possible without the constant encouragement from my parents, Julie and Rick (I am Richard Derias Treon IV), and my sister, Nikki Martindale. My friends, many of whom I consider family, were also instrumental in that regard.

My parents and sister are among those who read the first, (incredibly) rough draft of this novel. Others who read various drafts include my aunt, Tricia Lewis; my wonderful friend, Amber Guffey; one of my oldest friends, Katherine Ruth (who I will always remember as Kali Burris); my former colleague and friend Mollie Bryant; friend and fellow creative Jen Williams; and a few others I am surely forgetting. The importance of those beta readers cannot be overstated.

I also owe a debt of gratitude to all the language arts and journalism teachers I've had throughout the years, including Dawn Knobloch, Rosemary Parks, Melanie Hauser, and Dr. Maggie Rivas-Rodriguez. I apologize to you all for any errors. Yes, you did teach me better.

I am unbelievably grateful for the team at Black Rose Writing for editing and publishing this novel, which is the first I've ever completed. They went out on a limb with a new novelist, and I can't thank them enough for helping me realize a dream I've had for many years.

I would also like to thank all the colleagues I've had in journalism. Some of you had to put up with me as a peer, others as a subordinate. Then there are the poor souls who had to deal with me as their managing editor. You are the real heroes here.

About the Author

Rick Treon is a former newspaper reporter and editor. After graduating from The University of Texas at Austin with a bachelor's degree in journalism, Rick worked as a reporter for the *Fort Worth Star-Telegram*, as a reporter and editor at the *Amarillo Globe-News*, and was the managing editor of *The Kerrville Daily Times*. He now lives and writes in Texas.

Thank you so much for reading one of our **Psychological Thrillers**.
If you enjoyed our book, please check out our recommended title for your
next great read!

The Tracker by John Hunt

"A dark thriller that draws the reader in." *–Morning Bulletin*

"I never want to hear mention of bolt-cutters, a live rat and a bucket in the
same sentence again. EVER." *–Ginger Nuts of Horror*

View other Black Rose Writing titles at www.blackrosewriting.com/books

and use promo code **PRINT** to receive a **20% discount** when purchasing.